EVERY SAINT A SINNER

PEARL SOLAS

Dear Ann,
    Thank you for your
interest. I hope you find this
thought-provoking.
        All my best,
        Pearl Solas
              9/3/2021

**NIKSEN
BOOKS**

Published by Niksen Books

inquiries@niksenbooks.com

©2021 by Pearl Solas.

ISBN: 978-1-7368764-0-4

Printed in the United States of America.

Cover design by Owen Gent.

This is a work of fiction. While, as in all fiction, the literary perceptions and insights are based on experience, all names, characters, places, and incidents are either products of the author's imagination or are used fictitiously.

Names: Solas, Pearl, author

Title: Every Saint A Sinner, a novel/by Pearl Solas

Description: First edition. Niksen Books, 2021

For Father Tom Doyle, who tirelessly worked for justice from within

PROLOGUE

Though one day he'd be known as The Venerable and, later, The Blessed, on this day he was just Frank. He was about as exhausted and dejected as a "just Frank" could be. He shifted in the hard wooden chair and his sore, protesting lower back reminded him of just how long he'd been sitting there, staring at nothing. Hours. *Man*, he thought, *these chairs are torture devices*, and he considered whether he should request something more comfortable to accommodate the rare client who needed to sit across the desk from him, rather than on the plush couch at the far end of the office where he conducted his therapy sessions. Who was he kidding? If he went ahead with what he was planning, he wouldn't have any clients to accommodate. He wouldn't have an office.

He had been sitting in a guest chair, rather than his usual, more ergonomic perch on the other side of the desk, because it was closer to the locked filing cabinet. As he had done several times since he had taken this seat in the pre-dawn hours, he reached his hand toward the cabinet, then drew it back. Daylight had been steadily strengthening, and now it forced its way through the slats in the cheap blinds covering the window.

Soon other people who worked in the building would be arriving, and he would need to figure out how to hide his despair and get through the day.

Frank ran his hand over his jawline, feeling the salt-and-pepper stubble that had sprouted there since he had shaved yesterday morning. The tops of his cheeks were sticky with dried tears, and the skin around his eyes felt swollen and tight. He hadn't returned home after the police had patted him kindly on the back and told him he could leave—that they would take it from there. Instead he had come straight to the office. To what was in the filing cabinet. To do what he should have done years ago.

He'd woken in the night after having a vicarious dream. It was the second time in his life this had happened. Like the first time, there had been no mistaking it for something from his own subconscious. It was completely foreign, but vivid with detail, immediate. Also like the first time, the consciousness his dreaming self inhabited was female, the same female, in fact, although she was now a woman rather than a girl. Same agony, though. Same confusion and hopelessness. As it had decades before, experiencing her pain spurred Frank to action. He had leaped out of bed, accessed his client database to find her address, and rushed to her apartment as quickly as his shitty pickup could get him there. Though he had hoped against hope, his dream had, once again, revealed to him the truth. She was already dead by the time he got there. And so he had called the police and wept disconsolately while he waited for them to arrive.

At some point during the hours he had occupied the wooden chair, his weeping had ceased. The well of his tears, but not of his grief, had run dry.

"Right," he said as he stood decisively, forcing his stiff legs to straighten and waiting out the pins and needles. He removed the keychain from his pocket and found the match to the filing cabinet. He slipped the key into the lock of the bottom drawer, and pulled it open. Pushing the files forward, he felt for the small black box in the rear corner, wiping dust off of it with his hand, then turning the combination dial right, then left, then right again, hearing the faint click as the last of the tumblers slid into place.

He reached into the small safe and removed the only item it contained—an obsolete hard drive that was almost comically oversized in comparison to minuscule, modern USB drives. Frank placed the drive into the manila envelope on which he had written "Tavis" with a thick Sharpie. Now that it had come out of the safe, he could not return the hard drive to its hiding place. The die had been cast, and he would give the envelope to Tavis the next time he saw him.

As if on cue, a loud knock on the door shattered the silence of the office.

PART I

CHAPTER ONE

Veronica craned her neck and pulled down her rearview mirror, checking to make sure she didn't have anything in her teeth and that her lipstick hadn't bled into the small cracks that had recently begun to form around her lips. She wiped away the mascara that insistently deposited itself on the skin below her lower lash line by the end of every day. She ducked her head to sniff her armpits and frowned at the small circle of perspiration on her white blouse. She grabbed the suit jacket draped over the passenger seat and shrugged into it as she opened her car door and stuck out one of her legs. Not until her bare foot touched the warm asphalt did Veronica remember that she had removed her high heels to drive. Sighing, she reached into the passenger footwell, snagged the shoes, and stuffed her feet into them.

Her car hadn't had a chance to cool off in the ten-minute drive from her office, and Veronica felt hot and oily. The slight dampness in the places where her clothing met her skin made her feel like sausage innards stuffed into a tight casing. To an outside observer, however, the stylish but understated heel that emerged from the car, followed by a slim ankle and long, well-formed leg, the svelte body donning a fitted skirt suit, all suggested a cool, confident professional.

Veronica's heels clicked toward the door of Sacred Heart High School. As she approached, the door opened and a tween boy emerged, followed by a tall, striking, powerfully built man in a black suit punctuated with a bright white clerical collar.

"So sorry I'm late," breathed Veronica, giving the boy a quick embrace while he stood with his hands at his sides. "My deposition ran a little longer than expected, and I couldn't get ahold of Tom."

"No worries," said the priest, an easy smile spreading across his face as he ruffled the boy's hair. "Sean and I just talked about how he's adjusting to Sacred Heart, and he got caught up on his homework. I'd love to say I helped with it, but that math he's doing is beyond my skillset."

Wordlessly, Sean had begun to walk toward Veronica's car.

"Sean!" Veronica called after him. "Manners! Say goodbye to Father Paul and thank him for his help."

The boy looked up briefly from beneath his flop of hair. "Bye, Father. Thanks."

Veronica smiled resignedly at the priest. "Sorry," she said. "You know better than almost anyone, I'm sure, what this age is like. Someone takes your sweet, talkative child . . . almost too talkative . . . and replaces him with a monosyllabic alien."

Father Paul chuckled and waved away her apology. "He's a great kid. Scary bright. I'm sure this is all just a big adjustment for him."

"Thanks for being so understanding and for taking the time to help him transition. Tom and I really appreciate it. Somewhere in there," Veronica gestured toward the car, "Sean appreciates it too."

Deflecting her gratitude, Father Paul looked toward the

horizon at the dark wall of clouds distantly devouring the sunlit sky. "Looks like we're in for some weather tonight."

Veronica followed his gaze. The air had that oppressive weight that accompanies the collision of hot and cold fronts. She nodded her agreement. "It's that time of year. Well, I'd better get home and feed my brood before it hits."

"Of course. See you soon." For the first time during their conversation, Father Paul looked directly into her eyes. He bit lightly at his bottom lip and then smiled, bowed slightly, and turned back toward the school.

Before heading back to her car, Veronica paused briefly to allow her blood to cool. *Holy Thorn Birds,* she thought, *priests shouldn't be allowed to be that fucking sexy.*

"MEG, would you please bring me the salad bowl?" asked Veronica later that night, draining the water from the salad spinner and looking for a towel to dry her hands. Tom put his hand on the small of her back as he sidled around her to lift the lid on the simmering meat sauce.

Meg pushed up from the counter stool, every slouching step across the kitchen a silent protest at the injustice of being asked to help. Setting the table across the room, Avery rolled her eyes at her older sister.

"Thank you, daughter mine," sang Veronica as Meg thrust the bowl at her. As she grabbed the bowl, Veronica ensnared her eldest daughter's wrist and pulled her into a tight embrace. Meg submitted to her mother's affection, trying to suppress the smile that bubbled up through her practiced aloof expression.

Snuggling her nose into Meg's silky cheek, Veronica asked, "So what are your plans after tomorrow night's game? Are you going to stay awhile after you finish cheering, or are you going to bounce right away?"

"God, Mom. It smells like something died in your mouth. And nobody says 'bounce' anymore. At least *I* can't if you're saying it now." Meg extricated herself from her mother's hug.

"Ah, yes," piped up Tom in his best David Attenborough as he stirred the sauce and pasta on the stove, "the basic middle-aged white woman in her natural suburban habitat. Where slang goes to die."

Laughing in spite of herself, Veronica beaned a crouton at her husband's head.

"Hey, buddy," Veronica said to Sean as he entered the kitchen with wet hair. "Long shower, huh?" Veronica and Tom caught each other's eyes and smirked, remembering what their friend Melissa had said about the 45-minute showers each of her three sons had begun taking in their early teens. "Why don't you help Avery finish setting the table? Dinner's almost ready."

As they passed the dishes around the table Meg said, "Mom, Kelly said she can fit me in on Saturday to do a trial run of my hair and makeup for homecoming. Is that okay?"

"I assume what you're really asking is whether I'll pay for it. Did she tell you how much it would cost?"

"Well, no, but it's going to be so pretty! I found a picture of this updo that I just love and *nobody* else is going to have anything like it."

"Sounds very hair-odynamic." Veronica snickered at her own joke while Tom groaned.

"Lucky me!" exclaimed Meg in a falsely bright voice, "I get to have *two* parents who tell dad jokes!"

"You're such a twat, Meg!" shot Avery.

"Language, Avery!" Veronica fixed Avery with her best severe mother glare. "Just because someone *acts* a certain way sometimes doesn't mean that person *is* a certain way. Meg isn't a twat, she's just *acting* like a twat. And stop using that kind of gendered language—we women have enough problems without using derogatory slang for female anatomy to cut each other down."

"Sometimes you act like such a dick, Meg," amended Avery.

"Better," Veronica approved.

"Jesus, Ronnie," muttered Tom under his breath.

Veronica had just set the rolls in motion around the table when the singular sound of a tornado siren split the air. Tom's and Veronica's eyes met across the table. "I thought the storms weren't supposed to roll in until later," he said.

She shrugged and snatched the basket of rolls from Meg's hand, picking up her plate as she stood. "Grab your plates, guys, and let's go to the strongroom."

When the last of them had filed into the strongroom, Tom closed the door and switched on the battery-powered weather radio. They sat with their plates perched on their laps. The water table under their split-level home was too high for basements or for the tornado shelters favored in the area, so the Matthews family had settled for the strongroom alternative on the lowest level of their home: a concrete-enforced room with a steel door.

Veronica chose the seat next to Sean, who was leaning against the wall with his eyes closed, his dinner untouched atop his legs.

"Hey, buddy," she said, tucking his hair behind his ear.

"Hey, Mom."

"You doing all right? You've been pretty quiet lately."

"I'm okay. Just tired."

"You know, there's no reason you have to stay at Sacred Heart if it feels like too much. We said we'd try it, but you can always go back to the middle school and we can just do some enrichment programs if you feel like you want more."

"I know, Mom. Thanks."

Veronica finished her dinner and then absentmindedly rubbed Sean's back until Tom announced that the system had passed. Sean stood without a word, and Veronica's hand trailed down to where he had been sitting. Her fingers encountered a sticky dampness. She raised her hand and furrowed her brow at the rusty tinge covering her fingertips. She looked up at Sean just as he walked past the steel door. Her eyes widened at the dark, brownish-red stain on the seat of his pants.

CHAPTER TWO

Tavis Pereira shook rain droplets off his umbrella under the overhang in front of the emergency room entrance. The violence of the storm had passed—the ear-splitting thunder, eye-dazzling lightning, and gale-force wind that had torn shingles from roofs and branches from trees—but rain still ceaselessly dumped from the roiling clouds.

Tavis showed his badge to the triage nurse, who pointed out a white-coated man conversing with an elderly woman on a hospital bed surrounded by an imperfectly closed curtain.

Tavis walked over toward the doctor and stood a respectful distance away while the consultation continued.

"Dr. Selim?" Tavis asked when the doctor emerged from the cubicle.

Dr. Selim looked up from notating the chart in his hands, took in Tavis and the badge he proffered, and extended his hand. "Yes. Thanks for coming so quickly." He peered at the badge. "Mr. Pereira?"

Tavis nodded, and Dr. Selim led him into a small office, closing the door behind them.

"Mr. and Mrs. Matthews brought in their twelve-year-old

13

son, Sean, about an hour ago because of rectal bleeding so severe that the blood had seeped through his pants. They seemed to assume it was symptomatic of an illness, but it was obvious, on examination, that the bleeding was trauma-induced and required sutures. The boy isn't saying a word, and I didn't press him. I just called your office. The parents both appear to be completely gobsmacked. For what it's worth, I don't think they had any idea."

"Thanks. It's worth a lot. Did this appear to be a fresh trauma? Any signs of older or prolonged abuse?"

"The nurse can give you the digital images we took. Poor kid. I didn't see any bruising or irregularities on other parts of his body, but some of the tears are partially healed. Those that required sutures were quite fresh. I would say this wasn't a one-time incident."

Tavis looked up from his notepad. "Anything else you think I should know?"

Dr. Selim considered, then shook his head.

"All right. Please reach out if anything occurs to you. Can you show me to them?"

Dr. Selim led the way to a room with the words "Family Care" etched on the glass door. Tavis was relieved that, rather than the curtain-separated cubicles of the rest of the E.R., this room offered privacy for sensitive conversations.

Tavis introduced himself and shook hands with the haggard-looking parents. The boy lay curled up on the bed, facing the wall. When his mother reached up to rub his back, he twitched her off like a horse repelling a fly.

Tavis crossed the room and stood between Sean and the wall he faced. Squatting until his face was level with the boy's eyes, Tavis allowed Sean to take his measure before he started speaking. "Hello, Sean. I'm Detective Tavis Pereira with the Colberg Police Department. I think Dr. Selim and your parents told you why Dr. Selim had to call me. What can you tell me about how you got hurt?"

Sean closed his eyes.

Veronica Matthews again reached out for her son's back, stopping herself before she touched him. "Please, Sean," she pleaded, "please tell us who did this to you. Was it one of the boys at school?"

"I *knew* we shouldn't have let him move ahead so much," said Tom Matthews. "It doesn't matter if he could handle the academics. He was just not ready, socially, to spend his time with kids so much older."

Veronica's lips formed a tight line, avoiding a well-worn argument. Tom stood and paced. Sean opened his eyes and looked at his father, gazing at him with longing. His eyes held the despair of sudden rupture. He hungered to fix what had broken and return to the warmth of familiarity.

Tavis maneuvered the conversation into more productive territory. "Can you tell me what happened, Sean?"

When the boy remained silent, Veronica offered, "We've been trying to get him to talk to us since Dr. Selim explained what must have happened. Mostly, he's been like this," she gestured. "All we've gotten out of him is that something happened, that he didn't want it to happen, and he can't remember all of it."

Tavis's brow wrinkled. He considered a while before beginning hesitantly, "Veronica, Tom. I wonder whether Sean might feel more comfortable talking without the two of you in the room."

"Not a fucking chance," Veronica shot back. Tom resumed his seat with an air of finality.

"Okay," Tavis began again. "Sean, I know this is the last place you want to be right now. I know it's scary and embarrassing to talk about such personal things with your parents—not to mention with a stranger. Someone hurt you. Right?"

After a few seconds, eyes still squeezed shut, Sean nodded.

"All right. Can you tell me who hurt you?"

No reaction.

"Was it another student?"

A slight negative shake.

"You're doing great, Sean. Was it an adult?"

An almost imperceptible nod.

"Okay, Sean. Was it a teacher at the school?"

Sean finally opened his eyes and fixed them on Tavis. He nodded once.

"I *knew* it!" muttered Veronica angrily. "That Mr. Ronan has always rubbed me the wrong way."

"It wasn't Mr. Ronan, Mom," said Sean wearily, sitting up and hugging his knees to his chest.

"Well, then, who could possibly have done this to you?" asked Veronica, baffled.

Sean sighed deeply, more world-weary than any twelve-year-old should ever have reason to be. He faced his mother, his voice full of resignation. "Does it really matter, Mom? Will it change anything if you know? If I say, what happens then?"

Tavis fielded this one. "Sean," he said gently, "it *does* matter who it was. If he's a teacher, he could hurt other boys. Maybe he already has. If you tell us who it is, we'll keep other kids safe and make sure he's punished for what he did to you."

Sean turned his ancient gaze to Tavis. "And then what happens to me? Is everybody gonna know? What if people don't believe that I didn't want it to happen? He said I *did* want it." His voice broke and he looked at his father pleadingly, his mouth wide in a dry, silent sob. When he could speak again, he wailed, "Everyone will believe him instead of me!"

The dam burst and Sean shook with silent sobs. Uncertainly, Tom moved toward the bed and patted his son's back with his large hand.

"Well, let's start here, Sean," offered Tavis. "I believe you.

Your parents believe you." Tavis handed Sean the box of tissues on the counter. "I can't guarantee that nobody will know what happened to you, but we have a lot of tools to protect your privacy. We'll do everything we can to keep what you've told us as confidential as possible. I can't think of any reason the other kids at school would need to know about it. We're asking you to do something big and scary. I know that. But you can help stop this from happening to other boys. Men who do this usually don't stop with one victim. I know you're brave, Sean. Your parents and I will be with you every step of the way."

Sean searched his parents' faces. They nodded at him encouragingly. In a voice so quiet the adults had to lean forward to hear him, Sean said, "It was Father Peña."

"Paul?" exclaimed his parents in unison as Veronica's hand beelined to her neck to grasp the crucifix there.

CHAPTER THREE

Tavis knocked on the open door of Paul Peña's beautifully appointed and carefully curated office. Father Peña looked up from the papers on his desk, his brief expression of annoyance quickly smoothed over with a mask of polite curiosity. "Yes?" he asked with a raised eyebrow.

"Father Peña?" Tavis asked as he stepped into the room.

"That's me. What can I do for you?" He stood up from his chair and came around the side of his desk with his hand outstretched. He was tall and dark with a languid, feline athleticism. Seeing him face to face, Tavis understood the surprise Tom and Veronica Matthews had expressed when their son had named his attacker. It seemed unthinkable that this man would have a sexual interest in adolescent boys. It was also surprising that a man who exuded such vigorous traditional masculinity should have chosen to join the celibate clergy.

The men shook hands and then Tavis introduced himself and showed his badge. "I was hoping I might ask you a few questions to help with an investigation."

"Of course," Paul said smoothly, without an ounce of hesitation or trepidation. He closed the door and invited Tavis to sit. "How can I help?"

"Well," Tavis said, swallowing. There was a discomfort that always preceded informing someone that an accusation had been made against them. Tavis had been raised Catholic, and his own ingrained deference to the white collar around Paul's neck heightened his discomfort. "I wanted to ask you about allegations of sexual assault made by one of your students."

Paul barked out a short, harsh laugh. Tavis's surprise at this reaction registered on his face, and Paul put his palm out placatingly and said, "I'm sorry, Mr. Pereira. It's been a while since one of these has come up, but it's not unheard of. What happens is that students get infatuated with the charisma of their teachers, and when those feelings aren't reciprocated, and teachers try to let students down gently and explain why these kinds of things are not possible, students sometimes try to protect their egos by inventing physical encounters that never happened." He delivered this explanation with convincing ease.

"To make sure I'm clear, then, you haven't had 'physical encounters,' as you call them, with any of your students?"

"Absolutely not," Paul stated emphatically, looking directly into Tavis's eyes.

Tavis nodded and closed his notebook as if his suspicions had been confirmed. Paul relaxed further into his seat. "I really appreciate you taking the time to answer my questions so directly. We have to follow these things up, you know, even though, for guys like you and me, the thought of doing something like that with a man, let alone a teen boy, is enough to make you nauseous."

Paul's smile remained firmly on his face, but his nose twitched as if he had smelled something foul. "It's a common mistake. Most people misuse that word."

Tavis plainly had no idea what Paul was talking about.

"'Nauseous.' Most people think it means feeling sick. It really means to make sick. The word you're looking for is 'nauseated.'"

After an awkward pause, Tavis stood and held out his hand for a parting handshake. Paul smiled as he rose, his even, white teeth gleaming.

"We shouldn't need much more from you. The only other thing we'll need to clear you from our investigation is a DNA sample. Assuming everything's as you've said, I wouldn't worry about it. It's a formality."

"A DNA sample?" Paul's Adam's apple bobbed a few inches below his pearly teeth.

"Yes, we've recovered semen from the victim's underwear," Tavis said as he took out a sealed kit containing the cheek swab.

CHAPTER FOUR

More often than not, it's impossible for any third party to know, absent a reliable and corroborated confession by a guilty perpetrator, exactly what happened between two people with conflicting accounts. There's no perfect approach to investigation that unfailingly results in punishing the guilty and vindicating the rare defendant unjustly accused of sexually abusing children. Perfection's not possible in a paradigm that relies so heavily on the weight of one person's word against another's. Tavis and the Colberg Police Department's Crimes Against Children unit did their best, and they usually felt reasonably confident they had gotten it right. They could never be absolutely certain. But with Father Paul Peña, Tavis was positive he had gotten the right guy. In his hubris, Paul had never expected pesky evidence like DNA to bring him down.

The media attention surrounding Paul Peña's arrest caused other victims to come forward. Statistically, Tavis knew that the number of complainants likely was not even a drop in the bucket of the number of adolescents Paul had assaulted. The District Attorney decided not to prosecute a substantial percentage of the complaints because enough time had passed that statutes of limitation made those cases unwinnable. They had enough to go to trial on a handful of cases, including Sean Matthews's.

The Church had pressured Paul to accept a plea bargain to minimize the media circus, but his inflated perception of his own charm had led him to opt for a trial, where he expected to influence the jury to decide in his favor. But amid the rising tide of clergy-abuse reports in the media, and the collective anger mounting around evidence of the Church's failure to protect its flock from known predators, the jury proved immune to Paul's most winning efforts. They found him guilty on all counts after the briefest possible period of deliberation, recommending a sentence designed to keep him in prison for the remainder of his life without the possibility of parole.

Paul's choice of a public trial rather than a plea bargain and cooperating with the Church's efforts to settle quietly with the victims sounded the death knell for his priestly vocation. The publicity associated with his trial and subsequent conviction made the Church's decision straightforward and politically expedient: Paul was quickly removed from the priesthood, also known as defrocking, or laicizing. Because the process to laicize him had begun in earnest when Paul declined the State's plea offer, it was reasonable to suspect that the disciplinary measure stemmed more from the Church's embarrassment than from sorrow or remorse about the damage Paul had inflicted on vulnerable members of the Body of Christ.

Tavis knew he couldn't change what had happened to Sean or to Paul's other victims, but he felt that justice had been done. Tavis and the prosecutors were able to safeguard Sean's privacy through the trial, ensuring he gave testimony in a closed court-room and that the media never learned of his identity. In Tavis's experience, families weren't eager to sustain ties with the police officers who reminded them of dark times in their families' lives, so he wished them well at the end of the trial, certain that Sean's loving and conscientious parents would see him through the rough spots on his road to healing.

CHAPTER FIVE

"Good morning, sweetie," Veronica murmured as she opened the blinds in Sean's room.

Sean burrowed further into his blankets.

"Here's some toast to munch while you wake up. Would you like a little coffee? Dad will drive you to school today—he needs to leave in about 45 minutes."

Sean neither moved nor spoke. Veronica rubbed his back a little as she perched on the side of his bed. She looked at her watch.

"I'm going to have to leave, love, so I can take care of a few things at the office before I pick you up for your appointment."

One of Sean's eyes looked out at her from within his nest of pillows. His face held the mixture of dread and defeat that had become so familiar. School had become a place of foreboding to the boy whose remarkable academic prowess had always formed such a large part of his identity.

"Feeling like you can't face it this morning?" she intuited.

He shook his head, ashamed. "I couldn't get to sleep last night and I'm just really tired."

"It's okay," she said brightly. "Get a little more rest and I'll pick you up here for your appointment. Then we'll see how you feel about making it to this afternoon's classes. I'll call the school."

"Thanks, Momma."

Veronica leaned over and kissed her son's still-smooth cheek and tickled the whiskers that had sprouted on his chin. She would have to remind Tom to teach Sean to do a more thorough shaving job.

"We're due at Dr. Amerson's at eleven, so please be ready to go when I get here at ten-thirty."

"I will. Love you."

"Love you too." She closed the door.

AT 10:00 A.M., Veronica left the office, rushing out the door as she gave her secretary last-minute instructions about finalizing briefing and exhibits before filing that afternoon.

"I should be back here no later than one, so if you can get everything pulled together by then, I'll make sure it's perfect before we send it out the door."

"Got it."

"Thanks, Sal."

Flexing her talent for efficiency, Veronica decided to stop at the grocery store on the way home. It would be well-stocked and nearly empty at this time of day. Rather than the hour the trip would take during the post-work rush on her way home in the evening, she could buy everything on her list and be back in her car in 15 minutes.

As she drove toward home after the grocery-shopping whirlwind, Veronica thought about the morning's setback. In the more than three years since they had learned about the trauma Sean had suffered, navigating his mental health had been a roller coaster ride. At first, it seemed that changing schools had helped him move past the anxiety he had felt around the Sacred Heart building, but eventually the idea of attending classes, regardless of the physical location, the teacher, or the subject, had become overwhelming. Veronica and Tom had disagreed about how to respond to Sean's reluctance.

In Tom's opinion, the sooner Sean learned that life is about forcing ourselves to do things we don't want to do, the better. Veronica didn't disagree with his pragmatism, but she couldn't bear to force Sean to go to school when the prospect inspired such obvious dread. She called to excuse his absences on the many days he just couldn't face it. Each year, he had failed several classes, but had managed to pass just enough for promotion to the next grade. Now a senior at just over sixteen years old, Sean was on the final downhill slide of what had proved to be a miserable high school experience.

Veronica couldn't even imagine how things would have been if not for the army of mental health professionals, whose appointments accounted for a fair number of the excused absences she called in. After Sean's revelation about Father Paul, there had been cognitive behavioral therapy with trauma specialists and with other specialists focused on helping Father Paul's victims get through both testifying at trial and their reactions to Paul's conviction and sentencing.

When one of the specialists suggested the possibility that organic comorbidities of generalized anxiety disorder and clinical depression were exacerbated, but not caused by, Sean's trauma, Veronica sought out the best psychologists in Colberg specializing in treating these issues in adolescents. Semi-weekly sessions were added to talk therapy, and eventually, one of the psychologists suggested adding pharmacological treatment into the mix. Tom took the laboring oar and found the only psychiatrist in the tri-state area with the relevant experience and a waiting list shorter than two years, and when Dr. Amerson's schedule finally permitted, he began seeing Sean. The long process of tapering medications up and down led to the terrify-ing-sounding diagnosis of "treatment resistant depression." Sean, Veronica, and Tom were relieved to learn this diagnosis did not mean treatment was hopeless, but instead that Sean did not have the expected response to the drugs traditionally used to treat depression. So Dr. Amerson moved on to drugs used primarily to treat other conditions, such as psychosis or thyroid irregularities, but that also had proven effective with more stub-born cases of depression.

Sean had been tapering up on the most recent drug for the past six weeks, and Veronica was cautiously optimistic. Aside from this morning's hiccup, Sean had recently seemed more like his sunny childhood self than he had been since Sacred Heart. In fact, the evening before, he had been excited about family dinner. The girls had made their weekly sojourn from their college dorms across town, and Sean had taken out his old drawing materials and made silly caricature place cards for all of them. He had joined in the mealtime banter, at one point making Meg laugh so aggressively that the rest of the table thought she had choked.

As she and Tom cleared away the plates and washed the dishes, Veronica found herself closing her eyes by the sink in a silent prayer of gratitude. Coming up behind her, Tom set the dirty plates on the counter and slipped his arms around her waist. She turned to face him.

"Good dinner, huh?" he said, smiling down at her.

She beamed back up at him. "Are we finally getting our boy back?"

She leaned down and knocked on the wooden cabinet below the counter, and then twined her arms around her husband's neck, pulling him in for a kiss that surprised both of them with its sweetness and renewed novelty.

Turning onto their street, Veronica colored at the memory of that kiss. She resolved to look for a weekend when she and

Tom could book themselves into the B&B that had become their haven when they needed some uninterrupted couple time.

Veronica looked at the clock on her dash as she pulled into the garage. 10:40. Accounting for the five minutes she set it ahead to trick herself into punctuality, it was actually 10:35. The drop-dead time she and Sean needed to leave to make it to the appointment on time was 10:45.

She grabbed a load of groceries and hurried into the house, yelling as she entered, "Sean, I'm here! T-minus ten minutes, buddy!" Veronica dropped the bags on the counter and hustled out to the garage for another load. If she played her cards right, she could at least put the cold stuff in the refrigerator or freezer before she had to leave.

After she had stowed all the perishables, she looked down at her watch. "Two minutes, sweetie," she called up from the foot of the stairs. "I'll wait for you in the car."

She considered the groceries still on the counter. She could drop the non-perishables and paper towels in the storage area in the strongroom on the way to the car. Arms full, Veronica made her way to the strongroom and groaned in frustration when she tried the door handle and found it locked. She put down her load and prepared to stretch onto her toes to grab the key they kept on the door molding. She stopped when she saw the note taped to the steel door.

Momma,
I love you. The keys are in here
with me. Don't try to open the door,
just call the police. I'm sorry.

The light in the room contracted to a pinprick, and all Veronica heard was her own ragged breathing. Pounding on the steel door, she pulled her phone out and dialed 9-1-1 with violently shaking fingers. The line connected, she barely got out their address. She dropped the phone and alternated between saying "no, no, no, no, no" and shouting her dear heart's name. Not caring about its fruitlessness, she backed up several paces and launched herself at the steel door. She continued doing this until the police arrived and gently but insistently escorted her outside.

CHAPTER SIX

"How you holdin' up, kid?"

"Oh, you know," replied Veronica, wrapping her coat tightly around herself as a shield against the surprisingly bracing spring wind. "One foot in front of the other."

Her mentor took a long look at her, and they continued the walk back to the office from lunch.

"I've been worried about you," said Andy. "Not about your work—it's better than ever, really—but about you. You haven't really taken any time since . . . Sean . . . and I'm just concerned about how healthy that is. How is Tom managing? The girls?"

"Well, we haven't seen much of the girls lately. They're just across the city, but they seem to be coping by burying themselves in school. Probably for the best. I'm burying myself in work, and Tom's burying himself in baking . . . and eating."

"The board's offer is still open. If you need to take some time away, just say the word and we'll make it happen."

"Thanks, Andy. I really do need to work right now, though. It's the only thing that's felt at all sane. There is something I'd like you to take to the board for me, though."

"Anything."

"I've been doing some reading, and there's a fair amount of information out there about priests like Paul Peña. These priests' superiors knew what they were doing to children, but they hushed it up and just moved the priests to other assignments. Based on the number of victims who came forward against Peña, just here in Colberg, it's impossible that he wasn't doing the same thing wherever he was before. If he was, and the Church knew about it, then they are just as responsible for what he did here. For what he did to Sean."

Andy stopped walking and turned to Veronica. She averted her face from the overwhelming force of his concern.

"Oh, Ronnie. You know that nobody ever walks away from a lawsuit satisfied. Or vindicated."

Veronica looked down at her feet. "I just need to try to make somebody accept responsibility."

"Peña's in prison for the rest of his life."

"That's not enough. He's not the only one to blame. And he never actually accepted responsibility."

Andy sighed and rubbed his face with his hand. "I'll talk to the rest of the board. I assume you've already run a conflict check?"

"Yes. John Anderson did some work with the diocese years ago, but it was just some estate planning for retiring priests. We talked and he agrees there's no ethical concern."

"Under the circumstances, I doubt the board will stand in your way. I have no idea how Sandy Conlin will react, though. He's about as devout as they come, and he's going to hate the idea of the firm's name being associated with a lawsuit against the Church."

"Shit, Andy, *I'm* devout. *I* hate the idea of suing the Church. But we've all just trusted it to act in our best interests. If it's knowingly been placing wolves in our midst, then it needs to face the consequences."

Andy held out his palms and ducked his head. "I get it. I

suspect the board is going to want you to limit the resources you use. You'll have to do the brunt of the work yourself without much help from associates. Have you ever managed a lawsuit from the plaintiff's side before? I know we haven't done one together."

Veronica shook her head.

"Well, I met a guy at last year's ABA conference who brings these kinds of cases against the Church. I've probably still got his card back at the office. I'll find it and get it to you. Maybe he can give you some advice."

"Thanks, Andy."

"Good luck, kid."

ANDY'S CONTACT, Lane Gorman, turned out to be an invaluable resource.

"I'm not gonna sugarcoat it for you, Veronica. You're used to working for multinational oil companies, insurers, and global retailers. I went up against those kinds of behemoths earlier in my career and they got nothin' on the Church. You probably think the Church will approach a grieving mother with some sense of moral or spiritual justice or reconciliation. The sooner you get that idea out of your head, the better. The Church will hire lawyers who'll go to the mattresses as hard as you would for your best insurance client."

Veronica swallowed hard.

"You there?" Lane barked into the phone.

"Yes, sorry. I understand."

"Good. The Church always digs in on two tactics: statutes of limitation and discovery hardball. They'll have a statute of limi-tation motion filed so fast it will make your head spin. If they win there, you won't even get the pleasure of having them fight you tooth and nail before they'll turn over any documents in discovery. I've done some work in Colberg and, in all honesty, you're gonna have an uphill battle. The Church wins on statute of limitation grounds nine times out of ten. I'll send you the briefing we've done there and you're welcome to use anything that's helpful to you."

"Thank you. That's very kind."

"Don't mention it. We've gotten to the discovery phase a few times in Colberg. We have everything we've received from the Church in a database to paint a picture of the Church's practices throughout the country. I'll look and see if we have anything on your priest."

"Thanks again, Lane."

"Don't thank me until you get somewhere with it. Give 'em hell."

CHAPTER SEVEN

Veronica hung up the phone in her office and looked past the fluorescent light reflected in the large windows to the dark city beyond. Her fingers roamed the space of her bare leg, searching for just the right bump to pick and worry over.

Tom had been frustrated when she called to tell him she would be staying late at the office yet again to work on her response to the Church's statute of limitation motion. If the Church won, her fight would be over before it had begun. The Church decision-makers—who had known what Paul Peña was capable of, who had known what he had been accused of doing to adolescents in previous assignments, but who had chosen to transfer him to Sacred Heart anyway—would get off scot-free. All because of the idea that, if injured parties didn't act quickly enough to hold the responsible parties accountable, courts shouldn't waste their time with their claims.

Veronica only knew about the issues at Peña's previous assignments because, true to his word, Lane Gorman had searched his databases and found relevant files in the documents the Church had been forced to turn over in other lawsuits. Before sending the files to her, Lane issued a stern warning.

"Listen, Veronica, when the courts forced the Church to give us these documents, they put strict limits on what we could do with them. You *cannot* use them, or even refer to them, in court or in anything you file."

"I get it, Lane."

"I need to know I've been clear. You'd get me into hot water if you tried to use them. I'm only sending them to you so that you'll know what exists and what you need to fight for when you request documents from the Church. I'm trusting you, Veronica. Don't fuck me over."

As Lane had predicted, the Church's immediate response to Veronica's lawsuit was a request for the court to find that even if everything Veronica accused the Church of was true, she had simply filed the lawsuit too late to be allowed to proceed. The same day, Veronica received a call from the lawyer representing the Church. With smug confidence, he offered to settle for a pittance to avoid racking up attorneys' fees for a case that, he reasoned, Veronica must know had no chance of success. Veronica kept her cool long enough to politely decline.

He wasn't wrong about her chances, but Veronica had done her best with the state's unfavorable law. In a flash of creative brilliance, she had settled on a strategy that might just have a shot. Right before she called Tom to tell him she wouldn't be home for dinner, she had felt the triumph of finding just the right support for her theory. She shook off her exhaustion and set to work, weaving the authorities into her response in a way that would make the Church's smug lawyer choke on them.

CHAPTER EIGHT

"All rise for the Honorable Jeanine Stangl."

Veronica pushed back her chair and stood, staring straight ahead at the small, black-robed woman who emerged from the wood-paneled door behind the raised judicial bench, holding a coffee cup and a legal pad. She settled herself into the large leather chair and looked over her glasses at the courtroom.

"Be seated. We're here today in the matter of Matthews versus the Catholic Dioceses of Colberg and Granton. Counsel, please state your appearances for the record."

Veronica stood. "Veronica Matthews on behalf of the Matthews family as plaintiffs, Your Honor." She sat.

The lawyers on the other side of the aisle stood, while the cassock-clad representatives of the diocesan defendants remained seated. The voice of the lawyer with more silver in his hair boomed. "Grayson Greene and William Gordon for the defendants, Your Honor."

The judge looked at the mass of papers before her. The court reporter's fingers hovered at the ready over her stenography keyboard. "Before the court is defendants' motion. I've read all the briefing. Mr. Greene, it's your motion, so you may begin."

"Thank you, Your Honor. We won't bore the Court by regurgitating what's in the papers we filed. For the most part we'll stand on our briefing. Of course, the Matthews family has suffered a terrible, unimaginable loss. I know every person in this courtroom empathizes with Mrs. Matthews and her family . . ."

Shove your fake empathy up your arrogant ass, thought Veronica. She looked straight ahead.

"But even if the plaintiffs could somehow prove that my clients were responsible for the injuries sustained by Sean Matthews, or for his death—which, let's be clear, my clients do not concede and plaintiffs can offer no evidence to support— even then the law would require this court to rule in favor of my clients."

Greene moved to an easel that faced the judge and removed the covering that concealed the poster-sized diagram there.

"The plaintiffs allege that my clients negligently and recklessly supervised Paul Peña, and as a result of this allegedly unlawful supervision, Paul Peña sexually assaulted Sean Matthews. As the court is aware, plaintiffs had two years to file a lawsuit from the date the injury was discovered. If we go with the latest possible date of discovery—the date Sean Matthews's assault was reported to the police—plaintiffs' deadline expired here." Greene used a laser to point to a date on his timeline.

"Sean Matthews took his own life almost a year after that deadline, and the plaintiffs did not file their lawsuit until a year after that." Greene pointed to the respective dates on the timeline.

"As the court can plainly see, the plaintiffs simply filed their lawsuit too late, and the law requires you to rule in the defendants' favor."

Greene sat and the judge, satisfied that he had completed his remarks, inclined her head toward Veronica. Veronica wiped her palms on her pant legs and her voice, when it issued, betrayed none of her anxiety.

"Thank you, Your Honor. I'll also refer you primarily to our briefing with just a few comments. Mr. Greene is correct in two respects: Yes, the filing deadline is two years, and yes, it begins to run as of the date the victim discovers the injury. What Mr. Greene failed to discuss is that many courts have found 'discovery of the injury' to be different in cases like this. Courts around the country have recognized that, in cases of rape and sexual assault, children and adolescents cannot be held to the same standard as adults when it comes to discovery of the injury. They can't be said to have discovered their injury, for purposes of filing deadlines, until they have sufficient maturity to fully appreciate the effects of that injury."

Veronica took a breath. *Slow down,* she cautioned herself. *You're rushing.*

"For this reason, in many states, the two-year clock Mr. Greene pointed to with such impressive effect on his slick visual aid doesn't even begin to run until the victim is at least 18. In some states, the clock doesn't start until age 21. If Sean Matthews had lived," Veronica could not keep the quaver out of her voice, "he would still be several months away from his eighteenth birthday. Because he could have brought a claim in his own right, at the very least, his estate should be permitted to proceed with its claims against the defendants. We respectfully request that the court deny defendants' motion."

Veronica had begun to ease her way back into her seat when the judge asked, "Mrs. Matthews, how do you respond to the case cited in the defendants' reply to your argument? Doesn't it indicate that our state supreme court has already rejected the very argument you're making here?"

"Your Honor, it's important to understand how the facts of that case are different from the circumstances here. In that case, the plaintiff suffered a purely physical injury as a passenger in a car accident that happened when he was 14. He didn't file suit until after he had turned 19, and our supreme court held it was not proper to toll the discovery rule until he turned 18. That decision should not be binding here. The cases from other states referenced in the papers we filed explain how the psychological injuries sustained by sexually assaulted children are different from purely physical injuries, and why the victims cannot reasonably appreciate, or 'discover' for our purposes, the extent and impact of the injury until reaching the age of majority."

The judge wore a doubtful expression. "Well, counsel, our supreme court wrote: 'We reject the rule adopted by other jurisdictions that an adolescent plaintiff may be deemed not to discover his injury until reaching the age of majority.' That language doesn't really support the distinction you're asking me to make, does it?"

"Again, Your Honor, with respect, I'd urge you to revisit the cases outlining why these types of psychological injuries are different."

The judge pursed her lips and gathered the papers scattered in front of her into a stack, which she tapped on the table to smooth the edges. Then she leaned forward, resting her forearms on the bench in front of her as she addressed Veronica. "Mrs. Matthews, like counsel for the defendants, the court sympathizes with your . . . situation."

I don't want your sympathy, thought Veronica. *I want you to do the right thing!* Veronica rarely cried, but nothing stimulated her tear ducts like righteous anger that otherwise lacked an outlet. She felt her eyes prickle. *Not now!* she pleaded.

"As you know," continued the judge, "I am charged with upholding the law as it is, not as I might wish it to be. To opposing counsel's point, the allegations in your complaint are light on specifics and long on supposition. It's not clear to me why the Granton diocese has been named as a party to this lawsuit. Even if it were permitted to proceed, it seems unlikely that you would be able to make a case against the Church."

Veronica did not pause to check in with her internal cost-benefit calculator before jumping up. She was on the verge of losing, and if there was ever a time for a Hail Mary, this was it. "I can explain why we named Granton, Your Honor." The judge's eyes bulged at the interruption. With fumbling fingers, Veronica found the file she needed. "May I approach?"

"Go ahead," said the judge with poorly concealed irritation.

"The bishop of the Granton diocese, that man right there," Veronica pointed to one of the two cassocked men at the defendants' table, "knew of at least seven complaints against Paul Peña." Frenetically, Veronica laid out seven pieces of paper on the table before the judge. "He did nothing! All he did was transfer Peña to the Colberg diocese. Then, when Peña got to Colberg, . . ." Veronica rifled through her file for the evidence to support her next statement.

"Your Honor!" exploded Greene. Having finally recovered his ability to speak through his apoplexy, the empurpled lawyer shot up and shouted over Veronica. "This is completely improper! There has been no discovery of any kind in this case. May I see the documents she's showing you?"

The judge nodded. "Approach," she directed.

After a brief examination, Greene pointed to the numbers stamped at the bottoms of the pages. "Your Honor, these documents appear to have been produced in a number of different lawsuits. They certainly were not produced in this one. It is absolutely unacceptable for Mrs. Matthews even to have seen them, let alone try to use them here."

The judge fixed a stern glare on Veronica. "I have to agree, Mr. Greene. The court reporter will strike all portions of the record beginning from when Mrs. Matthews interrupted my ruling."

Gutted, Veronica walked slowly back to her seat.

"As I was saying," resumed the judge, "*regardless* of whether plaintiffs can prove their claims, we are not permitted to consider such proof. The law of this state is clear, and it does not permit the exception plaintiffs encourage us to adopt. Because plaintiffs' lawsuit was filed after the applicable deadline, we are obliged to grant defendants' motion."

The judge pushed her chair back so quickly that the bailiff scarcely had time to intone, "All rise" before she had disappeared through the door in the wood-paneled wall.

Spent, Veronica flopped back in her chair. She didn't stir until everyone at the defendants' table had packed their gear and left the courtroom.

As she prepared to leave, she saw Andy standing in the back of the gallery near the door. "Tough break, Ronnie," he said to comfort her, placing his hand on her shoulder. "You did the best you could with what you had to work with. What are you thinking about an appeal?"

"I'll lick my wounds, and then I'll probably file it."

"Oh, Ronnie. There's no way our state supremes are going to rule in your favor. Why throw good energy after bad?"

"It's my energy. I'll do what I want with it."

PART II

CHAPTER NINE

"Getting old is the worst. I used to think that, if money ever got *really* tight, I could put on a slutty skirt and go get some dates on The Point. You'd keep an eye on the kids, right?"

Tavis's wandering mind snapped back to the present and he covered his mouth and nose with his hand to keep coffee from shooting out.

"I mean, I guess it's still *possible*," she continued, smiling mischievously, leaning into her topic, "but at my age, I don't think this fat ass would make more money than, say, a part-time job shelving books at the library. Ah, there you are. Welcome back," she said as Tavis pushed air through his nose and shook his head in a half-laugh at her audacity. "I wondered what it would take to get your attention this time. I've already given you my dissertation on the Atlanta hip-hop scene, and I was about to move on to an article I just read about STDs in nursing homes. Old folks be gettin' freaky in their golden years! At least that's something to look forward to."

Gisela's twinkling eyes focused sharply as she observed her husband's attempt to reward her comedic efforts with a smile. It looked more like a grimace, with the expression of mirth moving no higher than the bottom of his cheekbones.

"Oh, *cariño*," said Gisela, moving around the breakfast table to massage the spot at the base of his neck that never failed to calm him. "Are you sure this work is right for you? Sure, it's important, but you're a mess."

Tavis sighed. "You know how I feel about this, Sela. I can't do much, but I can do this."

A news banner caught his attention and he peered at the nearly muted television playing on the kitchen counter. He picked up the remote and increased the volume to hear the local reporter standing in front of a nondescript house with peeling paint, brown grass, and drawn curtains.

"In breaking news, Eyewitness News 9 is here at the home where police received reports this morning of the sexual assault of a nine-month-old infant. According to sources within the police department, law enforcement was called after the child's mother discovered signs of trauma while changing the baby's diaper early this morning. Police have not made any arrests, but we're following this story and will keep you informed of further developments. Back to you, Lisa and Jim." The reporter's face caricatured an expression befitting the somber story she conveyed, but it was impossible to miss her poorly concealed glee at her assignment to such a sensational story.

"Fucking vultures," muttered Gisela as she took the remote from Tavis's hand and clicked off the television. "At least you won't be investigating that train wreck."

He pushed back his chair and crossed the sunlit kitchen, taking his breakfast plate to the dishwasher. "No," Tavis said, not even trying to hide his weariness, "*por lo menos* I don't have to do that."

CHAPTER TEN

In the wake of the Paul Peña trial, the Colberg diocese, like the rest of the Church in the fallout from the broader clergy abuse scandal, found itself walking a fine line between facilitating meaningful justice for victims and minimizing damage to the institution. The global Church did not decree canon laws or implement policies or procedures that weighed the balance in favor of justice—it didn't even work to even the scales.

Within the Colberg diocese, the bishop was quietly reassigned after it became common knowledge that he had been aware of allegations against Peña but had opted to minimize and conceal instead of holding Peña accountable. The new bishop, Eduardo Cólima, stepped in and addressed the issue head on. He committed publicly to formal internal investigations of every allegation of abuse, and to full cooperation and communication with law enforcement. Bishop Cólima needed a liaison who understood both the Church and law enforcement, who could be trusted to interact fairly and objectively with accusers, the accused, and anyone else who might have relevant information. The bishop's need and Tavis's own experience and calling seemed divinely aligned, and the bishop hired Tavis as one of his first official actions.

When parents or victims made complaints directly to law enforcement authorities, Tavis liaised with criminal investigators and with the applicable Church authorities to facilitate the criminal investigations and to conduct corresponding internal inquiries. When complaints were made exclusively within the Church, Tavis investigated before bringing, with Bishop Cólima's blessing, any substantiating evidence to law enforcement.

When Tavis first accepted Bishop Cólima's offer, he had felt competing loyalties: to the innocent victims, and to the priests he had been raised to believe were good and holy men, whose reputations shouldn't be ruined because of a few bad apples. Before digging into the work, Tavis had felt that his loyalties were pretty evenly balanced. He thought that the snowballing media coverage around the abuse scandal had, at first, served a useful purpose by exposing a sickness that thrived in darkness. But later, it seemed to Tavis that the media frenzy was feeding opportunists who saw the pendulum swinging toward believing accusers, even in the absence of evidence, and who jumped on the bandwagon to see whether they could cash in on a low-risk gamble.

Not long into his work, Tavis found himself needing to pray to maintain those competing loyalties so he could approach the job neutrally. It got much tougher to stay objective when, in case after case, the evidence corroborated victims' accusations. In a short amount of time, Tavis had learned to recognize two reliable patterns: if allegations against a particular clergyman received any level of media attention, the coming days often brought a number of calls to the diocesan center from unrelated individuals recounting uncannily similar details. If initial complaints were made directly to the diocesan center, without media involvement, investigations regularly yielded corroborating evidence and uncovered additional victims. Tavis soon discovered that, even if an accused priest had a clean record in the files maintained by the particular diocesan office in which he worked, when Tavis took Bishop Cólima's letter of introduction requesting accommodation to the diocesan office from where the accused priest had transferred, that office's file would often reflect that the transfer into the Colberg diocese had been motivated by the complaints of children or parents regarding sexually inappropriate behavior.

Seeing those priests' files and realizing, in case after case, that the priests' superiors in the Church had known about past complaints, and had just shifted "problem priests" to their next assignments without taking any steps to protect the flock in the new hunting grounds, wore Tavis's neutrality to the nub. Because many parents of abused children had complained only to the Church, and not to law enforcement, the Church's files were the only place to see the full story. The parents had trusted the Church to handle things, and the Church had "handled" things by applying band-aids to severed limbs.

ON THE DAY he first heard Frank Muncy's name, Tavis had been reporting to Bishop Cólima at the diocesan center for almost two years. Tavis liked to get to the office before most of the rest of the staff arrived. After filling his mug with the receptionist's inconsistent coffee—it alternated between lightly tinted water and a semi-solid sludge—he usually cleared his mind with a couple of games of computer Solitaire before diving into the day's tasks. He would get at least a solid hour of momentum under his belt before being distracted by the inevitable visitors who popped in on their way to or from the coffee pot.

These visits still surprised Tavis, especially because the office had been pretty standoffish when Bishop Cólima first installed him in the diocesan center. They thought Tavis was targeting priests they knew and admired, but most of the staff within the diocesan center eventually warmed to him and included him within the center's collegial culture. Tavis joked that he had won them over with his wit and sparkling personality, but the more likely explanation was that the remarkably observant bishop had noticed his exclusion and pushed the staff to extend a more welcoming hand. As with most of the bishop's actions, this effort was shrewdly calculated, not least because Tavis had to rely heavily on these people for the information and access required to conduct his investigations.

TAVIS'S INVESTIGATION into allegations against Father Francis Muncy began as so many others had: an outraged mother demanded that something be done about the pervert priest who had sexually assaulted her teenaged son.

During the intake interview with Dolores and her son, Dolores dominated the conversation to such an extent that Tavis had been forced to develop a strategy to enable the boy, Jeremy, to answer the questions posed instead of allowing his mother to answer. Jeremy explained that he had been volunteering at the diocesan food pantry, which Father Frank ran, and that although Jeremy's mother was supposed to pick him up, she had been "stranded." When using the word, Jeremy averted his eyes, suggesting that such mishaps happened fairly regularly, and that, resultingly, Jeremy often found himself stranded.

It had been dark and bitterly cold when the food pantry closed, and Dolores still had not arrived to drive Jeremy the five miles to their home, so Father Frank offered to give him a ride. On the way, Jeremy claimed, Father Frank stopped his small pickup near a city park.

"I don't know why he stopped the truck, but we were in a really dark place at the edge of the park and he sort of jumped across the seat and tried to kiss me," Jeremy blurted in a rush.

"Then he grabbed my crotch with one hand, opened his pants, and rubbed one out."

"I'm very sorry that happened to you, Jeremy. What did you do?" Tavis asked neutrally.

"I didn't know what to do. I was freaked out so I just closed my eyes, tried not to breathe, and hoped it would be over soon. He finished and I jumped out of the truck and ran home across the park."

WITHOUT DRAWING CONCLUSIONS, Tavis noted that, at parts of the story, Jeremy used language identical to the words his mother had spoken when she called the diocesan office to make the complaint. That in itself didn't mean much, but the series of events described by Jeremy and Dolores was also unusual in that, before the day in question, Jeremy had had no previous interaction with Father Frank. With adolescent victims, sexual predators tended to spend some time establishing a rapport with their targets as a means of making the victim's silence more likely. Also unusual was that, even according to Jeremy, it did not appear that Father Frank had manipulated a situation in order to be alone with the boy—he had simply reacted to Jeremy's need for a ride in dangerously cold weather. Upon completing the interview, Tavis assured Jeremy and his mother that their complaint had been heard, that he and Bishop Cólima took it seriously, and that the investigation would be rigorous and thorough.

CHAPTER ELEVEN

Before interviewing an accused priest, Tavis did as much background research as possible. As an agent of the Church itself, Tavis had access to records that the Church usually resisted providing in the context of civil or criminal legal proceedings. The guilty men often developed patterns of abuse so that, when historical allegations appeared in a given priest's file, there were usually striking similarities to the acts described in the present complaint. In such cases, verifying that the abuser had had access to the accuser during the timeframe in question went a long way toward satisfying Tavis that the evidence sufficiently corroborated the allegations to justify turning over the investigation to law enforcement.

From the outset, the allegations against Father Frank were different. Father Frank had lived and worked in the Colberg diocese for the past ten years, and the transfer into the diocese was the only transfer in his file. Father Frank had asked to move into the diocese to care for his sick mother, who had died within two years of his return.

Father Frank's file did not contain a single allegation of

improper behavior with children—or any other complaints for that matter. Most abusive priests tended to work in roles with close and regular proximity to children, but Father Frank's work provided very little opportunity for interaction with children. His primary responsibility was to administer the mental health clinic that served the diocese, and while he supervised therapists providing services to children, his own practice was limited to treating adults, with an emphasis on treating addiction. Father Frank's patients and their loved ones sang his praises from the rooftops. Apparently he had been an early critic of twelve-step programs in the face of mounting evidence about their low rates of long-term success. Instead he focused on approaches that acknowledged the complexity of addiction, that analyzed motivation and comorbid conditions, and that emphasized behavioral methods for managing urges.

Although the center served congregants from the diocese, it was part of a broader service initiative. As was often the case, the community had a greater need for mental health services than it had qualified professionals, so the center also served those unaffiliated with the Catholic Church. Many of Father Frank's clients came to him through referral from the criminal justice system. Father Frank was a priest, and he wore his clerical collar during sessions, but by all accounts, his patients appreciated that he did not impose dogma upon them. He never denied or hid his vocation, and he discussed the topic of religion if it was raised by a client, but he never introduced it. More than one of the clergymen and lay professionals Father Frank supervised told Tavis that Father Frank approached his work with the belief that "We can invest our work with Our Lord's compassion and grace without shoving our religion down our clients' throats."

The more Tavis interviewed those who knew and worked with Father Frank, the more farfetched the allegations against him seemed. Tavis was used to interviewing Catholics who spoke of priests with a respect and reverence that extended more to the office than to the man who held it. When these folks understood the context of Tavis's questions, they often became hostile to what they thought were efforts to ruin the reputation of the Church.

Again, it was different with Father Frank. Many of the people Tavis interviewed admired Father Frank in *spite* of his priestly vocation rather than because of it. With the secular media coverage of abusive priests and the Church's complicity, Father Frank had to work harder at building rapport with his clients. Like a used car salesman or a personal injury lawyer, Father Frank began each new client relationship with non-Catholics, and sometimes even with disenchanted Catholics, at a disadvantage, but his therapeutic gifts almost always overcame doubts. Even those who distrusted priests in general ended up liking and respecting him.

Many former patients of Father Frank were happy to meet with Tavis, and Father Frank's success stories were often so grateful for his impact on their lives that they had begun volunteering at the diocesan center. They were not shy about crediting Father Frank with their recoveries.

Father Frank was successful because he seemed to have an endless supply of the trait that most often causes burnout in mental health providers: empathy. Interview after interview built a picture of a man who never developed the thick skin that allows so many mental health professionals to maintain a separation between their patients' crises and their own lives. The outsized portion of empathy that initially motivates many mental health providers to pursue their work also makes new therapists agonize with their clients. Thoughts of their clients' struggles follow them home. Because it's impossible to live, long-term, in crisis mode, over time therapists' empathetic impulses evolve like the hands of a gym rat. The chafing of the empathic bar generates painful blisters and tears, which heal and tear and heal again with ever-thicker layers of skin until, eventually, strong calluses protect the hands from all but the most balls-out workouts.

The hardened empathy of mental health providers usually makes them more objective and perceptive, and it often helps them deliver difficult but important advice. The downside of calloused empathy, though, especially for inexperienced mental health clients, is that their provider does not fully appreciate the panic and crisis that led to finally showing up for help.

Father Frank's empathy never calloused. He lived in the blisters-and-tears state. He appreciated that almost every new patient was in a state of crisis: because their simmering anxieties had finally boiled over into full-blown panic; because their depression had reached such a deep valley that they could not seek the help they knew they needed, and so a loved one made an appointment for them; or because their substance abuse had reached a level that crossed paths with the criminal justice system.

In this kind of crisis, rigidly ending the first session at the scheduled sixty or ninety minutes, and hustling the new client out the door to greet the next patient on time, made many clients doubt whether the therapist truly appreciated their feelings of crisis, panic, and helplessness. Father Frank began demonstrating his empathy to new clients in dire straits, which felt life-threatening to them, by scheduling intake appointments in the last time slot of his workday. Rather than forcing an end to the session at a pre-ordained time, Father Frank explained that, while their future work together would need to be on schedule, their goal for the first session was just to get through the crisis, even if it required more time than a regular session.

This helped build rapport, and Father Frank fed those first

fragile sparks with dry tinder: body language that showed he was intently listening; space for thoughtful silences; questions that got to the nub of his patients' anxiety, fear, and shame; and advice that helped his clients understand the freedom in expressing vulnerability. He helped them feel less alone by relating their experiences to the universality of human existence, and he left them with a pinprick of light at the end of the tunnel.

Father Frank's clients made sure Tavis knew that those intake sessions never solved any deeply rooted problems, but they established trust and motivation for the hard work to come. Many of them reported that, after those first sessions, they had their first night of deep, uninterrupted sleep in a long time. Father Frank's own restless nights following intakes were usually filled with concern for the suffering souls that were now his responsibility.

A MAN less humble than Father Frank could have allowed his clients' devotion to ripen into a cult of personality. To provide balance to his investigation, Tavis spent a great deal of time searching online reviews for former patients with less favorable opinions of Father Frank. He couldn't find any, which made him suspicious.

Armed with his research, Tavis approached his first interview with Father Frank warily—ready to resist the charm of the smoothie who had developed such a fan club. His precautions didn't do much good—Tavis couldn't help but like the unassuming, somewhat awkward man, who radiated compassion free of judgements.

When he learned about Jeremy's accusation, Father Frank again bucked the norm by seeming less defensive than puzzled. He confirmed that he had given the boy a ride home when the boy's mother had been unable to pick him up from the food pantry. His denied the claims of contact quietly but firmly. After appearing to play back his interaction with the young man on an internal projector, considering whether anything in the interaction could have motivated the allegations, Father Frank said, "I only touched him once, accidentally, when I reached to adjust the heating vents on the dash. He reached up at the same time to change the radio station. It had been on NPR and he said he wanted to listen to music. Our hands bumped and the touch lasted less than a second."

Rather than calling Jeremy a liar, Father Frank seemed bewildered and, surprisingly, he said he had admired what he had seen of the boy's character. Against his own best interest, Father Frank said Jeremy had seemed responsible and trustworthy. Frank appeared to be working at a tough puzzle he wanted to solve in order to satisfy his own curiosity, rather than because the allegation threatened his vocation and the course of the rest of his life.

Frank mused, "He has a good heart. That was obvious even if just because, unlike most young people we see at the food pantry, he volunteered to serve instead of being ordered to by a court. He took the work seriously. He treated our guests with dignity, and he looked for additional ways to help without damaging our guests' pride. He seemed to understand how ashamed people can feel when they admit that they need help."

Father Frank exhaled forcefully and looked directly at Tavis. "So what now?"

"Well, I continue my investigation, including following up with Jeremy. When I'm finished, I'll report to Bishop Cólima. If my investigation corroborates any of Jeremy's claims, I'll recommend referral to the police, and then it will be out of our hands in terms of any criminal charges. It's up to Bishop Cólima what happens between you and the Church."

Father Frank inclined his head slightly to indicate his understanding. "How often do you turn the investigations over to law enforcement?"

Tavis kept his gaze firm as he answered. "In the two years I've been doing this for the Church . . . in every case. It doesn't take much evidence to move things along to the next level."

Frank nodded his understanding. Tavis asked a few more questions, and then he left.

CHAPTER TWELVE

Tavis took some time after interviewing Father Frank to pore over his notes and analyze what he had learned. He consciously tried not to make value or credibility judgments during the interview process, but afterward he allowed himself to test what he really thought about the interview subjects and whether their responses were believable and consistent. Then Tavis decided which subjects would need follow-up interviews, and he planned out the specific questions that would fill in gaps or expose inconsistency.

The case of Jeremy and Father Frank was unusual, and Tavis really had to work to separate his role from the admiration he had begun to feel, strangely, for both Jeremy and Father Frank. Pretending he didn't have those feelings made him less effective, so he acknowledged them and then put them in a box. Tavis had admired other accused priests before discovering unquestionable proof of their vile cruelty.

The Church had a knack for churning out clergy whose flawless public piety masked festering private lives. Like Father Frank, many of the guilty priests once had a following of those whose lives had been changed for the better by the priests' good works. Like all men, accused priests are complex creatures whose worst traits and deeds only tell part of their stories. The nature of child sexual abuse makes most people's skin crawl. That's why it naturally becomes what defines the people, mostly men, who are accused of the crime. Anything else they may be, no matter how good or helpful, is swallowed up in the label of "pedophile."

While the most important victims of the abuse crisis were the children, the damage didn't stop there. If they accepted his guilt, a disgraced priest's one-time admirers struggled with their confusion, with the sense that they were not the judges of character they had believed themselves to be—that their ability to sense danger and corruption had been flawed. They struggled with how to view the sacraments that had been administered by the fallen clergyman, and with whether to continue following any meaningful spiritual guidance the priest had provided. Other times, no amount of evidence could convince a priest's faithful followers that there was really a fire causing even the thickest, blackest cloud of choking smoke. These congregants simply could not square that the capacity for good and holy works existed within the same person who would sexually abuse a child. They had seen the good and holy with their own eyes, but they had not personally witnessed the abuse—and for them it was as easy as that. When the faithful defended guilty clergy, victims were further alienated from a community that could and should have offered comfort and compassion.

Bishop Cólima's directives were clear, and very little corroborating evidence justified a referral to law enforcement. It was enough that Father Frank confirmed that he had been alone with Jeremy in the car. It wasn't Tavis's job to judge credibility. His task was to gather any available relevant facts and pass the case along. Even so, to finish gathering available relevant facts, Tavis needed another meeting with Jeremy.

Tavis had suspicions about Dolores's influence over Jeremy's accusations because of the identical language the two had used. Tavis would have liked to conduct his follow-up interview with the boy without his mother present, but that was both against protocol and unwise, and anything Tavis learned would be tainted by the stain of potential coercion. So Tavis decided to visit the home without notice, which should reduce the possibility of Dolores coaching Jeremy. Tavis considered questions that would require Jeremy to give answers outside of anything his mother might have made him rehearse.

BECAUSE OF THE possibility that Tavis could be called upon to investigate any priest in the diocese—even, theoretically, Bishop Cólima himself—he couldn't turn to any of the priests in the diocese for spiritual advice or confession. Instead, about once a month Tavis made an hour-long drive to visit Father Stephen, a cloistered monk in a Trappist community outside of the diocesan hierarchy. The visits doubled as therapy. Father Stephen listened patiently while Tavis, without sharing identifying information, described the toll of the work; the gradual decline of his faith in the institution he had loved his whole life and that, despite all he knew, he continued to love; and his increasing difficulty trusting anyone wearing a clerical collar. Tavis struggled with this last bit, both because he knew the dangers of painting with a broad brush, and because his continued ability to do his job well depended on avoiding bias and on approaching each investigation with fresh objectivity.

Father Stephen was a helpful and sympathetic ear. He commiserated with Tavis's sympathy for the vulnerable children and adults who had suffered at the hands of trusted priests, and he expressed his own disappointment in the way Church leadership had compounded the injury. He exposed his own disappointment, shared by many of his clerical brothers, that his life of devoted service to God and to the Body of Christ had been reduced to a vocation viewed with suspicion and derision.

Tavis's visits to Father Stephen refreshed and renewed him because, after listening to and validating Tavis's despair, Father Stephen drew from a deep well of hope within himself. As Father Stephen prayed with Tavis, he thanked God for Tavis's unique skills and temperament, and for the vast majority of priests who continued to serve God faithfully in the face of broad suspicion and in accordance with their calling. Most importantly, Father Stephen's voice hummed with sincerity as he thanked God for his ability to use *all* things, even the suffering of the current crisis, for his good purposes. He asked God to fortify Tavis for his work, and to encourage Tavis with the awareness that his efforts accomplished God's purposes. Monthly meetings with Father Stephen were not a panacea, but they were the most effective method of refueling Tavis's depleted reserves of hope and purpose.

Tavis drove home after one visit as he neared the end of his investigation of the allegations against Father Frank. He thought about what he had to do before finishing his report for Bishop Cólima. He had come to believe that this was one of the super rare cases in which the allegations were completely fabricated. There were none of the hallmarks or patterns that had become familiar when a young person's claims were substantiated.

Even though it would mean a good man's name had been dragged through the mud, Tavis's mood was lighter than usual at the end of an investigation. Given the choice between potentially injured parties where child sexual abuse was alleged, Tavis would take a self-interested parent coaching a child to tell lies every time. Better that than a trusted adult in a position of influence using and damaging a child's innocence.

· · ·

As Tavis put the finishing touches on his interview strategy in the home office that evening, Gisela came in with two cups of hot tea and a plate of warm cookies. She set one cup in front of Tavis and then curled herself into one of the two comfortable armchairs in the room's reading nook.

"What a day!" Gisela sighed. "How was yours?"

"Weird."

In another marriage, such a non-response might have been interpreted as contempt or a rebuff to her overture of connection. Gisela knew, though, that Tavis drew clear lines around conversations that potentially touched on the details of his work. Gisela respected the boundary, never asking questions that would force him to choose between their deep intimacy and his professional ethics. As usual, she deftly maneuvered the conversation into waters that would not require a guarded response.

"Ceely told me today *que tenemos un,*" Gisela hunched her shoulders and threw up her hands to make air quotes, "'bourgeois lifestyle,' and, basically, world hunger, water insecurity, and poverty are our fault. I told her she can do her part by giving up her phone, her computer, driving the car, and the allowance she uses to buy herself clothes and lattes. She didn't seem to think that would make much of a dent."

Tavis chuckled and shook his head as he and his best friend basked in the shared glow of exasperation and admiration for their fierce girl's immature idealism. Neither doubted that their daughter Cecilia would improve many lives as she became more practical about how she channeled her innate compassion for the world's underdogs.

Tavis closed his laptop, collected his tea, and eased into the chair next to Gisela. "She's a pain in the ass, but she's a good girl. I'm still terrified all the time, though, Sela. I've seen too many good girls and boys try the things kids are supposed to try, but it turns into more than an experiment and they get stuck. A lot of times they get stuck because they're looking for an escape from thinking about how someone they trusted, someone older, hurt them in a way they didn't understand. What if someone hurt our Ceely? Most of these parents have no idea how to help their kids. How could we survive that kind of hurt to our girl? How would we be able to keep from driving ourselves crazy obsessing over what we could have done? To protect her, we almost have to think like one of these sickos. Who can live that way?"

Tavis closed his eyes, removed his glasses, and pinched the bridge of his nose in what Gisela recognized as a signal that he had retightened the release valve for externalizing his anxiety, and the struggle to make sense of his work would rage on internally.

Gisela resumed her steps in their long marital dance, in which she alternatively gave him permission to rest and lay down his work, and then fortified his courage to continue the good fight. She closed the space between them and wordlessly took one of his large, cool hands in her small, warm ones, and brought it to her lips. As she lowered his hand back to his lap, she began stroking his forearm with the sweeping feather-light touches of her finger pads that never failed to soothe him.

Tavis's unanswerable questions continued to spool. "Does knowing the truth and punishing the ones who put their hands on kids do anything to change the problem in the Church? Or is it just something we're doing for now—while there's so much attention and so much anger—and then when people get tired of hearing about it, will the Church just go back to its old ways? Will it know more about how to keep things secret to protect its good name? The Church has learned how much this black eye has hurt its reputation, and its collection plate, so what will it do in the future to avoid getting popped?"

Gisela's many talents did not include soothsaying, so she remained silent while his despairing questions hung in the air between them. She continued stroking his arm with feather-light brushes and, eventually, in spite of his uncertainties, Tavis felt himself sinking into the comforting warmth and strength she radiated. When, eventually, his eyelids began to droop, Gisela gently guided him to his feet and led him to their bedroom.

CHAPTER THIRTEEN

Dolores Ray's lovely mouth formed an "O" of surprise when she opened the door to Tavis's sharp rap. Clearly, she hadn't expected to see the Church's investigator on her front step.

Tavis smiled and "assumed the sale" by moving toward the open door as if Dolores had already invited him inside. As expected, ingrained manners and muscle memory moved Dolores's body to the side even as her face expressed surprise.

"Well, Mr. Pereira, I wasn't expecting to see you until next week," she said with her slight drawl in what always seemed to be a put-on style of speaking, as if she had practiced the breathy southern belle routine to near perfection. Her slightly higher-than-normal tone was her voice's only hint that the unexpected visit had unsettled her.

"Yes. Sorry for dropping by without calling, Ms. Ray. I had a few follow-up questions, and I saw Jeremy get home as I parked, so I figured this might be a good time to talk."

"Oh, I wish we could, but Jeremy and I have to leave—I was just waiting for him to get home." Like all the best liars, Dolores offered few details.

"It'll just take a few minutes, I promise. Then you both can be on your way."

"Well," Dolores consulted her trendy wristwatch, "all right. If you promise it'll be quick. I'll get Jeremy."

Dolores soon returned with Jeremy, who gave Tavis a friendly nod as he eased onto the spot at the other end of the couch on which Tavis sat.

"Thanks for talking with me, Jeremy. I know you have somewhere to be, so this won't take long."

Jeremy shot a brief glance at his mother, then assumed a polite and receptive expression as he looked at Tavis.

"I'm trying to wrap up my report for the Bishop, and to tie up a few loose ends, so I was hoping we could go through what happened one more time. We didn't record your statement before, and it really helps to have a recording when we make a referral to the police." Tavis took his phone out of his pocket, showed Jeremy the voice recording app, and set it on the coffee table between them. "I know it's painful to go through it again, but hopefully recording our discussion will make it so that you don't have to tell your story as many times to the police. Is that all right?"

Jeremy nodded gamely. "Where would you like me to start?"

"How about when Father Frank offered you a ride home?"

"Okay." Jeremy tilted his chin and looked up at the ceiling. After a few seconds, he began speaking quickly, without pauses or hesitation. "I was waiting outside for Mom while Father Frank closed up the food pantry. As he was locking up, I was moving around a lot to try to stay warm. He saw me looking at my phone, and he asked me if I had a way to get home. I told him my mom was supposed to pick me up but I couldn't get ahold of her. He asked where I lived, and when I told him he said it was on his way home and asked if I wanted a ride. We got into his old pickup, and we had to let it warm up for a few minutes because it was so cold outside. Boring people were talking on the radio, so I asked if I could find some music. I reached up to move the knob, but he was still moving the heating vents, and our hands bumped. He acted weird about it.

"The truck finally got warm and we started driving. When we got to Bishop Santana Park, he pulled over and parked in a dark spot under a tree. I asked why we were stopping, but he didn't answer. He just kind of jumped at me and tried to kiss me. I pushed at him, and he stopped trying to kiss me, but he put his hand on my crotch and then opened his pants and rubbed one out. Afterward, when he was zipping up, I got out of the truck and ran across the park to get home. I heard him calling after me, but I didn't stop. I was so freaked out. When my mom got home, she said she was sorry she'd been stranded. I couldn't stop crying, and finally she made me tell her what had happened."

As Jeremy spoke, Tavis followed along in his notes from his earlier interview and underlined several phrases that were identical to what Jeremy had told him before, and to what Dolores had said during her first call.

"Thank you, Jeremy, for going through that with me again. I know it's hard. I just have a few other questions. Do you know whether Father Frank's pickup was a standard or an automatic?"

Jeremy's eyes flew to his mother. She said, to Tavis, "Jeremy's only fourteen, Mr. Pereira, and we haven't started working on driving. Jeremy, while he was driving, did Father Frank have to keep moving a stick between the two of you, or did he just move a lever one time before he started driving?"

Jeremy gave it some thought, and then he answered, "He moved a stick the whole time he was driving."

Tavis smiled to encourage him.

"When the police start investigating, one of the things they'll want to do is to look at video footage. They'll probably ask people in the neighborhood if they have security cameras that would have recorded that night. They'll definitely look at the footage of the video cameras the City installed a few years ago in public places, like Bishop Santana Park. Do you think you can help me narrow which footage they'll need to look at by showing me the tree where Father Frank parked that night?"

Jeremy examined his hands. A deep red color creeped upward under his skin beginning where the collar of his shirt met his throat.

"He was crying and in a panic that night!" interjected Dolores indignantly. "I don't think we can expect him to point out a particular tree in a street full of trees."

"It doesn't need to be exact—the general area should be enough." Tavis turned his attention back to Jeremy.

"Did you notice, Jeremy, or do you remember, whether Father Frank is right- or left-handed?"

Jeremy studiously avoided looking at his mother, and began a halting response, "I-I think . . . I don't really remember, but . . ."

Dolores's voice broke in with authority, "I remember what you told me, sweetheart, you said that—"

"Ms. Ray, thanks for your help, but I really need Jeremy to answer these questions."

Dolores turned her head, but not before Tavis caught the venom in her eyes.

"Go ahead, Jeremy," Tavis encouraged gently.

Jeremy craned his head back and contemplated the ceiling, as if it held the answer.

Finally, with a slight shrug, he looked directly at Tavis. "He's left-handed," answered Jeremy certainly and correctly.

"But the reason I know that isn't because it would make more sense for him to have been left-handed to touch himself while he grabbed me across the truck with his right hand. I remember it from earlier that day, at the food pantry, when Father Frank was talking with an old woman who had teased him about being 'sinister.' Father Frank laughed, but I didn't understand the joke, so Father Frank told me that the word 'sinister' comes from the Latin for 'left,' and that there used to be a lot of superstitions about left-handed people. It was interesting." Jeremy turned his body to face his mother. With the steady exhale of a sniper, Jeremy released a stream of words. "He was actually really, really nice. I'd never met a priest, and he wasn't what I expected. He wore normal clothes, he let me pick the music for the drive home, and he didn't try to talk to me about church, or God, or anything like that. He was just a regular guy. A nice, regular guy. He told me I should take home a bunch of good food that they were going to have to throw away because nobody took it that day." With the shape-shifting mystery of early adolescence, Jeremy's face at once lost the extruding angularity of his burgeoning maturity, and a fat tear streaked down the soft cheek that suddenly seemed to belong to a much younger child.

Dolores scoffed prettily. "We didn't need food from a food pant—"

"Just *stop*, Mom."

The authority in her son's voice silenced Dolores.

"If the police find videos, they're going to see that I didn't run home across the park. He dropped me off in the driveway. He didn't touch me." Jeremy wiped the corners of his mouth with the pads of his thumb and ring finger. "I just said that because . . . because . . . we, I-I thought that all we hear in the news is that so many priests are lechy creeps, and maybe the Church would give us some money if a priest had done to me what they've done to all those other kids."

"Well, *Jeremy*! You told *me* . . ." Dolores's hand shot to her throat in search of absent pearls, a flawless southern belle as performed by a gifted actor. Jeremy silenced her with a look. The hardest part behind him, Jeremy now stared in a daze at the ground. "I'm really sorry," he mumbled miserably. "Please tell Father Frank I'm sorry."

CHAPTER FOURTEEN

W hen Father Frank opened the door to his office, his eyes were red-rimmed and bleary, but when he saw Tavis, he gave a warm smile and opened the door wider.

"Come in, come in, Tavis," he said, as he removed books from the chair nearest the door and gestured that Tavis should take a seat. "It's so nice to see you."

"I gotta say, Father, I don't usually hear that from someone in your position."

"Of course, but I know how important your work is and I admire your professionalism. How can I help you? I'm sorry I don't have anything to offer you to drink, but I had a long, rough night and I'm running behind today." Father Frank leaned forward in his chair, placing his elbows on his desk and resting his chin on his steepled hands in a posture of intent listening.

"Good news, Father. After a thorough investigation, there's no evidence to substantiate Jeremy's claims. Actually, the evidence shows the opposite. It appears that his mother had researched the Church's settlements with victims of abuse, and then she coached Jeremy to make allegations." Tavis briefly filled in Father Frank on the investigation.

"So what happens now?" asked Father Frank.

"Bishop Cólima has reviewed the notes from my interviews with Dolores and Jeremy, and you should expect there will be no further action against you after our presentation of evidence to law enforcement."

"And Jeremy and Dolores?"

"Well, that depends. The police can probably make a case for extortion. Bishop Cólima is willing to pursue this on behalf of the Church if you feel strongly about it. Another route he mentioned is for the Church to offer them pastoral care and counseling . . . from someone other than you, of course . . . although they're not Catholic so it's not clear they'd be willing."

"I'm not interested in being punitive," Father Frank said, "and I won't be responsible for seeking their prosecution. It's funny . . . I had the impression that young man was interested in the Church, and he should have the opportunity to see how it shows God's love and forgiveness."

Father Frank removed his glasses and rubbed his eyes. When he returned his arms to the desk, he exuded defeat.

"I don't get to deliver this type of good news very often, Father, but when I have it's usually been met with a little more enthusiasm," Tavis chided with a smile.

Father Frank raised his eyebrows and returned the smile half-heartedly. "I'm sure it is, Tavis. Thank you for your good work, and of course I'm pleased. Forgive my subdued response. As I mentioned, I had a tough night. I found out last night that a young woman with whom I've been working took her own life, and I'm finding it difficult to be enthusiastic today . . . even with your excellent news."

"Of course, Father," Tavis said, shaking his head. At a loss for words that might comfort him, Tavis shared Father Frank's suffering by sitting with him in silence.

After a moment, Tavis made his excuses and prepared to leave. As he rose from his chair, Father Frank, with his head bowed and his forehead resting on his steepled hands, spoke so quietly that Tavis almost did not hear him. "They're not wrong, you know."

"Excuse me, Father?"

"Jeremy and his mother. They must have somehow recognized what I am."

"I don't understand what you're saying," Tavis said, quickly resuming his seat with his heart pounding. "Are you saying that there's some truth to Jeremy's claims after all?"

"No . . . No. I never touched that boy. It wouldn't even have occurred to me."

As Father Frank slightly raised his bowed head, his bloodshot, anguished eyes peered up from under his brow and directly into Tavis's eyes, saying, "He's too old."

CHAPTER FIFTEEN

T avis remained glued to his chair as Father Frank began to unburden himself.

"What I am can't be explained by a bad childhood. My parents kept me safe and happy. Nothing bad happened to me, and I never even broke any bones. Sure, I had the usual cuts, scrapes, and splinters—all the result of playing in a protected neighborhood full of children roughly my age. I remember very clearly the only event that gave anyone even a moment of genuine panic about my safety.

"When I was seven, and playing near the bleachers at my older sister's softball game, a high foul ball hit me right in the head. I remember seeing my mother spring up from her seat in the bleachers in an attempt to reach me in the milliseconds before the ball struck. Because I had no idea the ball was coming toward me, I just thought her exaggerated expression was pretty funny. And then I was unconscious. A visit to the emergency room revealed a minor concussion, and my life soon returned to normal."

As if Tavis were his confessor, Father Frank continued to

describe his childhood. Although he couldn't have put his finger on it at the time, Father Frank later realized that his deep sense of security in childhood resulted from the careful structure his parents cultivated. It would have been easy enough to be carried along by the tide of seasons, holidays, school schedules, and activities. But Frankie's parents delighted in the flow of the seasons, in the art of balancing their busy professional lives with meaningful participation in the lives of their children and their community, and in observing traditions and milestones with creativity and enthusiasm.

From Frankie's perspective, this was simply how to live life. He began to realize it might not be as effortless as his parents made it appear when he overheard a conversation between his mother, Scarlett, and her friend one summer evening. "Seriously, Scar, how do you do it? I don't have a career, I can barely cook a grilled cheese, and it's all I can do to make sure my kids and their clothes aren't obviously dirty when they leave the house. How do you work full-time, raise kind, smart children, host most of our neighborhood functions, run the PTA, and still have energy to make every holiday an event? I feel like I barely have time to finish preparing for one holiday, which usually just involves making a dish to bring to your house, and the next thing that requires something of me is already upon me—and it all just comes faster every year."

Scarlett just waved her hand, deflecting the praise, as she leaned in to soothe her friend. "Oh, stop it, Kay. It's just a matter of how we're built to recharge. You need time alone with your thoughts to feel like yourself, so doing these kinds of activities and being 'on' around other people is stretching for you. But rather than using up my energy, planning and hosting events is how I recharge."

Frankie's well-educated parents were never wealthy, but they used their limited resources creatively to meet their family's needs and to project a carefree and unique style. As a small child, Frankie recalled observing his mother, looking particularly lovely before Sunday Mass, coloring a bleached spot on her black blouse with a permanent marker. When they were small, Frankie and his two elder sisters dreaded his family's regular visits to Goodwill. While their parents patiently sifted through an overwhelming amount of clothing and household goods to find hidden treasures, Frankie and his sisters played in the racks of musty-smelling clothing and whined in an attempt to hurry their parents along. As they grew older, Frankie, Amelia, and Emmy adopted their parents' enthusiasm for treasure hunting and for finding unique, quality items that cost virtually nothing. They listened to their parents' advice about seeking well-made materials and easily mended flaws. They delighted in answering compliments about particular pieces with, "Can you believe it? Three dollars!"

The fruits of the Muncy frugality were consumed almost entirely by the costs of educating three children at Saint Peter's Academy, which was both academically prestigious and a source of religious comfort for Scarlett Muncy, who prioritized steeping her children in the Catholic faith that meant everything to her. The Jesuit faculty at Saint Peter's had high expectations of its students, and required both critical thinking and concrete actions toward social justice. Scarlett feared her children would have missed these character-shaping values if they had attended the perfectly adequate public schools in their suburban community.

By adolescence Frankie had become a devout, compassionate boy with precocious insight into the motivations of others. His ability to apply information gained in one context to other, seemingly dissimilar situations earned him the admiration of his teachers, and his humility and humor gained him the good opinion of his classmates. Although almost all of his schoolmates considered Frankie to be a friend, the circle of children Frankie himself considered to be friends was intimate. He bonded with his closest friend, Jackson, over their favorite subject—technology—with both boys scrimping and saving to buy the most advanced computers they could afford. Their limited resources also went to paying off the telephone bills they ran up by dialing in to the electronic bulletin board systems that were popular at the time with tech-heads. Frankie and Jackson spent nearly every cent they earned from their part-time jobs at an ice cream shop to pay for time on the networking precursor to the internet. The computerized bulletin boards were incredible new tools that enabled them to connect with many others who shared their interests, and to trade information about topics that fascinated them.

Frankie's future seemed to be a cloudless forecast of familial, professional, and financial success. The outside world couldn't see, though, the dark and deeply troubling storm cloud looming over Frankie. He never felt more uncomfortable than when his friends or family teased him about girls and dating. They assumed every boy his age would be eager to date one of the many pretty girls in his life. And Frankie's good looks and quiet confidence did provide him with opportunities to date, which eventually he grasped in an attempt to distract himself from a budding awareness of the true objects of his attraction.

"THE FACT that I was a sick freak didn't just dawn on me one day out of the blue. I came to understand it slowly, over a series of years," Father Frank continued in a rush—a speeding freight train that could not be stopped.

In elementary school, Frankie had enjoyed the common-place succession of short-lived "girlfriends" among his contemporaries. In kindergarten, Frankie formed a close friendship with Suzanne. The two referred to each other as boyfriend and girlfriend, and they were inseparable during meals and at naptime. While eating lunch, they modeled behaviors they had observed in their parents: they served food to each other, made sure the other had everything they needed for their meal, and they cleaned up together. While driving to Suzanne's sixth birthday party, Scarlett asked Frankie how he knew he wanted Suzanne to be his girlfriend. Frankie shrugged and responded, "We were on our cots for nap one day and I looked over at her. I just knew she is my favorite friend."

As childhood progressed, Frankie participated in the ritual of sending and receiving "Do you like me? Check yes or no" notes. Like most elementary-school romances, these declarations didn't have much practical effect. There were a few awkward attempts at swinging together at recess. There were occasional aggressive hand-holding sessions that served more as a means of cementing the intention to be "boyfriend and girl-friend" than as expressions of affection. The children were usually too embarrassed by the implications of their relationships to speak to each other, so eventually one would send a break-up note to the other, there would be no further discussion, and a few days or weeks later, the cycle would begin with someone else.

Frankie and his classmates continued this sequence well into sixth grade. Near the end of that year, it began to shift. Boys and girls began to hone flirtation skills, and those who advanced more quickly were able to maintain actual conversations with members of the opposite sex. "Relationships" that previously lasted, at most, a few uncommunicative weeks began to extend to months of backchannel expressions of interest, telephone calls, shared lunches, jealousies, and emotional, attention-seeking break-ups.

Along with these psychological evolutions, their physical development also began to accelerate. Frankie soon found himself surpassed in height by all but the smallest girls. The pubescent girls first thickened and then stretched until, near the end of seventh grade, most of Frankie's female schoolmates seemed to be made entirely of long legs and budding breasts. Toward the end of middle school, the boys had begun their own sprints toward physical maturity. They grew several inches, sprouted acne and hair in awkward places, and teased each other about the wildly fluctuating pitch and timbre of their voices.

As a delayed bloomer, Frankie was at first disappointed that his friends seemed to be leaving him behind. Later in his life, he understood that he was bothered more by the fear of missing a shared experience than by his own delayed physical maturity. The truth was that his own small, youthful stature was convenient for maintaining the comfortable relationship pattern of elementary and early middle school with the girls who were still attractive to him: the girls who, like Frankie, remained small and undeveloped. Because of his own diminutive height, it seemed natural that his romantic attentions should be directed toward the girls who remained smaller than he was. That he lost interest in young women who had begun to rocket past him in height seemed natural and consistent with a healthy masculine desire to be the larger partner in a couple.

Because Frankie entered high school without seeming to be in any danger of experiencing puberty, he had no reason to question his preference for the girls in his class who, like him, were the smallest and least developed. He did not reflect on his subconscious distaste for the signs of physical maturity that his friends and classmates displayed so proudly. Frankie enjoyed spending time with his male friends, but he was also subtly repulsed by their pungent odors and by how they seemed to take every opportunity to wear tank tops that showed off the hair sprouting from their armpits like troll dolls in headlocks. He learned to fake enthusiasm for the constant and graphic discussions of the breasts, legs, and butts of the girls. Frankie's "fake-it-'til-you-make-it" approach assumed that his interest in these areas would eventually grow.

"That's not how things happened, though." Father Frank took a brief pause, with an expression that made him seem as though he were again inhabiting the confusion he experienced as a teenager. "When I finally started growing and filling out during the second half of my freshman year, things just got so much more uncomfortable and confusing."

His rapid gains in height pleased Frankie, but he considered many of the other changes he experienced to make him much less attractive than he had been before. Every day he shaved the hairs that grew on his face because he thought they made him look dark and unfriendly. He found the coarse hair that grew under his arms, on his lower abdomen, and in his pubic area to be disgusting, and he was particularly alarmed by the way in which it trapped odors. He tried to fix the problem by shaving in those places but, after experiencing the discomfort of razor burn and in-grown hairs, he began a nightly ritual of plucking any new hairs as they pushed up through his skin. This process soon became too time-consuming, so eventually he just began keeping the pesky hairs closely clipped. Frankie was also displeased by the way his growth hollowed his cheeks and sharpened his features. The girls at school seemed to appreciate the changes—many of them flirted with him—which made Frankie so uncomfortable that his evasions were interpreted as arrogance. In addition to the unwanted attention from his female schoolmates, grown women also paid attention to Frankie. He soon learned to ignore their sidelong glances. The attention confused Frankie, who did not see the attraction of his new angularity. Frankie himself hated the loss of his soft, clear skin and his rounded, full-cheeked good looks.

.   .   .

EVEN AFTER HIS OWN METAMORPHOSIS, he still couldn't match his friends' enthusiasm for their long-legged, high-breasted female counterparts. Not until the latest bloomers of his class had shed the soft roundness of childhood did the concerns lying under the surface begin to invade his consciousness. It wasn't that he lacked a sexual drive. He experienced physical lust and, like many of his friends, Frankie had begun to develop an interest in sexual behavior late in elementary school.

"The difference was," Father Frank explained, "that the objects of my friends' sexual interests evolved in lock-step as they and the rest of our classmates developed. My interests didn't change. They stayed the same. I never lost my attraction to smooth, soft skin, rounded faces, and bodies covered with peach fuzz rather than smelly, coarse hair."

Frankie first became consciously aware of his fixed attraction to children when, at 16, a neighbor asked him to babysit for her 9-year-old daughter. Frankie enjoyed playing with the child, and he was amused by her blatant attempts to manipulate him into allowing activities that her mother had explicitly forbidden.

At home in bed that night, Frankie found himself thinking about her sweet face and lively eyes. He was troubled. He had heard rumors of men with a creepy interest in children, and he remembered his friends mocking such "perverts" and other deviants. Frankie knew it was wrong, but he also couldn't stop thinking about his neighbor. When he was around other children, at church, or at his job, he found his attention fixed on them, too. The gender of the child was less important than the other traits that spoke to him: small stature, rounded features, hairlessness, and the uninhibited expressiveness that lacked the guardedness developed during adolescence.

In addition to consciously identifying his desire, and acknowledging that it was troubling and wrong, Frankie knew, instinctively, that it was not a problem that he could talk to anyone about. Ordinarily, when presented with an issue he could not resolve through his own efforts, Frankie would seek guidance from his sisters, his parents, or even the parish priest, Father James. Without having concrete evidence that any other person shared his strange attraction, Frankie's sense of self-preservation warned him that no confidante could possibly understand or sympathize with his plight, and that he would destroy himself by asking anyone for help.

Meanwhile, Beth's mother asked him to babysit more and more frequently because, she said, Frankie actually played with her daughter rather than relying on the TV. Babysitting was exquisite torture. While he enjoyed playing with Beth, and he often found himself gazing at her, he scrupulously avoided touching her unless absolutely necessary. When Beth, in her childish affection, launched herself at Frankie and hugged him, he escaped from the embraces as gently and quickly as possible.

Frankie tried to avoid his growing, unwanted obsession by exploring the expanding electronic networking world. It thrilled him to find a community that shared his passion for technology and all its possibilities. Being forward-thinking, Mr. and Mrs. Muncy encouraged his interest because they understood that, through his "hobby," their son was teaching himself skills that could serve him very well in an increasingly technological world.

"It was a really exciting time," Father Frank told Tavis, his eyes shining as he relived the memories. "Hackers weren't the criminals we think of today. We were puzzle solvers. We loved the idea of figuring out how to get useful information and then sharing it to make the world more accessible." Father Frank went on to explain how clever technology buffs had evolved from phone phreaking in the 1970s and 80s to trading harmless but difficult-to-find data in the 1980s and early 90s. Members of the growing virtual communities took documents and other information from their offline lives to upload and share with other members. Membership in these communities, and access to the information they held, was limited. A person couldn't join a network without knowing an existing member and having useful information to share.

In the early days, most of the information shared was only exciting because obtaining it required problem solving. As the electronic bulletin board communities expanded and diversified, some groups focused on pornography, and even these groups were often divided into specific fantasies and fetishes.

Frankie first encountered this facet of the virtual society after his hacking chops had earned a degree of respect that made his online handle sufficiently recognizable that he no longer needed to have a personal relationship with an existing member if he wanted to join a specific group. As a goof, Frankie and Jackson accessed some of the images shared in bulletin boards that traded in pornography. They didn't discuss their true reactions to the photographs—they just joked about the ridiculous expressions of the people pictured.

But when he was alone, Frankie found himself drawn back to the pornography boards. He wasn't aroused by what he saw, but he was interested in the images that were more amateurish and raw, that captured the participants in unguarded moments.

"I WAS ALMOST seventeen when I stumbled on the 'RealJailBait' folder on one of the porn boards. The children in the pictures were probably between six and ten. Although the folder was in a board that focused on porn and fetish, the images in the folder were not at all sexual. They were just snapshots of young boys and girls smiling, laughing, and playing in ordinary clothing.

"Young people today see graphic porn at earlier and earlier ages. Back then, though, it wasn't nearly as accessible, and I had seen much more than most people my age because of my digital presence. Even with all I had seen, the pictures of those kids, which didn't have anything to do with sex, were more exciting to me than explicit pornography."

Father Frank paused, and regarded the wall above Tavis, avoiding his face, gathering the strength to continue. Years of experience had taught Tavis to remain silent and mask his disgust with a sympathetic expression to encourage a perp to keep talking.

"For me, the best part was being able feast my eyes without bringing attention to myself. I couldn't stay away from it, and I felt a rush whenever new images were added."

FRANKIE HAD BEEN VISITING the folder for a few weeks when he received a message from the forum's administrator: "FraMu, I see you've been spending some time with RealJailBait." Frankie flushed with panic and shame. He knew administrators could see the content visitors accessed, but it was the first time his secret interest had been acknowledged by someone other than himself. Frankie continued reading. "I have some new photos I think you'll find interesting. I'm sharing with only a few like-minded friends with the understanding that you'll return the favor if something similar comes your way." Frankie closed the message and shut down his computer without responding, his brain sounding alarm bells.

Frankie's struggle with his better judgment lasted two full days until his curiosity finally prevailed. He responded simply, "I'm in." Later that evening, the administrator sent Frankie a new dial-in number and password, which opened a folder containing a series of image files.

After waiting what seemed forever for the first image to download, he was dumbstruck by the likeness of an angelic little girl, about six years old. Her blonde hair was so fine that the soft, loose ringlets at the uppermost layers seemed to reach toward the heavens in a halo-like effect. She wore a white nightgown that accentuated the overall impression of sweet inno-cence. Most breathtaking, though, was the stunning child's expression. She looked into the camera with such love and trust. Every photograph that followed was worth waiting for the download, and Frankie studied each image as it became accessi-ble. The series depicted the girl variously holding a portion of each side of the hem of her nightgown in her two hands, her arms straight down at her sides, and then she twirled and curt-seyed, and generally acted silly. Her expressions ranged from tight lips barely containing an explosive laugh, to a high head and outthrust hip that conveyed obvious pride in her pretty frock, to a head thrown back in laughter that showed a face less pretty than enchanting, with toothless front gums that were hidden in some of the other, more conventionally lovely photos.

Frankie found himself particularly drawn to a close-up image of the child's jack-o-lantern grin and dancing eyes, which conveyed pure joy. There was a small, faint heart-shaped birth-mark just below her left eye. Frankie stared at the photo for quite a while before moving on to the next image that had completed downloading. After a few more photos of the child alone, the camera appeared to have been mounted on a tripod because all of the subsequent images shared the same angle and perspective. A man, whose head was out of the frame, led her to a bed on which the camera focused. The last image before the pair reached the bed showed the little girl's legs raised in a care-free skip.

"I LOOKED at the pictures of what happened on the bed over and over. I knew that my body's reaction to what I saw was wrong, but I was so, so tired of fighting against it. Finally, I gave in. I stopped fighting and gave my body what it wanted. Afterward, my body felt sated and, actually, sleepy, but every other part of me screamed with horror and shame.

"I never had any doubt that the images I had viewed, and the pleasure I had taken in them, were an unequivocal moral wrong. Against this certainty, though, my brain tried to justify my actions, and it nagged at me and asked me to consider whether I was overreacting. Surely, if something were so wrong I wouldn't be able to access it so relatively easily, right? Maybe there were flickers of distress in some of the images, but in almost every photograph the little girl's expression showed nothing but love and trust. Could it be possible that the child had willingly participated? If so, was the activity really so terrible as our culture wanted us all to believe?"

In worrying over these issues as a tongue compulsively probes a loose tooth, Frankie allowed these louder justifications to drown out a much smaller, more still voice, which said that all of the expressions of love and trust appeared in the earliest images, and there were no shots of the child's face after she had skipped to the bed. Frankie's fragile and immature psyche was unused to participating in unvarnished analysis, so he clung to any possibility that what he had viewed represented voluntary, albeit culturally unacceptable, activity. And he comforted himself by insisting that regardless of the circumstances in which the photos were generated, he had not had a hand in making them. He had just observed the damage, if any, that had already been done, and that he could not change.

Frankie promised himself to think about the issue again when he was less exhausted. He saved the images to his external drive, stored the drive in a shoebox at the top of his closet, and cleaned all digital traces of the evening's activities. As he worked, Frankie reflected on his decision to save the images. He had done it almost instinctively, without forethought. What would he do with them? Would he turn them over to some authority figure? Even in his own overestimation of his integrity, Frankie admitted to himself that he would not tell anyone about them. No, the most unflinching aspect of

Frankie's personality, the core being that refused to allow him to delude even himself, acknowledged that he saved the images so that, when he had created a sufficiently rational argument to justify it, he could look at and take pleasure in them again.

After double and triple checking to ensure his electronic activities had been erased to the best of his ability, Frankie powered off his computer, crawled into bed, and promptly fell into a deep sleep.

CHAPTER SIXTEEN

L ike in most dreams, Frankie never had a clear moment of achieving awareness. Instead, the alternative consciousness revealed itself to him slowly; first, he had the sense of watching a far-off scene—like a play or a television show—and then the setting zoomed in until he was no longer in the audience, but a starring member of the cast. His individual will had been disabled, and he had no power to manipulate his own actions or other events. He simply looked out of eyes that he somehow knew were not his own, and passively and powerlessly experienced alien thoughts and sensations. Just after recognizing that he inhabited another consciousness, but before he could probe the mind he occupied, his independent thoughts were turned down, like a volume knob, to the lowest level above absolute mute. He had no choice but to live the scene from his host's perspective, without distraction from his separate, imprisoned mind.

Frankie's dream-self peered at its small, pale hand, which clasped a large, strong hand attached to a man navigating them down a steep flight of stairs.

. . .

I WONDER what kind of treat I'm going to get tonight!

I didn't get to see Daddy before Mommy said I had to go to bed, but Daddy woke me up when the house was quiet and dark, and he said it was time for a fashion show. Our fashion shows are so fun and funny. Daddy gives me pretty new clothes and then we go down to the basement and pretend that I'm a famous model and he's taking pictures of me for a magazine. He says silly things like, "You look maaahvelous, Dahling!" *or* "Blow your fans a kiss, Diva!"

When our fashion shows are over, Daddy gives me chocolate cake, or Skittles, or some other sweet treat Mommy would never let me have before bed because it would "rot your teeth," *and Daddy and I giggle about our secret play time. By then, I usually get pretty sleepy, so Daddy carries me to my room and tucks me in with butterfly kisses and he tells me I'm his beautiful little girl.*

I'm always so tired the morning after our fashion shows that Mommy gets flusterated with me. Her face gets pinchy as she helps me tie my shoes, and she pulls the laces too tight, or brushes my hair too hard, or says that I'm a big girl and I should know better than to make my bed in such a sloppy, "half-fast" *way. She says that I'm going to miss the bus and make her late for work again. I don't like it when Mommy is so grumpy, but secret playtime with Daddy is worth feeling tired and making Mommy's face pinchy.*

Tonight, Daddy woke me up by sitting on the edge of the bed and brushing my hair away from my face. When I was awake enough to see him, he reminded me to be quiet by smiling at me with his finger to his lips. I pushed off my covers and gave him a big hug, and he rocked me back and forth. After a little while, he pushed me back from him to show me what he had brought for me tonight. It was the prettiest nightgown I had ever seen, and I had a hard time remembering that I couldn't clap my hands together or I would wake Mommy. Daddy helped me out of my Strawberry Shortcake nightie, and pulled the new nightie over my head. It was soft and smelled so nice—a little bit like Mommy but different. Once my new nightie was on, Daddy asked if I wanted to bring one of my stuffies, so I chose Geraldine Giraffe, and we headed down to the basement for our fashion show.

Now Daddy is fiddling with his camera and with a stand he hasn't used before that has three legs. Daddy keeps sliding his camera into the stand until it clicks, and then he looks through the camera and moves it up or down or side to side. Finally, he nods to himself, takes the camera out of the clicky stand, and asks if the star is ready for her photo shoot. That's me!

We take some photos for a while, and I do all of my best poses and twirls, and Daddy says, "Beautiful! Gorgeous! Look at the camera, Julie!"

Daddy takes a lot *of pictures and then, after a while, he slides the camera onto the three-legged thing until it clicks, and he takes my hand and we walk over to the bed in the corner. Sometimes I take naps there when Mommy is working or exercising in the basement. I can't help skipping as Daddy takes my hand.*

Daddy asks if I want to do an extra special photo shoot, a kind that only the best and most famous models do. I clap my hands and say I do! I really do! Daddy frowns at me and says he's not sure if I'm ready for it, but when tears try to sneak out of my eyes, Daddy winks at me and says, "I can never say no to you, my girl, my sweet Julie."

Daddy says we'll have to have a costume change, so he helps me out of the pretty nightgown, and my Wonder Woman underoos, and then he folds the clothes at the foot of the bed. When he is finished folding, he looks at me and says, "Poor girl, you must be so cold! Come here and I'll warm you up before I go get your new costume."

I am shivery, so I take two quick skips to Daddy, and he lifts me into his lap, hugging me tightly to warm me up. Daddy sways back and forth, singing softly with his mouth against my hair. After a while, he begins petting me like I pet our dog, Claude. His big warm hand starts at the top of my head, goes all along my hair and then all the way down my back. It feels nice. I love being so close to Daddy.

Daddy has done a good job of warming me up, but I don't say anything because the petting feels nice, and I don't want to move my arms and legs. They feel heavy and comfortable. My eyelids feel heavy, too, and my eyelashes flutter against Daddy's shirt as I breathe in his clean smell.

I feel so sleepy that I don't even mind that we're not finishing our fashion show. Then Daddy lays me onto the bed and untangles my arms from his neck, like he and Mommy always do when they try to put me to bed without waking me up. I keep my eyes closed and let Daddy place my arms by my side, knowing the next step will be to cover me with a snuggly warm blanket. I don't realize that the blanket hasn't come until my skin gets a little prickly with cold. I hear some rustling at the end of the bed, and a zipper.

My eyes pop open as Daddy quickly pulls my legs apart and then I have to turn my head to the side to get a breath because Daddy is heavy on top of me. I feel something hard pushing against the place that Mommy and I call the puff-puff when she gives me a bath. I want to ask Daddy what's happening, but his chest is pushing down on me and I have to keep moving my face just to find an open spot to take a breath. Trying to breathe is the most important thing, but I forget about that when the thing between my legs keeps pushing so hard that it feels like I'm breaking and my head fills with yellow and red. My puff-puff is ripping. I finally catch a breath and, as it leaves again it takes a scaredy sound from my throat. "Be quiet!" *Daddy says in the low, angry voice he only uses with Mommy or when I've played with the toys on the special shelf in Daddy and Mommy's room—the toys Daddy's told me* "a thousand times are strictly off limits."

I can't see Daddy's eyes, but his voice tells me his bright blue eyes have those icy beams that turn Daddy into a stranger. A scary stranger. I know how important it is to keep the scary stranger calm, so I try my hardest not to let out the sounds that bubble up to my throat from the ripping and fire in my puff-puff.

. . .

*D*ADDY DOESN'T LOOK *at me when he uses a damp towel to clean me up and put my nighty back on me. He starts talking in that low, icy voice as he takes out a package from his bag. It's my favorite treat: Ring-Dings.*

"I can't give you a treat if you can't stay awake during our fashion shows." *He sounds so angry with me for ruining our secret playtime. He takes a Ring-Ding out of the box, opens the wrapping, and takes a big bite. He doesn't look at me as he chews, swallows, and then finishes it with a second bite. A few more drops slide out of my eyes, and Daddy looks over right when I'm wiping them away. I love Ring-Dings, but I don't care about them right now. I can't stop my eyes from leaking because I ruined the fashion show, and now Daddy's looking at me with squinty, angry eyes instead of wide, smiley eyes.*

"I'm sorry I fell asleep, Daddy," *I whisper.*

Daddy drops the Ring-Ding wrapper into his bag, zips it, and picks it up with his arm through the strap. He walks over to me and the ice in his voice melts a little as he says, "You'll do better next time."

CHAPTER SEVENTEEN

"When I woke up, I was breathing like I'd run a marathon, and I was drenched in sweat. At first I was relieved to realize it had been just a dream. The relief didn't last long, though, because I knew it wasn't like any other dream I'd ever had. It didn't have any strange inconsistencies of time, or space, or characters that dreams usually have. It had been linear, logical, and detailed. It had felt as real as it felt to be sitting in my bedroom after waking up. I had BEEN that little girl, Julie. I took out the notebook in my bedside table and wrote down exactly what had happened."

After he finished writing, Frankie remained in bed, paralyzed by the lingering intensity of the dream. He felt overwhelming waves of nausea, sadness, and guilt. As the ability to move his limbs gradually returned, he crawled across the bedroom to the adjoining bathroom, and vomited repeatedly into the toilet. When Frankie had exhausted the contents of his stomach, and had no more strength for the subsequent dry heaves, he collapsed on the hard tile and cried. The animal-sounding noises that came out of him terrified him, as did the rivers of snot and tears pouring from his face. Physically exhausted, he fell into a dreamless sleep on the bathroom floor.

After jolting awake again, all Frankie wanted was to escape back into sleep. Instead, he pushed himself off the floor, rinsed his mouth, and splashed his face with cool water. These simple actions had an immediate comforting effect and helped him feel human again. Instead of drawing his blinds and burrowing back under his covers, Frankie crossed himself and knelt by his bed to make a desperate plea to God. God had previously seemed distant and removed from Frankie's life outside of Mass and Confession. For the first time in his life, Frankie spoke to his Creator in words that had not been written by someone else or formalized into liturgy.

"I just asked God to help me," Father Frank told Tavis simply. "I told him I was lost. I was weak. I was . . . I am . . . disgusting. I told him how disconnected I felt from him, and how ashamed I was for him to see me that way. How ashamed I was to see myself that way. I told him I felt too weak and unworthy for him to bother himself about, but I wanted to be better. I wanted to control myself, but I couldn't do it without him. I prayed, 'If you're there, Lord, and if you can use even someone like me, I'm yours. If you care even for someone like me, please help me. Please help me. Please help me. Please help me. Please help me. Please help me.'"

As a professional who had encountered more than his share of evil, sick bastards, Tavis knew Father Frank had continued with his story, so far, because Tavis had not allowed his face or his body language to betray the revulsion he felt about what Father Frank had admitted to doing. But within Tavis, another fragile, nearly imperceptible, unexpected feeling began to take root. Intertwined with his disgust were tender shoots of sympathy for the confused kid who rightly felt alone in the world.

"When I woke up the next morning, I knew I needed to

commit to two things: First, I would never again contribute to or participate in any way in the harm of children. I knew I needed to avoid all contact with children, and especially to avoid time alone with them, because clearly I could not trust myself. Also—and this felt like it might be an overreaction—I promised to cut all ties with computers."

Maybe Frankie could have turned things around and used his love of computers for only wholesome purposes, but being honest with himself, he doubted it. Already, and even knowing what he knew, or thought he knew, about what had happened to little Julie, his untrustworthy brain was trying to find a way to justify taking another peek at the images he had saved. And if that was too much, it tried to convince him, couldn't Frankie just spend some time with the photos of other kids in the 'Real-JailBait' folder? No kids had been hurt making those pictures, right, so what was the harm?

Frankie nearly gave in. His body remembered and liked how it felt when looking at those photos. But before getting that drive out of his closet, or connecting to the bulletin board, he asked God to help him know and do what God wanted him to do. Thankfully, the answer was clear. Maybe other people could resist temptation, but Frankie *did* need distance from technology. He *did* need to avoid spending time in a virtual world where access to every desire he might have, was only a few keystrokes away. He might be able to resist temptation most of the time . . . when he felt strong, when the reasons for his commitment were fresh in his head, or when he remembered to ask God for help . . . but he needed to make it harder to give in during the times that would inevitably come when he felt weak.

When those times came, his best strategy was to repeat the spontaneous prayer for help he had prayed on his bedroom floor. As soon as he asked for help, he felt less alone, and he knew he could make it a little longer . . . at least until the next time he needed to ask for help. In the beginning, he had to repeat this process every few minutes. For a few days, he didn't leave his room—he told his parents he didn't feel well—and between periods of begging for help, he dismantled all of his computer equipment.

Eventually, Frankie didn't need to beg for help quite as often, and he experienced increasing periods of clear-headedness. The little girl whose experience he had shared in his dream never fully left his mind, and the disgust he felt at his body's attraction to the evidence of her destruction also stayed with him. He couldn't undo the role he had played in damaging her, as a consumer of her pain. Still, with the steady infusions of grace and resolve he continually requested and received, Frankie gradually healed. He asked his Helper for direction about how to live in his service, how to atone for what he had done, and how to prevent his unwanted attraction from ruling him and hurting others.

Frankie saw a solitary, lonely life stretching before him. He knew it was impossible to discuss his struggle with any other human being, that the risks were too great. He couldn't expect anyone to understand that he despised his inclinations, that he would do anything possible to kill them, and that he wanted to avoid, at all costs, the damage that would come from taking any action on those inclinations.

Though lonely, Frankie knew he was not alone. His invisible compassionate companion stayed close, constantly encouraging Frankie in his prison of shame and despair, and using Frankie's deep remorse as fuel for a service-oriented, redeemed life.

Frankie knew that he needed sacramental confession, but he could not bear the thought of any of the priests in his parish knowing the truth about him. So Frankie drove three hours to Ashford, where nobody knew his name, face, or voice. He visited a church and made a full confession to an unseen priest behind the screen in the confessional.

The priest spent a long time with Frankie, asking probing

questions, raising important concerns, and cautioning him about the dangers of believing he could resist his desires without professional assistance. Eventually, the priest seemed satisfied with the sincerity of Frankie's repentance and his commitment to change, and he assigned Frankie penance and granted absolution.

Frankie left the unfamiliar house of worship with his remorse intact, but he had replaced much of his shame with a motivating hope. He did not delude himself into believing he had been "cured." He faced the future with clear and pragmatic eyes, recognizing that he would struggle against his sexual desire throughout his life, but also appreciating the reasons he had to hope.

"God helped me understand that there was no law requiring me to allow this aspect of my personality to dominate my thoughts or my actions. I knew that, in spite of my best efforts to avoid it, there would be times of temptation. I also knew, because I had proof of it, that I was, and am, capable of making disastrous choices if all I rely on is my own willpower. Fortunately, I also had experience with touching the faintest outlines of the help that was available to me for the asking, and I knew that source of strength was more than sufficient," Frankie explained to Tavis.

After completing the sacrament of reconciliation, Frankie transformed dramatically. He ripped off the band-aid and began running, without delay, the race that had been set out for him. Because he had no business putting himself in situations involving regular interactions with children, Frankie quit his job at the ice cream store, and the next time his neighbor asked him to babysit he told her his schedule had changed and made babysitting impossible. Frankie resolved to direct not just his actions, but also the eco-system of his thoughts, into paths of empathy and righteousness, which required him to maintain his distance from children.

Not until taking these steps did Frankie realize how consumed he had been by thoughts about children. But he developed new mental pathways through physical separation and a commitment to asking for divine assistance whenever he needed it. As with anything, the results were not perfect, and troubling, obsessive thoughts still sometimes invaded his mind, but there was enough improvement to encourage Frankie to continue.

To avoid falling into old patterns, Frankie devoted himself to spiritual development and academics with an appetite that bewildered his parents, his teachers, and his priest. He pestered Father James regularly about the philosophy or insight of whatever he was reading, and Father James suggested the seminary might be the best place to seek answers to his many questions. Frankie considered this suggestion carefully, but he didn't think himself ready for that commitment.

FRANKIE GRADUATED high school and enrolled in a well-respected liberal arts college in a neighboring state. After a few false starts in choosing a major, Frankie's fascination with his introductory psychology class led him to pursue a degree in the field. Examining the complex and often counterintuitive workings of the brain fascinated him, and he jumped in with enthusiasm.

Frankie was also drawn to psychology because he wanted to understand what was wrong with him. He understood the term pedophilia applied to him. Like most people, Frankie assumed that, because the label applied, he might be hardwired to hurt children.

"As much as I wanted to fight against that part of myself, and not to hurt anyone," he said to Tavis, "I was afraid I was really just delaying the inevitable because I was a monster who would eventually act according to my evil nature.

"Thank God, literally, for my abnormal psychology course. More than anything since God comforted me on the floor of my bedroom, that course gave me hope for the future. There was a unit on sexual deviancy, which explored a number of paraphilias, including pedophilia. I learned that the media often oversimplifies the condition and uses the same broad brush to paint all individuals on a spectrum. One example is the commonly understood definition of pedophilia. Culturally, pubescent and post-pubescent adolescents are children, but the clinical definition of pedophilia is limited to sexual attraction to pre-pubescent children.

"By far the biggest relief, though, was learning that those of us who are cursed with that attraction aren't necessarily doomed to act on it. Obviously, it's tough to get data about pedophiles who never commit offenses against children. It's the same reason I could never talk to anyone about it when I admitted to myself what I am. We have every incentive to keep our struggle secret because not guarding that secret with our lives will cost us our lives—either literally, or in terms of ruining us within our communities. This is why the public only hears about pedophiles who act on their attraction. We learn about the harm they have caused to children, either directly or by consuming child pornography, only when they are caught."

As Father Frank continued, Tavis realized he had no idea how long he had been sitting in his office. Tavis had the same common understanding about pedophiles. He had spent so much of his career catching them that it was hard not to assume that all pedophiles hurt children.

Father Frank was cut short by a light tap at the door, followed by a prim woman in late middle age opening the door and poking her head in.

"I didn't want to interrupt, Father Frank, but we're getting quite a back-up out here. Can I give folks an idea of when you'll be able to see them?"

Father Frank smiled sadly at the woman. "I'm sorry, Schelle. I'm not going to be able to see them. Please tell them I'm dealing with an unexpected crisis. In fact, you should probably cancel my appointments for the rest of the week."

The woman opened her mouth as if to speak, and then quickly closed her mouth. She nodded once, and then reached for the doorknob with one hand while her other hand moved in search of the crucifix hanging from her neck.

"Oh, and Schelle?"

She stopped the door in its path and raised her eyebrows expectantly.

"I hate to ask, but would you please bring us a couple of waters and cups of coffee? I think we're going to be in here a while longer."

"Of course, Father," she said briskly, shutting the door. Her shoes clicked on the floor as she sped away to complete her tasks. Tavis wondered what she thought they were discussing. He wondered if she would have willingly granted any favor to Father Frank if she knew what he had been confessing.

As if they had never been interrupted, Father Frank continued like a dam that had burst.

"Like I was saying, it's impossible to gather accurate statistics, but we know that many people who fit the clinical definition of pedophilia are empathetic and socially competent, and never act on their impulses. We also know that many people who commit sexual offenses against children and adolescents don't have a sexual preference for those age categories. Many of those offenders are not, clinically, pedophiles, hebephiles, or ephebephiles."

"Sorry to interrupt, Father Frank, but those last two words are Greek to me."

Father Frank laughed at Tavis's unintentional joke. "No, I

apologize, Tavis. I assumed they would come up in your work. A hebephile is attracted to pubescent adolescents, and an ephebephile is attracted to post-pubescent adolescents."

Father Frank continued. "Where was I? . . . Oh, right. In that unit about paraphilias, I learned that while many pedophiles act on their attraction and sexually abuse children, the majority of people who commit sexual crimes against children are not actually pedophiles. These individuals are motivated by a completely different set of factors, and there's usually an alignment of antisocial tendencies, opportunity, and lack of impulse control. A predisposition to antisocial behavior is the most common denominator in incidents of child sexual abuse, which means that more offenses against children are committed by anti-social individuals who are not clinical pedophiles than by those of us who fit the clinical definition."

The explanation interested Tavis in spite of himself. Father Frank took a pad of paper out of his desk and drew a Venn diagram. In one circle he wrote "Antisocial Tendencies." In the other, he wrote "Pedophilic Attraction," and in the overlapping center, "Archetypal Predator."

Father Frank explained the relative rarity of this combination, which represented the greatest danger and created the framework for the archetype of the serial child rapist—wholly lacking in empathy and resistant to treatment or reformation. "Some of the most frightening real-world examples of individuals like this are Albert Fish, Earl Bradley, and Jerry Sandusky. These are the men who haunt parents' dreams and inspire the most shocking books and TV shows. Our culture is revolted by characters like this, but they also generate a deep fascination— the type of train wreck from which we, as media consumers, can't look away. They make it easy for us to believe that all people who commit sexual offenses against both pre-pubescent children and pubescent or post-pubescent adolescents are pedophiles, that all pedophiles commit sexual offenses against children, that all pedophiles are immune to treatment, and all pedophiles are just slaves to their compulsions. Accepting this framework makes us feel justified in viewing pedophiles as the lowest form of life in our society.

"It's no wonder, then, that those of us who recognize some of this within ourselves, who are ashamed of it and know the harm we're capable of causing, who don't want to hurt anyone, and who would do *anything* to change ourselves, realize that our only choice is to tell no one. We can't seek therapy because, even if we're clear that we never intend to harm children, we can't guarantee that therapists won't decide they have a duty to report."

WHEN FRANKIE WAS IN COLLEGE, and had already resigned himself to a lifetime of shame, isolation, and secrecy, learning more about the nature of his condition gave him hope. He was grateful for confirmation that, although responsible for his actions, he had not chosen the object of his sexual attraction. Even more encouraging: evidence that he did not have to give in to a compulsion and that he could live a purposeful life.

Frankie felt even more sure about his commitment to living in the service of the One who had pulled him from danger, and who promised redemption and purpose. Frankie's studies led him to thank God for giving him the nurturing childhood and the tools that had socialized him and that would give him power to resist the compulsion or apathy that might result in acting on his sexual desire.

FATHER FRANK WARMED his hands with his coffee cup and looked at the black liquid thoughtfully.

"I would have loved to put that night when I was sixteen out of my head forever. To live as if it had never happened. I needed to remember it though—both the part that had felt good and the terror and confusion that went along with understanding what that little girl had gone through so that I could feel good. I needed to associate those sensations so that if I was tempted to seek out more photos or videos in search of that pleasure, I would remember what the price would be. I needed to keep that price before me, and that's why that hard drive has gone with me wherever I've gone. I doubt the technology to access the drive still exists. At least I'm sure it's hard to come by. I haven't tried to look at the images, anyway—that's not the point. I keep the drive with me as a reminder of how I contributed to that child's suffering. Of why it's so important for me to maintain habits that remind me of God's promise that I'm not doomed to be a person that takes pleasure in damaging others."

FRANK FINISHED his Bachelor's and Master's degrees, moved back to Colberg, and started working as a therapist at his home parish's Catholic Charities. He admired the director's ability to manage the overwhelmed and understaffed center with compassion and pragmatism. The mental health clinic was just one part of the larger center Father Anthony directed, but he made all members of the team, including Frank, feel like valued partners in the fight to bring health, safety, and community to those suffering from soul-crushing depression, anxiety, substance abuse, and combinations of these and other invisible illnesses.

"Father Anthony met briefly every week with each staff member, and I treasured these opportunities to observe and learn from a man in whom God had so beautifully integrated religious devotion with action-oriented compassion. Because of these meetings, I found myself led to a calling I hadn't seriously considered since high school. Under Father Anthony's guidance, I started praying for discernment about whether God was calling me to ordination. The more I prayed about it, the more certain I became that the call was genuine and, at Father Anthony's suggestion, I attended a week-long retreat at a Trappist monastery about an hour away–"

"I know it," Tavis interrupted. "I visit there pretty regularly."

Father Frank smiled, "Then you know what a perfect place it can be for uninterrupted prayer and reflection. While there, I read Saint Teresa of Ávila's *Interior Castle*, and it felt like the opening passage had been written just for me. I keep it with me always."

Father Frank rolled up his sleeve and showed Tavis his forearm, where, in ornate script, was a tattoo of the words, *Strength arising from obedience has a way of simplifying things which seem impossible.*

"Those words clarified God's promise to use me as I was, and to fill me with hope and strength in spite of my flaws and my temptations. I left my retreat with a quiet, solid certainty that I had received a divine invitation to a life of ordained service."

After ordination, Father Frank continued providing therapy through Catholic Charities, but in another state. Through his work, Father Frank went deep into understanding patients' realities, and he offered them the relief of being seen at their cores. He let them know he valued them in spite of—and, often, transformatively, because of—who they were. The extraordinary empathetic bond allowed his patients to trust Father Frank, and they grasped onto his suggestions like lifelines. Father Frank served in that community for several years, until his mother's failing health motivated him to transfer to the Catholic Charities center in Colberg, where he had worked for more than a decade by the time Tavis crossed his path.

"It's sometimes draining, but my life has been joyful. I have had the opportunity to serve suffering people. It's my love song to the benevolent being who lifted my chin and kissed my face when I was at my most broken and suffering. The God who replaced my unwanted obsession by filling me with compassion; who replaced shame and self-hatred with clear purpose. I've lived my entire adult life gratefully certain that I have been rescued from my own worst impulses, and this certainty has allowed me to live my life in the sweet spot of success—at the intersection where significance, interest, and talent meet."

CHAPTER EIGHTEEN

"Listen, Tavis," blurted Father Frank, "I'm about to break every ethical rule in the book by discussing this with you, but the client is dead and it can't hurt her. Anyway, for reasons you'll understand in a minute, I'm pretty sure I won't need to worry about keeping my license after today."

Those who relied on Catholic Charities for mental health treatment, including treatment for drug and alcohol dependence, came to the agency through a number of avenues. The Church both supported and relied on the resource, but the agency also accepted referrals from other public and private social agencies and from the criminal justice system.

Father Frank began to describe the day, less than a year before, when he had set aside his last appointment to intake a new patient referred through the local drug court program. The program allowed nonviolent drug offenders to erase convictions from their records by completing the program's requirements, including therapy designed to strengthen cognitive behavioral coping techniques developed in previously completed inpatient drug treatment programs. Therapy also helped participants develop defenses against the temptation to return to familiar, destructive patterns of behavior.

"I had read my new patient's file to prepare for her intake, and it was pretty standard for drug court referrals. There was a familiar story of brushes with the law beginning in her mid-teen years that got more serious over many years, and that led, finally, to a serious arrest. The client had completed in-patient treatment, and was ready to begin the therapy and community service requirements."

When Father Frank opened the door to his office to let her in, he noticed she was tall, but carried herself to take up as little space as possible. She kept her head down even as she sat on the sofa, so at first all Father Frank saw was a disheveled tumble of black hair, pale skin, and layers of dark clothing.

She sat down, glued to her phone, and Father Frank told her it was important to keep their sessions free from electronics. She didn't answer, but killed the screen, tossed the phone into her bag, clasped her hands together on her knees and, for the first time, lifted her head to look at Father Frank.

Father Frank's voice trembled with the memory, "It was the shock of my life."

One of her eyes was still covered by the hair that had obviously been dyed black to cover a very light shade of blonde. The other eye, though . . . the other eye was clear and blue, and it pierced Father Frank. He would have recognized her by that eye alone. But had he needed further confirmation, there on the cheekbone just below her eye was a small, heart-shaped birthmark.

THE MAN who had been calmly, rationally sharing the deepest secrets of his life with Tavis disappeared briefly, replaced by a man who sat before Tavis in extreme distress.

"Obviously, I was freaking the fuck out! I didn't allow myself to stare, though, or to betray myself with any other body language. I bought myself a moment by looking down at the file on my lap. The name I had been reading in that file before she arrived took on a whole new meaning, and I couldn't help but wonder what game God was playing with me now. I closed the file, set it on the table next to me, and started the work." He snorted in disgust. "I thought I was being so righteous and obedient."

Father Frank told her he had read the file forwarded by the court, which told him one side of the story about why she was there that day. "I'd like to hear your story, Julie," he said. "It will help me know what you expect of our time together, and what you hope to gain through our sessions."

Julie leaned back on the sofa and ran her fingers through her hair. She hugged herself. "I'm here because it's part of what I have to do to stay out of prison. I expect that we'll feed each other as much bullshit as we can get away with. I hope to gain whatever paper proves I've been here."

This attitude was pretty common for Father Frank's court-referred clients. It was mind-bogglingly disturbing for Father Frank to know such personal information about her childhood —knowledge that would usually take at least several sessions for her to trust him enough to share with him. A part of him insisted, in a whisper, that this patient was not for him, and that it was unethical to continue meeting with her for a minute longer. But his pride shouted over that small voice of conscience, positing that Julie showed up in his office because God wanted him to help her. He told himself that her presence was a divinely appointed opportunity to reconcile his specific sin by working wonders of healing in her damaged soul. That voice won, and Father Frank relaxed into his chair to begin the familiar process of building trust between them.

. . .

OVER THE COURSE of the next several months, Father Frank and Julie built a rapport that led to exploring the factors motivating her drug use and other destructive behaviors. Father Frank was gratified when, after completing the sessions required by the drug court, Julie asked to continue working with him. Julie trusted Father Frank enough to try out several of his techniques and suggestions for managing her triggers. It took much longer for Julie to share what he already knew had to be at least one significant cause of the soul sickness that led to her self-destructive choices. Father Frank carefully avoided revealing that he knew anything other than what she had told him. Instead, he waded with Julie through the chaos of her own perception of her motivations.

To Julie, her issues with drug abuse represented choices she had willingly made and weaknesses she could overcome if only she pulled herself up by her bootstraps, imposed some self-discipline, and tried harder. Julie believed that drug abuse (and, really, most mental illness) was a matter of choice and a sign of weakness. With this attitude, she initially resisted therapy. Under Father Frank's empathetic guidance, however, Julie took her first steps toward sharing parts of herself that she believed to be proof of her freakish defects. Father Frank met her revelations with compassion, understanding, and reassurance that she was not alone in her fears.

Eventually, Julie was ready to discuss the years of rape she had endured as a child. When she was in her late teens, the FBI arrested her father, even though she had never said a word about what had happened. Until then, she hadn't known about the wide circulation of the photographs and films her father had taken of her. On that day, she learned that the whole world could see what she had previously believed to be her private and secret shame.

It had taken Julie a long time to talk about the issue because she had understood the purpose of the therapy was to address her drug use, and she genuinely believed that the issues were separate, or at least only very loosely related. She prided herself on her resilience and she believed that the trauma of her early life was over. She considered the door on that period to have closed firmly and finally when her father was killed in prison within a few months of his arrival.

When Julie finally began to share how she had been robbed both of her childhood and her privacy, she was not much interested in identifying a connection between her childhood trauma and her escape into substances in adulthood. Rather, she was seeking the unburdening that comes with verbal confession of deep shame. Father Frank had been trustworthy with some of her less-secret thoughts—listening with attention; avoiding expressions of shock or judgment; offering compassion; and challenging Julie to go deeper. This willingness to gently but firmly call Julie on her bullshit went further to foster her trust and respect for Father Frank than any coddling could have done.

Julie began sharing the story that had dominated her childhood by unemotionally reciting the facts. Father Frank guided Julie through the ripples those experiences had made throughout her life, and the manner in which her drug abuse might be tied to her desire to escape the pain she didn't have tools to confront. Julie discovered, with Father Frank's help, that there was a certain degree of peace that came with acknowledging rather than running from the pain, and developing strategies other than escape into drugs when the pain overwhelmed her.

In exploring the dancing partners of self-blame and shame, Father Frank thought about how he could best drive home exactly how powerless Julie had been over the abuse she suffered. Rather than approaching the vulnerability of her six-year-old self through the faulty lens of her own memory, Father Frank tasked Julie with volunteering in the center's daycare program, where she spent some time with kindergarteners. She wasn't used to spending time with children, and was surprised by how easily they placed trust in authority figures. She began to see the truth behind her father's scoldings that almost always followed his abuse: her father did not use her body because she had behaved badly. He had manipulated her and ensured her silence by foisting his own shame onto her small shoulders.

This shift in perspective made Julie angry. She had not previously spent much energy being angry at her father. Instead, she kept her cool by saying her childhood was history that couldn't be changed by thinking about it in the present. Julie considered this approach to be proof of her mental toughness, of avoiding the trap of "victimhood," and of "getting on with life." Until her work with Father Frank, Julie had not realized how hard her subconscious had worked to avoid thinking about her experiences and how they had affected her. She finally began to accept that much of her reason for using and abusing substances was to escape the grief and anger that seeped in through the chinks in her psyche's armor.

With gentle compassion, Father Frank supported Julie through examining what she had endured and reconsidering the experience through the lens of adult perspective. Father Frank bore witness to the intense emotions evoked by such an examination. The process was messy and difficult for both of them, but their commitment to the work increased as they progressed together.

"I thought we were making real progress," Father Frank told Tavis, with tears running unchecked down his cheeks. "If I hadn't been such a self-important asshole, I would have seen the writing on the wall during our session last Thursday."

"I CAN'T LOOK people in the eye when I walk down the street," Julie had told him. "Sometimes I'll see men and I can tell they recognize me. The worst are the guys whose eyes light up. They bite their lips or smile at me like we share a secret . . . and I guess we do. Sometimes, their eyes just get wide and they look surprised and a little ashamed."

Father Frank kept his mouth shut. It was therapeutically reasonable to let her continue without offering comment, but his more selfish motivation was controlling the expression on his face.

"Fuck." Julie ritually ran her bone-thin hands through her dirty hair. "Why do so many people have to know?"

Father Frank cleared his throat and offered, "Have you thought about taking ownership of the fact that it's public?"

Responding to Julie's baffled expression, he continued, "Just hear me out. So, you can't unring the bell—what's out there is out there. But you can use the fact that it's public to control the narrative. People will want to hear your story, and your strength in the face of what you've endured. You could turn something terrible into something good by using that platform to advocate for and encourage other children in similar situations."

Julie's brow furrowed, and she leaned forward in her seat, remaining silent for a few moments while she allowed the suggestion to sink in.

"I get what you're saying," she began slowly, "but no fucking way am I doing that. It would be like ripping myself open over and over again."

"It could be like that at first," he agreed, "and I certainly don't think it's something you'd be ready for anytime soon. Maybe, though, it's something to chew on as we continue our work. My constant prayer is for God to show us how he will redeem the double tragedy of your abuse and the fact that troubled souls used your injury for their own purposes. I don't know, but maybe it's even possible for God to use your resilience to change the behavior of those men you sometimes happen across. Perhaps, even, it's worth hoping that your refusal to remain a victim will lead to their reformation and redemption."

"Uh, Padre . . ." Julie spat, her initial stunned silence giving way to anger. "The last thing I give two shits about is the redemption of those sick fucks. It's hard enough to care about my own. It's hard enough to care about getting out of bed in the morning, about brushing my teeth, about putting one foot in front of the other. Most days my first thought is what a relief it would be if this were all over. Usually when I wake up in the morning, I spend a little time imagining how right it would feel if someone just stuck a knife right into my heart. I don't want to do it myself, but I have this feeling that, if someone would just do it for me, it would be like coming home."

The words hung in the air between them. Right when he opened his mouth to ask for more information about Julie's specific ideation, Schelle knocked on the door and popped her head into the room. "Sorry to interrupt, Father Francis, but your 2:30 appointment has been waiting for about five minutes."

"Thank you, Schelle, please tell him it will be a bit longer, and we'll make up the time at the end, or we can reschedule if he can't wait."

As the door closed, Father Frank steepled his fingers and rested them under his chin as he tried to find the right words.

"Julie, have you ever hurt yourself, or tried to?" he asked, searching her face.

Julie laughed dismissively, and Father Frank knew the spirit of deep sharing had disappeared. "Don't worry, I'm not going to off myself, it's just a weird thought I have sometimes. There's a certain comfort to it. Listen, you have another appointment waiting, and I'll be late for work if I don't leave now."

Julie stood, and he closed the distance between them as she reached for her backpack. They shook hands. "Thanks, Father. I feel like shit now, but if I've learned anything from hanging out with you, it's that later I'll end up feeling relieved to get this stuff off my chest."

"Julie," Father Frank said, his voice tight with concern, "as you can understand, I'm concerned about the thought you shared, and I'd like to spend some time with it as soon as possible. I don't think we should wait until next week to discuss it— please ask Schelle to schedule you as soon as you're able to come back. We'll shift other appointments to accommodate you. In the meantime, if you do have any thoughts about harming yourself, please call me right away."

"You bet," quipped Julie lightly as she slid her hand from between his, clicked her tongue, shot him finger guns, and moved toward the door. On her way out, she called over her shoulder, "See you soon!"

He did not see her soon.

FATHER FRANK, arms resting on his desk and cradling his head, looked up at Tavis, anguished and exhausted. "I never should have tried to treat her," he said in a voice filled with self-loathing. "Every rule of professional ethics told me that, as soon as I recognized who she was, I should have found a way to refer her to another provider. In my self-importance and pride, though, I thought I could fix her, and that there would be a certain divine poetry in someone who had been one of the instruments of her harm being used as a tool of her healing.

"An emissary of Christ—what a joke!" Father Frank nearly choked on the words as he tore at his clerical collar and tossed it on his desk. "I didn't even pray about whether I should proceed with her treatment. It just seemed too perfect to be coincidence, so I jumped right in. I lied to myself and told myself I could help her, but really it was all about me: about how I could ease the guilt I've felt every day since I woke up from that dream and knew exactly what she had suffered, and how I had used her suffering to get myself off."

His haunted eyes hardening with grim purpose, Father Frank picked up a manila envelope from the credenza behind him and slid it across the desk to Tavis. Tavis was surprised to see his own name written in bold Sharpie.

"I've kept this drive with me for well over twenty years. I haven't had the equipment to access its contents for nearly that long, but I've kept it to remind me of how dangerous I can be if I let down my guard and forget that I need God's help. In my arrogance, I thought I was only dangerous in that particular way."

Father Frank placed his head in his hands. After drawing several deep breaths, he nodded toward the bulky envelope on the desk between them. "Take it," he whispered.

"You know what will happen if it has the pictures you say are on it, right?" Tavis asked. "And you've taken it to other states. That means mandatory prison time."

Father Frank barked out a bitter laugh. "People like me always know the legal risks. I know the consequences. I didn't touch Jeremy, but I'm certainly not innocent. It's time to pay the piper and to give Julie at least a small part of the justice she deserves. I should have done it a long time ago."

Tavis sat in his seat in silence, attempting to come to terms with what Father Frank had told him. In all his years, Tavis had never encountered an offender who saw himself so clearly or who voluntarily faced the consequences of his actions. His experience had given him the ability to recognize manipulation and the signs of a target's unhealthy interest in children. Father Frank had not tripped any of those alarms. He had not structured his life around access to children even though, as a priest, it would have been easy for him.

Tavis couldn't get his head around the idea that, just when his investigation proved the accusations against him were false,

Father Frank shared evidence of his decades-old crime. There was no reason that the secret couldn't have stayed a secret forever, but he chose to share it with someone he knew had a duty to report it to the police. Tavis felt completely unprepared for the direction the meeting had taken.

But there really was no choice to make. Tavis stood, took the package from the desk, and left.

PART III

CHAPTER NINETEEN

"Please sit down, Father Frank," said Caroline, motioning to the empty seat across the desk from her. The priest entered the room, obediently sat, and looked at her expectantly.

"Getting right to it, I wanted to talk one-on-one about the reactions you're having when Paul shares during group. It seemed like you had a tough time today."

"He's just a disgusting human being."

"I can appreciate that," murmured Caroline sympathetically.

"I really don't understand why you even run group sessions with these types of offenders. Everything I've read indicates they have a huge potential for what I'm seeing with Paul. Rather than contributing to a constructive group—where participants share honestly and also gain strength and encouragement from hearing about tools that have been useful for others—some members of this group seem just to be interested in stoking our collective sick fantasies. Paul is completely unrepentant; he just wants to brag about how successful he was in every area of his life—even at hurting boys and getting away with it."

"I respect your professional opinion, but I'm going to have to ask you to trust my experience in this setting and with this category of offenders. You're right about the potential pitfalls of groups like this, but we're fortunate to have an added dynamic that, in this case, makes the possibility of meaningful therapeutic progress much greater. I think you can be my secret weapon."

Caroline waited a few seconds before wading in again with carefully chosen words, "Frank, I'll be as straight as possible. I'm going to ask something of you that is not fair, and maybe it's even a little bit unethical, but I hope you'll listen to why I think it's for the greater good, and that you'll give it some serious thought before deciding."

Frank nodded for her to continue. She cleared her throat.

"You are right to conclude that this group is not likely to be very helpful to *you*. Unlike almost every other offender I see in this place, you had developed a healthy means of dealing with your urges long before you came here. And I know you fought hard for what peace you have. Participating in this group is always going to be dangerous to your equilibrium. Even so, I'd like you to keep going. After I explain my reasoning, if you choose not to continue, we can move forward with private sessions, and I'll recommend that you be permitted to stop participating in the group."

"Go ahead," said Frank, leaning forward in his customary posture of attentive listening.

"You are such a rare example of someone who is open about your condition that I think you can be helpful in a way that no other well-meaning mental health expert, who does not share your disorder, can be. I certainly can't. You are one of the rare proofs that there are exceptions to the stereotype. You can't be the only person with your condition who has not only found a means of successfully battling your urges, but who has also lived as a well-adjusted member of society. But you are the only one I know who has ended up in prison.

"Usually, the people who seem to be well-adjusted but find

themselves in prison turn out not to be well-adjusted at all—they're just really good at masking how anti-social they are until they're caught with their collection of child pornography. In your case, the blameworthy portion of your crime happened before you developed the disciplines that enabled you to be a helpful contributor to the world. Even more remarkable, in light of the stigma associated with your condition, you voluntarily disclosed both your disorder and your crime. This almost never happens."

Caroline took a deep breath, "I know it's a lot to ask, but I also know you chose a life of service before coming here. You've demonstrated you can make the difficult decisions your conscience demands. I think you can hack this if it will make a real difference to the quality of life of these men. It should also go a long way toward protecting children when these offenders' sentences are complete. Basically, I'm asking you to continue living a life of service."

When Frank finally spoke, his voice was husky and dark, "What if I don't want to serve these men? Would God really ask me to get this close when I've fought so hard for distance? I dedicated my life to God and to serving others in his name to keep myself from thoughts that these men share. I know we're not supposed to bargain with God, but that's what I did. And I was fine for so long. You're just asking too much . . . surely God's not so cruel! I don't want to spend a minute more with those men than is absolutely necessary—especially with that fucking animal Paul Peña. Of course I believe, intellectually, that God is willing and able to forgive them and to redeem their sins, but surely he can do it without me. How effective can I possibly be if, every time I'm near Peña, my skin crawls?"

"Maybe it's about modifying your perspective. One reason your practice was so successful was because of your empathetic gifts. I've done this work for a long time, and I still have to consciously put a damper on my own empathetic responses so I can keep doing the work without burning out. I can only imagine the strain that giving free reign to that empathy must have placed on you during your practice. In this case, it might be time to open those taps again. Like many of us who interact with those who offend against children, you've probably tried hard not to place yourself in their shoes. Your foot is the right size and shape, though, and I think you're strong enough to handle the consequences. If you do, you won't be able to help seeing past the horrible things they've done to the broken people they are.

"Take Paul, for example. I'm not talking out of school here because he has shared much of this in group. Unlike you, he doesn't have an innate sexual preference for children. Also unlike you, he did not have the cultural or environmental training to understand exactly how unacceptable his behavior is. In fact, his own history of sexual abuse as a child probably led him to believe that it is just a part of life that powerful men impose themselves on those weaker than they are.

"Paul was raised by a family that emphasized the surface of things—as long as the public image is maintained, all manner of horrors can happen in the dark. He didn't internalize the concept that society works best when individuals value the good of the community more than they value satisfying their own desires. So, Paul appreciates avoiding scandal, but he sees no incentive in the general concept of avoiding antisocial behavior. If he sees an opportunity to take something he wants at a nominal risk, his background has conditioned him to take it regardless of how it may negatively impact others.

"Because your family raised you to value community and service, when your condition manifested, you came to the conclusion quickly that what you desired is antisocial, you understood the potential criminal implications of acting on such desires, and, most importantly, you appreciated the impact that acting on your temptation would have on the children involved. Paul understood the criminal implications of his behavior, but he lacked the other socialization tools that you took for granted."

As Caroline finished her pitch, Frank picked up the stress ball on the desk between them and examined it with unwarranted intensity for several seconds. "My impulse is just to say 'no,' and leave it there. I heard you, and who knows, maybe you're offering me a way to continue to serve God, even if it is in the most uncomfortable possible way. Give me some time to think and pray about it? I promise to work on shifting my attitude toward Paul to a genuine 'There but for the grace of God . . .' approach."

"Of course. I wouldn't expect anything else," said Caroline, whose warm smile and even teeth lent beauty to her otherwise plain features. She stood, opened the door, and nodded to the guard, who accompanied Frank out of the medical wing.

CHAPTER TWENTY

Frank fought through the paralysis of deep sleep, attempting to surface. A strong hand shook him insistently, while a strained voice occupying the singular range of a shouted whisper urged, "Father Frank! Wake up! Wake up!"

Frank struggled to find his bearings as he bolted upright in his cot. The urgency of his rouser's tone caused him to bypass his waking ritual of, first, realizing where he was, then why he was there, and finally, experiencing the despair that accompanied those realizations. Daniel, the young new guard, was in his cell. "What's happening?" Frank croaked.

"The doc needs you in the infirmary right away," Daniel said, eyes wide and voice breathless.

Frank did not waste time asking for a reason. Instead, he swung his legs over the side of the cot, put on his pants, and splashed some water on his face. Then he and Daniel trotted through hallways and courtyards toward the infirmary, their quick pace punctuated by short pauses as the guard station buzzed them through locked doors.

When they arrived in the infirmary, Frank was surprised to see Yvette, the resident physician, sitting in a chair with her head in her hands. When she heard Frank's and Daniel's approaching footsteps, she raised her head and quickly assumed her customary expression of professional impassivity.

Yvette rose from the chair and extended her hand to Frank. "I'm glad you're here, Father," she said. Her habitually calm voice contained a strained quality that betrayed her anxiety.

"How can I help?" Frank replied.

Yvette cleared her throat. "Paul was brought into the infirmary a short while ago with severe injuries. Our team has done what we can to address most of his discomfort, including setting a few broken bones and stitching the deeper cuts. He doesn't appear to have any serious internal injuries, and he's conscious and alert. He asked to see you. If you're willing to sit with him, I'll just remind you that because of his injuries, it's important to avoid agitating him. Will you visit with him?"

"How was he injured?"

Yvette rubbed her temples with her finger pads. "He was beaten in the shower. He was alone when the guard who brought you here found him, and he refuses to identify whoever attacked him."

Frank moved his head in two staccato nods, ran his hand through thinning hair, and said, "Well, I guess you should take me to him."

Although prepared by Yvette, Frank nonetheless had to exercise rigid control over his facial expression when he saw Paul's bruised and battered body and face. Frank forced himself to look directly into Paul's single functional eye—the other was completely swollen shut. The "good" eye was less white than yellow, and had a bright red broken blood vessel.

"Will you please help me drink some water?" Paul croaked.

Frank complied, noting an unprecedented humility in Paul's tone. When Paul had finished drinking through the straw that Frank held to his parched and split lips, Paul said, "Thank you. And thanks for coming."

Waving aside Paul's thanks, Frank held his face in the compassionate expression he had cultivated during his long professional practice. He knew Paul was most likely to get to the reason he had requested Frank's presence if Frank kept his face attentive and his mouth silent.

Paul focused his yellow and red eye on Frank and rasped, with effort, "I need to make my confession."

Frank paused before beginning, gently, "Of course I'll hear your confession, but first perhaps we should discuss why you feel such urgency. I won't insult your intelligence by pretending our relationship is not contentious. Would you feel more comfortable waiting for Father Matt? He'll be here the day after tomorrow. I know you've been through something terrible, but Dr. Yvette didn't appear to be concerned that you have any injuries that won't mend."

This unassuming acknowledgement of Paul's implicit fear of imminent death caused Paul's eye simultaneously to well with tears and to widen with naked terror.

"I don't think I'm going to make it, Frank. I know what Dr. Y says, and I'm sure both of you believe I'll recover, but there's something very wrong. I just know it. Yes, I'd prefer to make my confession to Matt—but I don't think I have long enough to wait and I can't risk it."

Frank looked at the man he had loathed—the arrogant and vain man who embraced all that Frank had struggled to eradicate within himself. Frank took in the handsome face that had been disfigured, the strong body that was now broken, and his disdain weakened against the force of his innate sympathy for any soul in pain. This sympathy was as inextricably a part of himself as his unwanted sexual desires. Instead of trying to gather the wary reserve he had intended to maintain, Frank's voice unconsciously warmed as he placed his hand over Paul's and said, "Let me get my stole."

After he had secured the stole and said the prefatory blessing, Frank waited with unhurried expectation.

The usually cocksure Paul began with halting confusion, "I .. . I'm not sure I've ever made a genuine confession before. Hell, I'm actually pretty sure I never believed in God the entire time I wore the collar. I basically just said whatever I needed to say to convince my confessor that I was repentant about some minor infraction. Really, though, I was never bothered by anything I had done. I sure as shit never confessed the really juicy sins— the ones that landed me here."

Paul licked his dry lips and Frank, anticipating his thirst, lifted the water to the injured man's mouth. Paul took another long pull from the straw before continuing.

"I never cared about forgiveness of my sins or removing any impediment to my relationship with God because I neither had nor wanted a relationship with God. My goal was winning admiration and power. I learned early in life that the collar was a direct path to those goals, and my vocation would provide me with the materials for what eventually became my favorite pursuit. I had ready access to an endless supply of naïve young men who thought I was a hero.

"Making regular confession was just another part of the game I played. Repentance and reconciliation didn't figure into my algebra. I crafted confessions like works of art—just the right mix of introspection, remorse, and yearning for justification through faith—and then, I flawlessly *performed* those confessions. I could tell when my confessors had been moved by my performances, and seeing their response to my 'humility' felt like winning. One can never know what's going on in another person's head, but they *really* didn't know."

Paul's words had come in a torrent. While he paused to take a labored breath, Frank interjected, "Acting as your confessor, it's certainly interesting to hear how much you enjoyed manipulating confessors and mocking the sacrament. At the risk of beginning down a road of circular logic like Vizzini from *The Princess Bride*, what you've said so far begs the question: Why should I continue to participate in what you've just told me is probably a sham? How do I know you're not manipulating me like you manipulated all those other confessors?"

Paul attempted a few deep breaths. Every movement confirmed that his barely subdued terror remained. Unexpectedly, he barked out a harsh laugh. It ended as abruptly as it began when Paul felt its painful consequences in his damaged ribs. "It's really fucking ironic that my motivations for confession are questioned the only time they've ever been genuine."

Paul continued in a low, flat voice, "You can't know for sure. You should proceed as if my intent to manipulate you is a real possibility. I guess I can only offer this comfort: If my desire for repentance and reconciliation is not real, it's on me and not on you. Even though I didn't take the sacrament of ordination seriously, please just do what your vows call you to do: bear witness. Be the tool that helps me connect with God and trust that he'll sort out my motivations."

Paul adjusted himself to alleviate his discomfort, and continued, "I know Dr. Y doesn't believe my situation is as serious as I know it is. But holy fear of imminent death can bring even the biggest cynic to true belief and genuine repentance. I'm not one of those deathbed penitents who hedges his bets on the off-chance that God exists. I've been ordained, honored, admired, disgraced, and defrocked, but I've never experienced certainty of the reality of God until a couple of hours ago. Having come into contact with that presence and that reality, I can't live a second longer, and I certainly can't go to what's after this life, without at least trying to wash the stains on my soul."

Frank again assumed an expression of patient encouragement, and he nodded for Paul to continue.

Paul furrowed his brow with uncertainty, "I know I've facilitated this process a thousand thousand times, but I just don't know where to start."

Frank responded, "If you believe time is short, why not start with the deepest stain?"

"Might as well jump in," Paul agreed. "Obviously, we both know why I'm in this place, but I'm not sure that's really the deepest stain. I mean, it's not like I *raped* any of those young men, and they *were* young men. They weren't little boys. They were past puberty, past the age of reason, and they made a choice. I never forced anyone. Sure, there was some seduction involved, but they enjoyed that part as much as I did."

Frank was stunned by Paul's entrenched defensiveness, and took a moment to collect his wits. He had counseled many grown men who, as adolescents, had been gutted by abuse and manipulation that, according to Paul, they had "chosen."

Frank struggled to maintain the pastoral demeanor required of him in his role as confessor, and though he kept the volume of his voice low, he couldn't completely remove a steely undercurrent as he asked a series of questions to explore Paul's unrepentant declaration. "Didn't you say earlier that power was one of your primary motivations for pursuing the priesthood?"

"Yes."

"And I'm right to assume that, like many of us who chose this vocation, you first perceived that power as a child through the lens of the unquestioning deference that our Catholic communities and families bestow on priests?"

"Sure."

"So, of course, you knew that the balance of power between you and these boys was not equal. I'm not just talking about the differences in age. These boys were conditioned from birth to see your collar as the symbol of God's wisdom and power on earth, and to trust your judgment as approaching infallibility. Is that about the measure of it?"

Paul, perceiving an uncomfortable trap, weighed his words carefully, "Well, yes, but ..."

"If you're honest, isn't it true that what excited you, more than the physical pleasure, was not 'seduction,' as you called it, but exercising the power that came with your vocation to confuse and bend these boys to your will?"

Paul swallowed painfully. He had heard these arguments before, but they had never resonated as deeply as when he was confronted with the imminence of his mortality and the possibility that, sooner than he expected, and much sooner than he was prepared to accept, he might have to confront the One who would slice through his justifications and self-deception to the enormity of the damage he had inflicted.

Frank did not relent. "Isn't there a word for using influence and vastly unequal power to coerce sexual gratification?"

Paul looked at Frank pleadingly. "I know what you want me to say, Frank, but I can't say that word."

"If you are genuinely repentant, you must face the reality of your actions. Refusing to say 'rape' doesn't alleviate your guilt and, in the same way, using accurate language for what you did doesn't aggravate your crimes. The beauty of the sacrament of reconciliation is that you might feel a lightening of your spirit if you stop using evasive language to describe your sin. Sin is exactly what it is."

Paul nodded, and then immediately winced at the sharp movement. "Maybe I'll just start by describing what I did, and then we'll see whether it's important to label it."

Frank raised an eyebrow, but waited in deference to Paul's preferred approach. Paul cleared his throat, "Shortly after I began teaching, I realized how interesting I was to these young men. I remembered something similar from my own days as a student—the magnetism of a gifted teacher. These boys had such shining eyes, and they fell all over themselves to be useful to me or to have a little of me to themselves. These were the standouts among their peers. There were also weaker, less popular boys who acted similarly toward me, but they didn't interest me and I never encouraged them. I loved it when the leaders of the class sought me out because they thought they could go far with my guidance. At first, there were no sexual overtones to these relationships—I just enjoyed the ego stroke.

"My first young man really *did* make the first move. After he graduated, all bets were off. At first, I limited my physical attentions to students like him. Eventually, though, they began to bore me because it was too easy, and they were too emotional when it was time to move on. It required energy I no longer wanted to spend. So, I began to choose boys who were more firmly on the heterosexual end of the spectrum. It was more of a challenge, but the seduction was so much more exciting! I've heard about some men shortcutting this process with physical force, but that felt like cheating. There was an art to cultivating the patience and discipline that would mold red-blooded American males who didn't have an inkling of homosexual tendencies into pliable participants who would do whatever I asked.

"There was a fairly typical pattern. What started with purely platonic activities and attention gradually moved to extremely subtle innuendo, to increasingly overt expressions of my interest, to making the first physical overture. It was fascinating to watch their reactions change from innocent pride in receiving my attention, to confusion, to dawning awareness, to mild revulsion tinged with concern about disappointing me, to resignation. I liked that these relationships had a natural life cycle. I didn't have to worry about the unpleasantness of a lovesick admirer. When their time at the school ended, they were ready to move on, and so was I—it was tidy and satisfying."

Frank saw how Paul's good eye shone as he re-lived his exploits, and he made no effort to disguise his disgust. "Well, I don't think you're manipulating me. I believe you accurately described how you used these boys, stole their innocence, and spat them out when you were finished with them. You know that describing the facts surrounding your sin is only one of the requirements of confession. You're basically bursting with pride, and I don't see an iota of remorse."

Paul thoughtfully chose his words. "You're right," he agreed, "I've never been sorry. But maybe there's the start of a shift. I don't want anyone else to know this, so I'm invoking the seal of the confessional, but the man who assaulted me was one of my young men. I didn't recognize him at first—it looks like he's lived a rough life since our time together, and he looks much older than his actual age—but he revealed himself during the attack. There was a rage and disgust that I never would have thought he was capable of.

"I didn't spend much time thinking about the nature or impact of my April-September relationships—neither of us was old enough for me to think of them as May-December relationships. I knew, intellectually, that while they were beneficial to the young men in terms of networking, they probably caused some psychological damage. I never had to see that damage, though. It probably shouldn't have, but the vehemence of this man's anger shocked me. He repeated several times that I ruined his life. If I'm being honest, I can't be sure that being aware of the level of damage he believed I caused would have changed my behavior, but maybe it would have. I don't know.

"For the first time, though, I have some concerns about the harm I may have been responsible for. Maybe I'm not yet a true penitent, but I feel like I'm on the road. It scares me, but I really need the opportunity to go further. I'm willing to start the journey, but I'm afraid my body will fail me before I reach the destination."

Frank inhaled deeply and fixed his gaze on the crucifix in his hand.

"I appreciate your honesty. I can't imagine you're trying to manipulate me about not being repentant. And you know I can't grant absolution without repentance, but I'll walk the road with you. For tonight, let's end with a prayer."

Frank laid a light hand on Paul's head and began, "Heavenly Father, whose ways are not our ways, thank you for being the compassionate and loving force who redeems all evil acts. While we grieve over the injury done to Paul's body, we are grateful for the work of reconciliation you've begun in him. Grant him the strength to reflect unflinchingly on his actions with a mirror of truth. Help him to see and understand, with your understanding, how his sins have damaged others and have distanced him from you. Grant him the endurance to run the race you've set out for him, as the author and perfector of his faith. Bring him into genuine relationship with you and with the community of your holy Church.

"Dear Lord, give Paul relief from his physical suffering so that he can focus on the hard work of seeking you and atoning for his sins. Grant him the grace and courage to love and serve you with gladness and singleness of heart. Holy Comforter, grant Paul the peace that passes understanding. Ease his fear of imminent death if doing so will help him avoid distraction as he seeks relationship with you, and the repentance and reconciliation you desire for him.

"For myself, Lord, please use me in accordance with your will to best help Paul toward your righteous wisdom, empathy, and love. If my sharing in any portion of Paul's suffering will further your purposes, Dear Lord, I ask that, in accordance with your will, I may share his burden.

"In the name of Jesus Christ, the Blessed Virgin Mary, and all the saints, we humbly pray. Amen."

Frank raised his head to see Paul's single, discolored eye fixed on him. "So, you're not going to grant me absolution tonight, then." He said it as a statement rather than as a question.

Remorsefully but resolutely, Frank said, "No, Paul. I'm

encouraged you're moving toward repentance, but I can't, in conscience, grant absolution where repentance doesn't yet exist. I'll be here to help you get there, though."

"And what if I die before we get there? You're content to let me die like this?"

"Again, Paul, your wounds are severe, but Dr. Yvette seems confident you'll make a full recovery. We have time to do this hard work, and to do it right. Maybe this will be a comfort: Remember the prayer for those 'whose faith is known to God alone.' None of us knows all the implications of that idea, but I like to think of it as God's ability to redeem and relate with people who have not explicitly repented or professed their faith, or who may not even be consciously aware of their own faith. It's extremely unlikely, but if you die before making a full, genuinely repentant confession, and receiving absolution, even then, God is capable of completing the work he has started in you."

Seeing that Frank would not be moved, Paul turned his head and closed his eye. Frank placed a gentle hand on Paul's, and gave it a pat. Frank's prayer that Paul would experience the peace that passes understanding appeared to have been answered powerfully and affirmatively, and Paul's heightened anxiety gave way to the morphine-like effect of that peace. He drifted toward sleep. Just before losing consciousness, Paul heard Frank say from the doorway, "I'll come see you as early in the morning as I can."

Neither man knew, of course, that Frank would be in his own sickbed the next morning.

CHAPTER TWENTY-ONE

The first curious features on which Paul's attention focused were his hands. They were folded in his lap, and they were so strange that he raised and examined them. They were smooth, fair, unmarred, and, most surprisingly, young. Paul knew these hands did not belong to his dark-haired, nearly fifty-year-old self. As one does in a dream, Paul acknowledged the strangeness and then mentally shrugged and accepted that these unfamiliar hands were his.

As his awareness of his surroundings expanded, Paul recognized that he was in his office at the parochial school where he had spent the most fulfilling part of his career. Lucid enough to recognize he was dreaming, Paul marveled at the level of detail his mind conjured in furnishing his familiar, lavish office. The shades of fabric on the draperies and the sumptuous chairs were remarkably precise and vivid. His brain even supplied the stubborn ring at the corner of the desk from when a careless student had failed to use a coaster.

Paul enjoyed revisiting these surroundings—running his unfamiliar hands over the familiar, polished surface of his desk, breathing in the soothing aroma of the books that lined the substantial bookshelf, and standing up to peer at the many framed photographs of himself with various dignitaries.

While he contemplated a photo of himself with a devout Senator who had donated generously to the school, the office door opened to admit . . . himself. Paul was struck dumb by the strange dislocation of observing himself from outside of himself. His other-self smiled sardonically and said wryly, "I see you've made yourself at home, Joshua." His other self winked to take the sting out of any perceived rebuke.

The words added a strange overlay of memory to the perception of Paul's dream self, and in addition to realizing he was observing himself from the perspective of fifteen-year-old Joshua Phillips, he now remembered this precise encounter. He recalled how he had surprised Joshua exhibiting a somewhat unexpected degree of familiarity while waiting in his office. As the *déjà vu* suggested the rest of the meeting to his consciousness, he experienced a vague trepidation.

Through Joshua's eyes, Paul watched himself cross the room, an easy, white-toothed smile offering forgiveness for Joshua having overstepped himself. As Paul clapped a strong hand on his shoulder, Paul-as-Joshua smelled Paul's subtle aroma of soap and aftershave, and Paul's hand remained on his shoulder as he began telling the stories behind many of the photos Joshua had been examining. Throughout the conversation, Joshua felt a low level of unease about Paul's persistent proximity and lingering physical contact. An outside observer wouldn't necessarily have detected anything improper, but Joshua had a vague sense that he and Paul were standing slightly too close together. Joshua's discomfort was heightened when Paul subtly brushed against him while reaching across to direct attention to a photo hanging on the far side of Joshua.

As if he sensed Joshua's disquiet, Paul said abruptly, "Well, enough of that, Josh. You didn't come here to listen to me relive the glory days. Have a seat and we'll talk about what you can be doing now to make sure that, by the time you're applying to colleges, you'll have an impressive list of achievements and glowing letters of recommendation."

Joshua obediently moved across the desk to take a seat, relief mixing with eagerness. He appreciated the interest Father Paul had taken in him over the past several months, and he knew that the boys Father Paul previously mentored had their pick of the best colleges. Joshua wanted to be a science major, and thrilled at the thought of participating in the most advanced scientific research at the most prestigious universities.

And he wasn't just in Father Paul's office because he wanted help getting into a great college. He enjoyed being around Father Paul and he was honored that Father Paul had taken an interest in him. If he had recently begun to feel twinges of anxiety during their increasingly frequent meetings, he didn't dwell on it. Instead he shoved those emotions down deep— where feelings belonged, according to his family's culture.

Even if he had chosen to explore his unease, Joshua probably would not have been able to pinpoint its source. Father Paul had been generous with his time and his talents. In addition to his charisma, Joshua had come to appreciate Father Paul's incisive intelligence and wit. As Joshua's appreciation for Father Paul grew, Father Paul's interest in Joshua's success also seemed to grow—he invited Joshua to accompany him to the school's ritzy annual fundraiser, advising that such networking opportunities eventually could yield impressive letters of recommendation.

If Father Paul sometimes stood closer than was comfortable, and if his hand sometimes lingered too long after an encouraging pat on the back, Joshua didn't dwell on his confusion. He had no context for an interpretation that would give him cause for overt alarm. He was not so sheltered that he was unaware of pedophilia and homosexuality, but he thought of pedophiles as men who preyed on small boys—boys too young and weak to resist—and homosexuals as effeminate men who had no affinity for masculine pursuits like sports. Father Paul was confident, ruggedly athletic, and dominant. And he implicitly acknowledged Joshua's own heterosexuality by asking him about the girls he liked. Father Paul also supplied the same strange encouragement that Joshua's parents and other adults exhibited: a sort of perverse biological pride in what they perceived to be his ability to attract a flock of girls and to "play the field." Of course, these same parents never would have offered the same encouragement if their daughters had demonstrated the same capacity.

Father Paul and Joshua passed a pleasant and productive half hour discussing Joshua's school list and his progress on a number of tasks Father Paul had assigned. Finally, they decided on a plan for tasks to complete before their next meeting.

As Father Paul and Joshua were finishing up, Father Paul took a set of keys from his pocket and opened the credenza near where Joshua sat. As he reached in to extract a bottle of scotch and two crystal tumblers, he asked, "Any big plans for the weekend?"

Joshua explained that he planned on an early night because he had a track meet the next day and he was scheduled to participate in five events. He was also going to see the new Kevin Harlow film, which had received great reviews. No one who had seen it would talk about it with anyone who hadn't, so as not to give away any spoilers. He had already bought the tickets.

"Who are you taking?" asked Father Paul with a knowing smile as he handed Joshua one of the two tumblers containing three fingers of amber liquid. Joshua flushed slightly, both because a large part of his excitement about the movie plans related to the fact that he'd asked Kendra Scott to join him, and because he wanted to keep his cool during the unprecedented experience of sharing a drink with Father Paul. Joshua wasn't a stranger to alcohol—he had drunk beer with his friends at parties, and he had gigglingly joined his friends in taking swigs from their parents' liquor bottles. It was new and unexpected, however, for a grown man to casually hand Joshua a glass in the same manner as he might offer a drink to a colleague.

Joshua tried to strike the right balance between sufficient gravitas and nonchalance. Unconsciously, Joshua adopted the expression and body language he had observed when his father's friends accepted drinks at parties: he nodded his thanks almost imperceptibly, and then crossed one leg over the other so that his right ankle rested on his left thigh, while draping his arm over the chair's armrest and leaning back into the seat with a slight slouch as if to say, "Whew, what a week—time to take a load off!"

If Father Paul was amused by Joshua's studiedly casual approach, his face did not embarrass Joshua by betraying anything but relaxation and camaraderie. In the part of his dreaming brain that was Paul, he recalled being amused and impressed by Joshua's moxie—the insouciance with which he accepted the drink had been such a departure from the other boys. Paul had needed to look away and pretend to be distracted by reaching down to address a non-existent fleck on the carpet to avoid chuckling when Joshua's first taste of the scotch appeared to be closer to a gulp than a sip. He remembered imagining the surprise Joshua must have experienced.

Indeed, Joshua nearly choked when the slight burn and foul taste registered. But he steeled himself, and relaxed and then constricted his throat to swallow the unpleasant mouthful. He observed the small sip Father Paul pulled from his glass and, after recovering while they further discussed his weekend plans, he mimicked Father Paul's draws. The reduced quantity made the scotch significantly more palatable, if not actually pleasant.

Joshua and Father Paul slowly drained their glasses, passing another thirty minutes of conversation. The scotch warmed them, and Joshua felt a general sensation of well-being spread through his body. The earlier slight misgivings about Father Paul disappeared, and he just felt grateful for Father Paul's assistance, and proud of his own sophistication.

When both glasses were empty, Father Paul took Joshua's tumbler and opened the credenza, saying, "Time for one more?" Although Joshua needed to get home to do the homework that would otherwise get lost in his busy weekend, he grinned and said, "Why not?"

Joshua and Father Paul began their second drinks, which Joshua noticed were somewhat more full than the previous had been. Joshua settled back into the comfortable leather armchair and took a sip as if he'd had years of practice. He asked about Father Paul's time at university, and was surprised to learn that, while in college, Father Paul had not been a particularly serious student—he had managed his academic responsibilities, but in a way that left plenty of room for his fraternity, parties, and, most surprisingly, girls.

The last admission surprised Joshua and made him feel honored to be taken into Father Paul's confidence. "Really?" he asked, "You dated a lot of girls in college?"

"I'm not proud of it, but more than 'dated,'" Father Paul admitted wryly. "I didn't always treat those young ladies with a great deal of respect."

"How about you?" asked Father Paul. "Any special girls on your radar?"

The question caused Joshua to flush. "There is a girl," he conceded.

"Does she like you back?"

"I don't know," Joshua groaned. "Sometimes it seems like she does, but other times she basically ignores me." Joshua explained his confusion about Kendra's conflicting signals, and his excitement for Saturday night's date. His inhibitions were relaxed because of the alcohol, and were further relaxed with his new understanding that Father Paul had not always been a celibate cleric. Maybe he actually understood the alternate despair and elation caused by the mystery of the opposite sex. Joshua shared more of his feelings about Kendra—how her attention warmed him, her indifference left him desolate, and her beauty drove him to distraction. Joshua's description of Kendra's physical charms became more enthusiastic than his internal filter would have allowed if he had been sober, and he noticed, without alarm but with a flicker of amusement, that his last few words had been somewhat slurred. He considered repeating the slurred words more slowly to demonstrate that he was not drunk, but then he remembered what he had actually said. He'd been crude and inappropriate. To a priest. A priest who held a great deal of influence over his future. Coloring deeply, Joshua stammered a hasty apology.

Father Paul merely chuckled and reached for Joshua's empty glass, setting it and his own nearly full glass on the desk.

"Listen, Josh," he said, patting Joshua on the knee, "it's natural for a young man like you to have these feelings, and to express them. What's unnatural is to keep them bottled up and to pretend they don't exist. For men, especially, it's important to have an outlet for these urges, or we run the risk of being unable to focus on our work and other responsibilities."

Joshua gulped and nodded, unable to do more to express his gratitude for Father Paul's understanding. Father Paul's hand remained on his knee, gently rubbing back and forth as he said the words intended to ease Joshua's discomfort.

"I assume, based on what you said, that you haven't been physical with Kendra. Is that right?

Joshua's eyes widened, and he nodded.

"Have you been physical with any other girls?"

Joshua remained mute as he shook his head.

Father Paul nodded knowingly, as if he were a doctor who had been given the final piece of information necessary for a definitive diagnosis.

"Sometimes, when we're new to all of this, it's helpful to be able to explore and experiment with people we trust." As he spoke, Father Paul's short, gentle strokes extended from Joshua's knee to his upper thigh. Joshua froze at the rapid, unanticipated, and unmistakable escalation.

The persistent, subconscious apprehension broke the surface of Joshua's awareness, and he could no longer avoid Father Paul's intent. The knowledge confounded him. He couldn't square the way Father Paul was rubbing his leg with what he knew about the unimpeachable nature of priests and their wholly holy calling. These contradictions would have been too much even for his sober brain. And Joshua was anything but sober. He was frozen by confusion as Father Paul's hand traveled further up Joshua's thigh, brushing lightly over his crotch. To Joshua's horror and further puzzlement, he realized he had an erection. Still paralyzed by shock and indecision, Joshua remained silent with his gaze averted. Father Paul's hand returned to Joshua's crotch and stroked with determined pressure.

Joshua continued to work to unlock the puzzle of what was happening. Father Paul wasn't just a priest, a chosen conduit with a direct line to God, he was an important man with wide-ranging connections. These facts contrasted with Joshua's long understanding that sexual intimacy between men was unnatural and sinful. And Father Paul had explained he was doing a kindness for Joshua—helping to overcome his inexperience so that he would be better prepared for physical interaction with women. Surely Father Paul, who was wise and worldly, had a better understanding of this than Joshua did.

Joshua continued to struggle with these contradictions as Father Paul pulled him to his feet. Joshua found that his legs were unwilling to support him and, as if anticipating this, Father Paul supported Joshua's weight by bending his knees, wrapping his arm underneath Joshua's armpits, and leaning the boy against himself.

With one arm occupied by supporting Joshua, Father Paul's other hand continued to stroke Joshua's crotch outside of his pants, and then he unbuttoned Joshua's trousers and, with a smooth movement, slid the pants and underwear down his legs. Joshua murmured something incomprehensible as Father Paul took hold of his penis, and his confused brain gave way as his body reacted to the unprecedented and inescapably pleasurable sensation. With a shudder and a flush of shame, Joshua's body betrayed him as he climaxed.

After the physical release, Joshua, on the precipice of losing consciousness, was unable to move as he felt Father Paul drape him gently over the desk. He did not fight the blissful unconsciousness that overtook him within seconds.

Joshua was startled back to semi-consciousness by a pain that was at once agonizingly sharp and steadily achy. His face pressed against the polished desk, Joshua could not regain clarity of thought, but what wits that remained identified what was happening to him with a sickening horror. The same as before, he could not will his body to move or to resist, and the only protest he was capable of was a long, low moan.

Willfully misinterpreting, Father Paul leaned down close to Joshua and whispered in a voice ragged with exertion, "I knew you wanted this as much as I did."

A tear slipped from Joshua's eye as his body reflexively retched, and he returned, gratefully, to painless unconsciousness.

WHEN JOSHUA NEXT AWOKE, he was no longer drunk, but his head throbbed and he was desperately thirsty. He flexed his fingers and moved his arms to test the responsiveness of his limbs. As his wakefulness increased, Joshua noted the room was in deep shadow save for a lamp blazing from Father Paul's desk. At the thought of Father Paul, Joshua reddened with shame. He sat up on the couch on which he'd been sleeping, and gingerly removed a blanket with which Father Paul had apparently covered him.

"What time is it?" Joshua croaked.

Father Paul looked up from his paperwork and beamed at Joshua. "A little past eleven. I called your mother and told her you were helping me with a time-sensitive research project and would be home late."

Father Paul chuckled, "I'll bet you have a doozy of a hangover—we'll have to take it a little easier on the scotch next time."

Joshua stared down mutely at his pants. He couldn't remember how they got back on.

"Why don't you run along—I know you have a busy weekend ahead. I'll look forward to hearing about the date with your young lady. Let's plan to meet at the same time next week to talk about our progress on the goals we set today." With that, Father Paul returned his attention to the paperwork before him, and Joshua knew he had been dismissed.

Joshua stood up and suppressed a wince. Wordlessly, he gathered his jacket and his backpack from where he had placed them when he entered the office what seemed a lifetime ago. He fumbled with the lock on the door—when had it been locked?— and then he closed it quietly behind him. He maintained composure until he reached the bike rack where his bicycle was, and then he just stood there in a stupor, leaning against the bike rack for support, a barrage of unanswerable questions assaulting his mind.

Had he, as Father Paul suggested, wanted such a thing to happen? What signals had he given to make Father Paul think he did? If he didn't want it, why did his body betray him when Father Paul touched him? Was he gay—a state of being that he and his friends found to be so disgusting and ridiculous that it was the punchline of their locker room jokes? If he wasn't gay, why didn't he fight back? Obviously, he couldn't tell anyone, but what if his friends somehow found out? Why had Father Paul acted as if nothing had happened? Should Joshua do the same thing? Would the same thing happen when they met again next Friday?

His parents didn't have the first idea about how to apply to state schools, let alone to the elite universities on which Joshua had set his cap. Without Father Paul's guidance, Joshua could not hope to leap the admissions hurdle, let alone putting together a feasible scholarship package. At the moment, he wanted to distance himself from Father Paul, but what would that mean for his dreams?

An even more complicated truth struggled to rise to the surface: He had so long admired and wanted to emulate Father Paul—what did this say about him? And, even in the midst of his confusion, he still cared about Father Paul's opinion of him, and craved Father Paul's approval.

Joshua was a person of action. He never remained paralyzed with indecision when confronted with a problem. Instead, he developed plans and attacked them. But Joshua had no idea where to begin formulating a plan for this situation. Worse, the person whose advice he valued the most was the problem. Joshua felt nausea rise within him once again. He rushed to the grass nearby and his stomach emptied itself of its contents. He unlocked his bicycle with the precise movements that characterized his usually orderly mind, but then buried his face in his hands, crying out in gulping, gasping sobs.

CHAPTER TWENTY-TWO

P aul woke himself with the sobs that had carried over to his body from the dreamworld. He breathed deeply to calm himself as he returned to the awareness that, in fact, he occupied his own body and mind instead of the body and mind of Joshua Phillips. Paul hadn't spared a thought for Joshua in years. But now, having lived within Joshua's experience, Paul couldn't lie to himself any longer. He couldn't tell himself that Joshua had been a mature young man when they had known each other. He had been a child who had had no point of reference for his encounter with Paul, and no skills to extricate himself from the situation.

For the first time, Paul caught a glimpse of the enormity of his actions. Regarding his "seductions," Paul experienced a new emotion: shame. By inhabiting Joshua's perspective, Paul internalized what he had been told but had never before appreciated —that Joshua and, Paul now realized, all the other boys had neither the capacity to give consent nor the tools to refuse him.

Dwelling within Joshua's perspective laid bare another lie Paul had repeated to himself so often that he had come to believe it. The substance Paul added to the boys' drinks did not simply relax them and remove their inhibitions. In combination with the stiff drinks, it impaired their awareness and rendered them incapable of resistance. The lies fell away, and the truth to which Paul had willfully blinded himself looked him full in the face: Paul had not seduced those boys—he had raped them.

Once he was confronted with the truth, Paul experienced horror at the enormity of the damage he had inflicted over many years. For the first time, he wept for the pain he had caused rather than for his own perceived persecution. Not used to feeling guilt, the sensation was crushing and inescapable. Paul was certain that, now that it had broken in, it would dig in like the most unwelcome of guests.

The immediacy of the dream and its aftermath had been so consuming that Paul hadn't taken in his surroundings, as one usually does upon waking. When his weeping had run its course, he felt that hollowed-out, soul-scrubbing effect following uncontrollable sobbing. It was only then that he realized he had not awoken in his usual bunk. He considered the dim, sterile light of his strange surroundings, and the circumstances that had landed him in the prison hospital came flooding back to him. But it seemed as though the situation had changed vastly from when he had drifted into the sleep from which he feared he wouldn't awake: though his eyes were puffy from weeping, both were fully functional.

Paul took further stock of his body and was surprised to note an absence of pain. Reasoning that the medical staff must have put a powerful opioid in his IV as he slept, Paul felt his body and his face with his hands. In addition to the ease with which he was able to move his broken limbs, Paul was mystified by the smoothness of his face. It contained none of the lacerations or swelling from the severe beating he had endured a few short hours earlier.

Paul began shouting for the attendant, for the doctor, for anyone within earshot. When the duty nurse ran in breathlessly, she started upon seeing Paul sitting up in his bed without any cuts or bruises. In an urgent tone, Paul said, "I need to see Father Frank right away."

Unconsciously responding to his imperious tone, the nurse replied, "I'll call Dr. Yvette."

While he waited, Paul removed his casts and bandages, and slid to his knees on the floor.

Yvette, rushing in a few minutes later, found Paul in this prone position, alternately praying, weeping, and laughing as his emotions alternated between intense grief and shame as he remembered his dream, and confusion, amazement, and gratitude for his remarkable healing.

When Yvette touched Paul's shoulder, Paul looked up with red-rimmed but shining eyes. "It has to be a miracle, Doctor," began Paul in a rush. "My body has never felt better. I need to see Father Frank right away."

Yvette maintained a thoughtful silence, as if she needed to see Frank herself. "We'll send someone to bring Father Frank, but first, let's take a better look at you."

The doctor began checking Paul's current condition against the inventory of wounds she had catalogued less than twelve hours earlier. Every single one of the lacerations, broken bones, bruises, swelling, and potential sources of internal bleeding she had noted seemed to have disappeared completely. Although Yvette was a woman of lifelong faith, and she attended her respectable, stolid Episcopalian church semi-regularly, her religious inclinations knew their place. While she conceded the theoretical possibility of divine intervention, she placed such possibilities firmly behind explanations that relied on observable, replicable scientific reasoning. The further Yvette's examination of Paul progressed, the more she had to subdue competing sensations of wonder and panic as the foundations of her comfortable worldview suffered indelible cracks.

As Yvette prepared the paperwork for new x-rays of Paul's ribs, a guard entered the room in a flurry, his face ashen.

"It's Father Frank," blurted out the man. "You need to come right away."

Yvette's long training took over and she responded unhesitatingly to the panic in the guard's voice. Almost before she realized it, she had put down the camera she was using to document Paul's condition, and had taken two long strides toward the door. Hesitantly, the guard nodded toward the camera and said, "You might want to bring that."

Wrinkling her forehead and thinking to herself, *What in the world is going on?* Yvette had a presentiment that whatever was happening with Father Frank related to Paul's astonishing recovery. She hastily retrieved the camera and followed the guard at a trot.

When Yvette left, Paul resumed his prostrate position on the floor, praying. He alternately thanked God for his physical improvement and wept because of his new awareness of the gravity of his sins. He did not know how long Yvette was absent, but he felt a shift in the air around him upon her silent return.

Paul was surprised to find that Yvette's face mirrored his own—swollen and blotchy from crying. Paul raised himself from the floor and sat on his bed patiently. Rather than joining him at the bedside and resuming her examination, Yvette sank into the closest chair and rested her forearms on her thighs, her face a shifting mask of grief, confusion, and disbelief.

When she was finally able to collect herself enough to speak, Yvette cleared her throat. Her voice lacked the authority that she'd learned from holding her own for many years among the prisoners. She sounded much younger and more fragile. "Father Frank has died," she said simply.

Paul sat in stunned silence. "What? . . . How?" he finally asked.

In a voice raspy with grief Yvette replied, "The guard found him in his cell this morning, looking like he had been severely beaten. He was still alive when I arrived, but he died as we were moving him from his cell to the prison hospital. The autopsy should clarify some things, but I suspect he died from internal bleeding."

"When . . . Who . . . ?" Paul stammered.

"We don't know," Yvette answered. "He went back to bed in his cell after visiting you late last night, and as far as we know only the guards had access to him between then and this morning. Of course, they're being questioned, but I would be surprised if that yields anything. It was the strangest thing . . ." Yvette broke off, shaking her head as if to clear it.

"It was the strangest thing," she began again, "but Father Frank's injuries looked identical to yours. His left eye was swollen shut, he had the same lacerations to his face and arms, and I think his autopsy will catalog injuries that match the injuries you had last night. How does something like this happen?"

"I don't know," answered Paul truthfully. "I mean, obviously . . . God . . . but I don't know how, and I certainly don't know why."

After a brief and incredulous silence, Paul asked, "Have you called in a priest to say last rites for Father Frank? It would be important to him."

Yvette nodded without speaking, lost in thought. A few minutes later, she spoke again, "He was still conscious when I arrived, and he spoke to me as we were moving him here."

"What did he say?"

"He was obviously in a lot of pain, but he didn't seem afraid or upset. Instead, he was . . . joyful? He was insistent that nobody had beaten him. He said . . . he said that his injuries were proof that God loved him and that God was willing to use even imperfect people for great things. He said I should tell others what I had seen and heard. He also asked me to pass along a message to you."

Yvette paused to locate a glass and water, and Paul waited impatiently while she took a long drink. After she had finished, she continued, "He said that God wants to use you, too, and that your imperfections make you perfect for God's purposes. He said not to squander your new knowledge. Does that make any sense to you?"

Tears that had been eager all morning once again escaped from Paul's eyes and raced down his cheeks. "It makes all the sense in the world," he affirmed. "When Father Matt finishes with last rites, will you please ask him to come and see me? I need to make my confession."

Yvette observed the difference between when Paul requested to make his confession to Father Frank the night before, and his current request. Although he had obviously been in a great deal of pain the previous evening because of his physical injuries, Paul's request for Father Frank's presence had had an urgency borne of terror. A different motivation was manifest in this morning's request. He asked to see Father Matt with an air of hope, and his eyes shone with wonder and purpose.

Yvette's head reeled from the whirlwind of the previous twelve hours, and from the inexplicable phenomena the morning had presented to her. "Absolutely," she said, "I'll let him know." She pulled the clipboard from the end of Paul's bed and retrieved her camera from the chair where she had set it down.

"Shall we continue?"

PART IV

CHAPTER TWENTY-THREE

As Dr. Yvette had predicted, Frank's autopsy revealed the cause of death to be exsanguination resulting from a liver laceration. This particular injury did not match the injuries Yvette had treated and documented with respect to Paul the previous evening, but in every other respect, the medical examiner's written observations of Frank's injuries were consistent with, and in fact eerily identical to, Yvette's notes on Paul's injuries. Yvette surmised the liver laceration would have been revealed if she had access to the right imaging equipment.

One of the many surprising aspects surrounding Frank's mysterious death and Paul's remarkable recovery was that the events did not generate larger ripples of attention. The story was not widely publicized because the prison had an interest in containing the news of a mysterious death of a prisoner within its care. As Frank had no living family willing to maintain contact with him, the prison did not have to contend with pressure from that quarter. The Church had its own reasons for containing the story. The institution's public relations machine, always leery of miracle claims, was particularly circumspect regarding an unexplained phenomenon in which the primary participants were priests convicted of sexual crimes against children.

But those who had been affected by the events, or who had observed them firsthand, couldn't help but talk about what they had witnessed. They soon learned, though, that most people dismiss fantastic stories they haven't personally experienced. Even the previously unblemished credibility of observers like Yvette did not lend much weight to the remarkable tale, and Yvette watched her own stock drop with each telling—her audience averting its eyes in embarrassment at what they perceived to be her delusion and newfound religious fervor. Even friends and colleagues Yvette knew to have their own religious inclinations were uncomfortable discussing the subject with her, and their faces feigned polite interest while their eyes did not quite conceal concern for Yvette's mental health.

As had Yvette before the event with Paul and Frank, her friends and colleagues preferred their church (and, by extension, their God) to stay in its place. For the most "religious" of them, it was a forum for gathering, socializing, and networking, and for others with only nominal religious affiliation, it was an occasional obligation. Their faith memberships were perhaps most helpful in allowing them to identify where they stood in the endless categorizations of "us versus them," and bolstering their feelings of belonging and superiority. Even the regular churchgoers among Yvette's circle of acquaintances, who were steeped in language regarding God's omnipresence and omnipotence, did not translate the concept of such power into their daily lives.

Absent a plausible scientific explanation for the events, Yvette continued to believe she had witnessed a miracle. Yvette was baffled by God's motives in trading the life of a good, though flawed, man for a man who had been such a willing instrument of evil. Yvette didn't see evidence that the miracle had transformed Paul into a valuable member of society, or in this case, the prison community. Instead, when he was not required to be out of his cell, Paul spent all of his time on his bunk, sobbing.

Just because Yvette didn't observe an improvement in Paul did not mean he hadn't changed profoundly. Part of the reason Paul wept was because of his confusion and grief about Father Frank, whose joyous selflessness, as reported by Yvette, baffled Paul. The bigger reason for his constant tears, though, were the dreams that inundated his sleep and haunted his waking hours. He did all he could to avoid sleep. Even so, inevitably, eventually he succumbed to what his body demanded, and the resulting dreams were visceral, intense, and singular in their theme. Paul experienced, from the adolescent perspective of his victims, the sexual violations Paul had inflicted upon them. He inhabited their naivete and trust of priests; he experienced their confusion, pain, and shame about the acts into which Paul forced and coerced them; and he lived within the ever-present, stomach-churning sense of betrayal.

In his dreams, Paul so often saw his own face twisted in manipulation and lust that in waking life, his reflection became repulsive to him. For most of his life he had been unable to pass a reflective surface without admiring his own pleasing features, but he began covering the polished sheet of metal that served as a mirror in his cell, and avoiding the other mirrors within the prison's walls.

Because Paul continued to refuse to identify his attacker, he was housed in a single-person cell within the protective unit. Other than the solitary walk in a small, secluded courtyard for an hour each day, he passed his time praying or speaking with Father Matt, the prison chaplain.

While Yvette did not believe that Paul was using the remarkable gift he had received for any higher purpose, Father Matt had a different perspective. Paul was, admittedly, spending a great deal of time in seclusion, but that time alone was not wasted. Before the Event, Father Matt's interactions with Paul had been infrequent and unpleasant. Paul had postured and attempted to exert hierarchical dominance over Father Matt. Father Matt had reminded Paul, as gently as possible, that Paul was no longer a priest and that his time might be better spent repenting for the crimes that had landed him in prison and resulted in defrocking. Paul had responded by raising his chin defiantly and arguing that the process that stripped him of his status as an ordained priest had been illegitimate. The two men hadn't had much to say to each other after that.

But the Event significantly altered this dynamic. In his terror and grief, Paul requested a visit from Father Matt and, with unprecedented humility, Paul began making his confession. As with Saint Augustine, a single session of confession was grossly inadequate for Paul to detail the extent of his sin or to adequately express the depth of his remorse. Paul and Father Matt understood that this confession would be an ongoing process that would take as long as it took. After it became apparent that his dreams would continue to plague his sleep and recall specific instances of abuse he had inflicted, Paul and Father Matt decided to allow God's messages, in the form of the dreams, to shape each confessional session. Father Matt scheduled time to visit Paul every day, and every day, Paul described some new horror he had inflicted on a young man who had trusted him to be God's representative on earth.

The stories that Paul shared haunted Father Matt but, paradoxically, they also gave him reason to hope. Father Matt had heard the confessions of other men who had sexually abused children and adolescents and, like Father Frank had done with Paul in the medical ward, he had occasionally been forced to suspend confessions because of a demonstrable lack of true repentance.

His current sessions with Paul were markedly different, however. The confident, arrogant priest who had refused to acknowledge the validity of the process that had defrocked him, and who had not accepted that he had raped sexual "partners," had been replaced by a broken man with tormented eyes. Paul's previous physical fastidiousness, which he had maintained even throughout his pre-Event incarceration, deserted him. A life-long adherent to rigorous physical exercise, a healthy diet, and meticulous grooming, Paul had lost all interest in food and exercise. He became unkempt, and his increasingly sallow skin, declining weight, bedraggled hair, and stale odor contributed to a general impression of wretchedness and despair. Anyone meeting Paul for the first time would have found it impossible to believe he had been a respected and admired member of the community only a few short years before.

During the daily confession, Paul could not wait to verbally shed the misery of whatever particular instance of abuse had been recalled to him during the previous night's dream. While Father Matt had good reason to keep up his guard around Paul, he was convinced of the sincerity of Paul's confession and repentance. Paul no longer justified his behavior, nor saw it as a consensual activity between willing participants—those scales had been ripped from his eyes. Paul had taken the secular consequence of imprisonment in stride, but he was undone by the perfectly proportionate form his divine discipline had taken.

Father Matt did what most compassionate priests know they are called to do. Even though he had mixed feelings about Paul, he bore witness to his suffering. On the one hand, Paul, and those like him, had damaged countless innocents and had sullied Father Matt's beloved Church. On the other hand, the same aspects of Father Matt's nature and faith created space for a deep well of compassion for Paul's suffering, even if—perhaps especially because—it had been self-inflicted.

Another aspect of the process to which he bore witness, which filled Father Matt with wonder, was the perfect mechanism through which God worked his transformation in Paul. The biblical metaphor of a "hardened heart" had so accurately described Paul before the assault: he was unrepentant, arrogant, and wholly lacking in sympathy. Father Matt would not have wished the suffering Paul had inflicted upon anyone—even Paul himself—but he appreciated how effectively Paul being forced to inhabit his victims' perspectives engendered remorse within Paul's heart. It was working to soften Paul's heart for whatever purpose God intended.

And Paul's heart *had* become tender. At first, although he had the intellectual honesty to acknowledge that experiencing for himself the damage he had inflicted was a just consequence, his pity was primarily self-focused, and he bemoaned what *he* was being forced to endure. In the course of the extended sacrament of confession, however, Father Matt witnessed a gradual shift in Paul's sympathies. Over time, Paul stopped lamenting the merciless onslaught of dreams and his inability to be comfortable within his own mind. He began focusing on his victims' misery and expressing anxiety for their mental suffering. Because of the limited scope of his dreams, he did not know exactly how his crimes had altered the course of his victims' lives, but he experienced enough of their pain to know it could not help but take root deep in their psyches.

Father Matt observed this shifting center of gravity with interest and hope. The confessions continued to be emotionally exhausting for both men. At the end of each confession, when it would have ordinarily been time to assign a penance, Father Matt could not conceive of a discipline more likely to further carry Paul on the path to repentance, forgiveness, and reconciliation than the process God had already devised and implemented. He ended each confession with a straightforward, "Keep dreaming, and sin no more."

The process felt interminable both to Paul and to Father Matt, but after many hundreds of dreams and confessions, the dreams stopped. After his first night of dreamless sleep, Paul woke feeling rested for the first time in over a year.

CHAPTER TWENTY-FOUR

The morning after that first, blessed, dreamless sleep, Paul was on his knees in his cell, trying to make sense of the purpose of his recent experiences, and coming up short. If the purpose had been to fill him with guilt, shame, and remorse, then it had been accomplished in spades. But to what end? Paul could not use his remorse constructively within the walls of the prison.

"Stop feeling sorry for yourself," a voice behind him chided.

Paul had not heard the cell door open, so his head jerked up to see who had interrupted his contemplation. Sitting backwards in the metal chair by the door, his legs straddling the seat and his arms resting casually on the chair's back, was Francis Muncy. Paul thought he may have been hallucinating. He closed his eyes, then opened them again, and still Frank sat, looking at him with some amusement.

"Of course I'm not physically here, but I'm going to keep projecting into your brain until you hear what I have to say."

Paul found he could not look away from Frank. He had never believed in the existence of incorporeal spirits, and he certainly had never expected to see one, much less hold a conversation with one, but he discovered that he had, apparently, harbored expectations of how an otherworldly spirit would appear. Contrary to his belief that there should be some visible aura, or inner luminescence, or that the imperfections that marked Frank in life would be erased, Frank appeared solid and . . . ordinary. It was like the smoothing features on high-end televisions that made subjects appear uncomfortably close. Frank was the opposite of ethereal. He looked much as he had the last time Paul had seen him: somewhat pale from insufficient sunlight, rather too thin, and prematurely aged.

Only Frank's eyes, the windows to his soul, betrayed some hint of the wealth of the new horizons available to him. They were bright and clear, shining with peace, joy, and hope— without any trace of the somber anguish that had inhabited them in life.

"God has big plans for you, you know," remarked Frank, directing a warmth toward Paul that contrasted starkly with the iciness characterizing Frank's manner toward Paul while he was alive.

Paul, haggard from his months-long sleeplessness and suffering, simply glared at Frank broodingly.

"I mean it," said Father Frank. "Stop feeling sorry for yourself. You've been given a gift beyond measure."

"If God changed our places so that he could torment me with my own actions . . . it's been some gift." Paul could not keep the bitterness from his voice.

"I can see why you might feel that way, but these unpleasant experiences serve an important purpose. Do you remember me telling you that I would be with you as you did the work of seeking genuine repentance?"

"Of course. I remember everything about that conversation."

"Well, where do you think you are on that path?"

Paul considered. "If repentance is the same thing as being overwhelmed with remorse and shame, then I repent. I understand now how I tried to justify myself, and how I lied to myself, in order to continue doing what I wanted without being annoyed by an active conscience. So, yes, I'm remorseful and I repent. But so what? God 'forgives' me? What does my being forgiven do for the kids I hurt? It's pretty unsatisfying to claim forgiveness for myself and then call it a day."

Frank smiled like a teacher whose struggling pupil has finally grasped an elusive concept.

"This is the part that gives value to your recent suffering. You needed that tempering to see beyond yourself and to gain the perspective that would lead you to genuine repentance. I hear you saying that you repent, but that you're unworthy of forgiveness because you can't undo the damage you caused. You're right. You are unworthy and you can't undo anything. But here's the beauty—forgiveness, like so many of the best gifts in life, never comes because we deserve it. If we got what we deserved, it wouldn't be called 'forgiveness,' it would be called 'justice.'

"If God's love is for everyone, then it's also for you. If God's mercy and forgiveness are for everyone, then they're also for you. If God's reconciliation is for everyone, then it's also for you. How much more valuable are those precious gifts when we know, beyond doubt, that we do not deserve them? And how much more energetically are we willing to work for God's purposes when we know that we can never hope to repay his generosity?

"I told you God has big plans for you. You need to go into his work with a small glimpse of how he feels for you. He doesn't give you his forgiveness begrudgingly, and when he grants you a role in his ministry of reconciliation, he doesn't do it hesitantly. He's not forced into this choice because he promised to extend his forgiveness to the whole world and, unfortunately, that world includes someone as miserable as you.

"No, Paul, he extends these gifts to you because he delights in *you*. He knows every atom of your body, your mind, and your soul—much better than you could ever hope to know yourself—and still he delights in you. His love for you is what has made your choice to separate yourself from him, through your selfish and revolting sins, so painful for him, and it's what motivated his extraordinary efforts to bring you back into relationship with him.

Frank spoke with a quiet certainty and awe infused in every word. He crossed the room to where Paul sat with his head in his hands, still overwhelmed with self-loathing.

"Stop feeling sorry for yourself," Frank repeated for the third time, the love in his voice removing the sting from his rebuke. "You are so loved. He *knows* you, Paul. Knowing you, he still chooses you. Choose him, and he will redeem even the evil choices you've made and, in his divine creativity, use them for his good purposes."

Paul's voice broke as he responded, "That isn't even possible. You don't *know* how I used those boys—how I destroyed them. That can't be used for good."

"Oh, ye of little faith," rebuked Frank, his features darkening as, for the first time during their encounter, he invoked the words of his Master and filled the room with his otherworldliness. "Who are you to say what is or isn't possible for the God of creation? Is anything that happened with you and me 'possible'? His ways are not our ways, and thank God for that."

As quickly as it appeared, Frank's anger faded. "It's hearing about the things that shouldn't be possible that gives us joy and hope. You feel discouraged right now, but when God did the impossible with you and me, and with how he's been refining you since then, he paved the way for you to have that joy and share it with others.

"It's like that beautiful passage in Luke's gospel. Jesus had just healed the sick and raised the dead, and he told the disciples to go and tell John the Baptist about what they had seen and heard. I've always thought Jesus wanted to encourage John, in his work to amplify God's message of love, with concrete news of God's immanence and power. You need to answer that same call. Go find the people who need the encouragement you're in a unique position to give. Tell them what you've seen and heard.

"I understand, Brother, that it feels like a daunting task. Even with all your intelligence, you don't see what shape his redemption could possibly take. Here's the beauty: you don't need to see it, or to plan it, or to control how it's implemented. He does all of that heavy lifting. He's the landscape architect. He just wants you to plant the flowers according to his design, and then to enjoy their beauty."

"How will I know where he wants me to plant them?"

Frank chuckled. "This is going to be a challenge for your pragmatic, take-charge mind, but you'll need to wait, seek relationship with God, and keep yourself open to his instruction. It probably won't be as straightforward as this conversation, but when you know, you'll know."

"Now," Frank said in a business-like tone that signaled a shift, "get some rest. You need to re-charge for what's to come."

Paul bowed his head to hide the flood of tears that had welled up on account of the hope Frank's words had inspired. When he lifted his gaze, he discovered that he was, once again, alone in his cell. He was exhausted. But pushing his fatigue aside, Paul eased his knees onto the cement floor to pray.

CHAPTER TWENTY-FIVE

J.P. was a big, hard motherfucker. At least, that's how his
fellow inmates described him. For more than ten years, as
he served his time, he crafted a quietly menacing physical
and psychological presence. The combination of his height, the
musculature he honed for hours each day, and the tattoos that
covered his arms and neck and face, rendered him singularly
imposing. Other men took pains to stay out of his way, giving
him a wide berth while he lifted weights during his daily exercise regimen. The only person to observe him on the day Paul
returned to general population was the guard responsible for
monitoring the area.

J.P. was taking a brief rest after putting up a set of back
squats that would have staggered most of the other inmates. He
visibly blanched when he saw Paul enter the yard. All of the
inmates had heard some version of Frank's sudden death and
Paul's stunning recovery, but it had been easy to forget the
rumors of a miracle during Paul's long segregation in the
protective unit.

As Paul walked toward the squat rack near where J.P. rested,
J.P. observed with incredulity that, while Paul was significantly

thinner than he had been during his previous time in the general population, he was unmarred and did not walk with the limp one would have expected based on the severity of his beating.

Instead, he glided with a smooth, upright gait infused with a serene dignity that replaced his previous arrogant swagger. When he got close to J.P., Paul dropped to his knees. Looking directly into J.P.'s eyes while his own brimmed with tears, Paul said, "Oh, Joshua. I won't ask you to forgive me, but I am so sorry for hurting you."

J.P. couldn't have said what he expected when he saw the approach of the man he had known in another life as Father Paul, but it certainly wasn't this. J.P.'s face remained impassive, but his surprise at Paul's words caused him to sit heavily on the nearby weight bench. When he was finally able to speak, the words came from deep in his throat, like a growl, "You'd best move the fuck on, old man."

"I will," Paul assured, swallowing his fear. "But first, I have to say some things to you."

The words gathered velocity as J.P. stood and glowered over Paul. "Even if you beat me again, I need to say these things to you. I know I have no right to talk to you about God, but God requires this of me regardless of my fear. You need to know that you did nothing, absolutely nothing, to cause what I did to you. I manipulated you into believing that perhaps you sent signals to which I responded, but that's just not the truth. I intentionally took advantage of your youth, and of the fact that you trusted me, admired me, and relied on me as a priest and as someone who could help you reach your goals. I abused your trust, and I actively encouraged you to believe what happened was your fault.

"I am so sorry, Joshua. Now that I've said what God required of me, I'll add that I won't try to speak with you again. But if you ever need anything from me for any reason, I'm here."

The guard responsible for the fitness area watched the interaction with interest, but was not close enough to hear the men's words. He watched J.P. wipe the sweat from his face as he towered over a prone Paul. When he removed the towel, J.P.'s eyes were blazing so dangerously that the guard, his instincts honed with long experience, began running toward the men and requesting back-up through his shirt-mounted walkie. J.P. punched Paul forcefully one time, and then put up his hands.

"You'd better tell that old faggot to stay away from me!" J.P. called out to the guard running toward them. Then he dropped to the ground as the guard demanded.

WHEN PAUL MET with Father Matt the next morning, his eyes shone, though one of them was bruised and swollen. Paul didn't mention J.P.'s name, but he explained that one of his victims resided within the prison, and he described what had happened.

"I knew God wanted me to talk to him," he explained. "This man expressed his anger, which I understand, but I have no idea what the long-term impact will be. This hurt, obviously," he said, pointing to his face, "but I feel a little lighter. I don't *deserve* to feel any relief from my guilt, I know that, but accepting responsibility and apologizing—genuinely apologizing . . . it felt important. It felt right."

Father Matt spoke slowly and thoughtfully, "I'm concerned about you imposing yourself on your victims in any way. I know you've been praying for discernment, and you've been working to align yourself with God's will. If what you did yesterday really was responding to God's call, then that probably explains why your burden feels lighter. You can't do much to ease the suffering of your victims, but there has to be some healing value to owning your responsibility."

"Do you think . . ." Paul began, and then his sentence trailed off as he worked through the maze of his thoughts. Father Matt waited patiently.

"Sorry," Paul said, coming back to himself. "I was just thinking I would like to offer the same apology to everyone I hurt."

Father Matt considered silently before speaking, "It's a good thought, but it's also a real can of worms. How would you go about contacting them? Ideally, they are in therapy, and an unsolicited communication from you could derail progress they've made toward healing. And if they're not in therapy, the risk is greater if they don't have a healthy framework to process the intense emotions hearing from you would certainly evoke."

The two men sat in silence for a few minutes, each struggling to find an approach that would allow Paul to offer apology and take responsibility without causing greater harm. Finally Father Matt said, "Let's continue to think about it and, most importantly, let's ask God to align us with his will. If it's something he wants to happen, he'll clear a way."

Paul bowed his head as the young priest began to pray, invoking God's presence, requesting clarification of God's will, and pleading for God's strength.

CHAPTER TWENTY-SIX

That night, Paul experienced a dream of similar intensity to the ones in which he occupied the perspective of those he had raped. Like his other dreams, it began with a scenario that had actually occurred—it was a meeting he had attended with the bishop when, years earlier, he had been transferred to a school in a different part of the state. The parents of a couple of his students had made the usual complaints, and he had been hauled before the bishop like a recalcitrant child.

The bishop's sharp features arranged themselves in weary exasperation as he looked up at Paul from the file lying open on the desk between them. Like the administrator he was, Bishop Fallin appeared to perform a number of calculations before he addressed Paul.

"You've made a real mess, Paul," said the bishop, removing his glasses and rubbing his eyes.

The bishop began cleaning his glasses with a nearby cloth—examining them for any residual spots or streaks. He remained silent until he was satisfied and then, as if his weariness had simply fallen away, he resolutely replaced his glasses and focused sharply on Paul. "Fortunately, we know how to handle messes like this and, God willing, we'll have you back to using your talents for God's Church very soon. For the next six months, you'll be at a treatment facility in Connecticut. We'll classify this as a medical leave of absence. You will complete your treatment shortly before the beginning of the Fall term and, by that time, I'll have a new assignment for you. You will not be a headmaster to begin, but we will expect you to make the best use of your administrative and fundraising talents. Of course, it goes without saying that we must never hear of this kind of trouble again."

"Of course, Your Excellency." Paul knew what the bishop wanted to hear. "I've made a full confession and I'm confident that, with the help you've prescribed and God's grace, I'll put this problem behind me."

"Make sure that's true," said the bishop icily. "You're dismissed."

In his dream, Paul stood and turned to leave, and when he looked back before reaching the door, the wall behind the bishop seemed to stretch back into infinity, and in the endless space behind the bishop stood a faceless crowd of Church hierarchy, including bishops, archbishops, cardinals, and even Popes, all wearing the most sumptuous accouterments of their stations. Many of the vestments were historical, and others reflected the styles adopted in countries throughout the world. In a single, united voice, these Church leaders spoke, though only the bishop's lips moved: "We'll clean up your mess. We've done it before. Keep your mouth shut and don't embarrass us again."

THE DREAM LINGERED with him throughout the following day. His meetings with Father Matt had decreased in frequency from every day to a couple of times per week, and for the first time, he was glad not to have an appointment scheduled that would allow him to unburden himself of a troubling dream. Paul wanted time to unpack this particular vision before discussing it with Father Matt. Like the dreams that had led him to repentance, Paul did not doubt God had sent this dream for a purpose.

He considered what had occurred after Bishop Fallin gave him that slap on the wrist. He had put in his time at the "treatment center," which had been more like a restful retreat filled with clergymen who had committed similar offenses. Upon completing treatment, he attacked his role at the new school to which he had been assigned, and his teaching and fundraising talents soon led to a position of influence comparable to the one he had occupied before the bishop had imposed his tepid discipline.

It wasn't long before he began abusing his students again. After his "treatment" and reassignment, his number of victims more than doubled what it had been before. His superiors never asked about his medical leave, and he suspected his immediate superior was not even aware of the previous complaints about his sexual appetites. Paul was able to continue enjoying his "seductions" with impunity until the Matthews family took their complaint directly to the police.

Although Paul had begun his prison sentence stripped of everything he held dear, he had refused to accept the validity of his laicization. In the early days of his prison sentence, Paul debated the issue with Father Matt when the latter visited the prison to minister to the inmates. During these discussions, Paul relied on his extensive knowledge of Church history and tradition to run rhetorical circles around the young cleric.

Paul had defended his position with arrogance and obstinacy, but there was some validity to his assertion that he was a convenient scapegoat in a much larger wheel of blame. While Paul had physically committed the crimes that landed him in prison, there was an argument to be made that the spiritual damages caused by his crimes were compounded because the abuse had been facilitated by the Church's willful blindness. The Church had chosen to avoid scandal instead of securing the physical, psychological, and spiritual well-being of the children in its care.

As a result of the Event, Paul's arrogance had fled, and he no longer believed that his right to claim the priesthood had survived his crimes. As Paul waited for God to reveal how he could become the promised tool of redemption and healing, his thoughts often returned to the role of the Church in the whole sordid mess. Paul accepted responsibility for his own actions, and had no interest in avoiding or shifting blame. Even in the midst of his self-loathing and shame, however, his newfound intellectual honesty led him to the inevitable conclusion that, with awareness of his past behavior and absent solid evidence of reformation, the Church leadership's calculus appeared to have been as simple as concluding that scandal must be suppressed at all costs, and Paul's success as a fundraiser and school administrator was more valuable than preventing him from causing additional destruction.

While serving his sentence, Paul had followed the clergy-abuse crisis as it continued to unfold, first in the United States and Ireland, and then throughout the world. The larger scandal was consistent with his own experience. At an institutional level, those with authority over abusive priests often trans-planted the offender into a similar environment without mean-ingfully addressing the behavior itself. This tactic, in conjunction with an exertion of spiritual pressure on complaining parents, who almost always brought their griev-ances to the Church rather than to the police, allowed the Church to appear to have addressed the issue while avoiding publicity disasters. The band-aid would hold until complaints began to surface in the problem-priest's next posting, and the shell game would resume.

That the same pattern manifested across the globe made it reasonable to conclude that the practice was tacitly, or even explicitly, authorized up to the highest levels of the Church hierarchy in Rome. As investigative journalists attacked the issue of who in the Church knew what, and when, the inference of Vatican complicity became even more difficult to avoid. A prime example was Marcial Maciel Degollado, the long-time head of the Legionaries of Christ, who had been a rock star fundraiser with rare access to the Pope despite decades of substantiated allegations of sexual impropriety and abuse of many dozens of the boys and seminarians within his broad sphere of influence.

Protecting the vulnerable appeared to be the exception rather than the rule as the Church closed ranks around its priests. The Vatican even went so far as to issue written instructions mandating absolute secrecy around the investigations and ecclesiastical trials of priests accused of abuse, impurity, or obscenity.

When increased public knowledge of the breadth and depth of the clergy abuse scandal caused allegations and discovery of corroborating evidence to snowball, the Church followed neither its Teacher's tenets nor its own sacramental underpinnings: making full confession; demonstrating true penitence; and being willing to forego physical riches for spiritual treasure. Instead, it acted as any other besieged corporate behemoth: it engaged the best lawyers and hired-gun experts. As the many wounded lambs in its flock began to air their sufferings in the courts, though the Church held evidence to corroborate a staggering number of the allegations, it remained firmly in its trenches, using its formidable legal weapons, which were perfectly acceptable in the secular context of litigation, to resist discovery of substantiating documentation.

The Church's other primary tactic was to rely on statutes of limitation to argue that, even if evidence existed *to prove* that a priest had perpetrated abuses for years, and even if there was evidence *proving* Church leaders knew of such proclivities before assigning the man to the parish where he later abused little Suzie or little Johnnie, Susan and John had been adults for some time before hauling the Church into court. They simply had waited too long to hold the priest and the Church accountable. The hypocrisy was rich because the Church's own doctrine never considered the mere passage of time to be a basis for absolution. Victims whose wounds would always feel fresh were prevented from seeking secular, civil justice, just as they had been denied justice in ecclesiastical and criminal contexts.

Even the few victims permitted to proceed to trial, where they were awarded staggering verdicts, were not "made whole" by the money they received. At best, they took some comfort from knowing that the juries' verdicts acknowledged their suffering. Those verdicts affirmed what the victims knew intellectually but had difficulty accepting emotionally because of the conditioning inflicted on them by their abusers and the aggressive defense adopted by the Church: what happened to them was not their fault, and the people and institutions to which their care and safety had been entrusted had failed them.

Before reaching trial or jury deliberations, many victims expressed a willingness to forego the opportunity to impose substantial financial damages awards against the Church if only the Church and those men within her who made abuse-facilitating decisions, would simply admit their blame and offer sincere apology. With only the rarest of exceptions, and never at the highest levels, the Church declined these opportunities. Instead, it retreated to secrecy and protection of its institutional power and wealth.

And so a battle raged. On one side stood the growing army of those who were breaking their silence, and trying to hold the Church and her human instruments to account. On the other side stood the individual men who comprised the institution—

steeped in tradition and notions of their own infallibility and that of their superiors. To protect their institution, they ordered defensive measures that surely would have disgusted the author of their faith. Caught in the breach were clerics like Father Tom Doyle, who at the expense of his own career within the Church, came down on the side of the abused.

CHAPTER TWENTY-SEVEN

After so fittingly being called to account for his own behavior, Paul's tenderized heart bled afresh on behalf of those who had suffered.

Surprisingly, in the midst of his despair and frustration about what he could possibly do to reconcile the hurt, Paul also felt stirrings of joy like shoots from bulbs breaking the surface of spring soil. He had been drudging through a spiritual waste-land for so long that he had accepted it as reality. With awe, he began to explore the well-watered garden of relationship with his Creator. His heartbreak for those he had hurt never left him, but his anguish had a dancing partner: the peace of knowing God had fully forgiven him after a confession that blasted the deepest, darkest recesses of his damaged psyche with cleansing light. Paul's gratitude for this transformation motivated him, out of love, to serve the remarkable being who excised even the metastases of sin that had seemed guaranteed to destroy his soul. His gratitude was coupled with a need to identify and perform any acts, however meager, that could in some way atone for the damage he had caused.

Meaningful acts of atonement were slow to present themselves, and as Paul continued to meditate and wait for divine
instruction, his need for an outward display of his internal
remodeling was forced into micro-expression. The charismatic
personality that had been larger than life, and that never missed
an opportunity for carefully calculated self-promotion à la "the
humble brag," had learned to find joy in quiet, seemingly
insignificant acts of service. Paul began volunteering for the
most dreaded work and, rather than reviling the drudgery or the
filth, doing unpleasant tasks carefully and well filled him with a
sense of contentment and accomplishment that he'd never experienced, even when he had been doing the high-flying and
"important" work that had won him acclaim. When Paul saw a
fellow inmate's need that he was able to fill unobtrusively and
anonymously, he filled it. When he witnessed the strong preying
on the weak, he made what intervention he could, heedless of his
own safety. As a result, Paul took more physical abuse than he
would have taken if he had kept to himself. To him, though, the
wounds that resulted from serving others were a cause for joy.

Even though remarkable changes had occurred within him,
Paul was still human. As all men, he was imperfect and retained
all of the flaws that had so long held pride of place in his life.
What had altered was Paul's reaction to his imperfections.
Before, Paul had made extraordinary efforts to deny, obscure,
and avoid responsibility for anything within himself that could
be perceived as an imperfection. But the Paul who knew himself
to be wondrously loved despite his flaws was clear-eyed about
his shortcomings. Rather than dwelling on these disappointing
aspects within himself, Paul practiced a sort of spiritual judo.
He did not resist his imperfections with the force of his equally
imperfect will. Instead, when confronted with a troubling self-
awareness, Paul accepted the truth of the flaw, asked for God's
assistance in overcoming the obstacle, and expressed gratitude

to God for his faithfulness in continuing the work of his creation within Paul.

In this way, rather than suffering the debilitating shame and paralysis of the soul that would have come from obsessively examining his wretchedness in a spiritual mirror, Paul experienced the freedom that came, as C.S. Lewis wrote, from using the mirror to reflect, not himself, but God's perfect mercy, timing, and strength.

As Paul made himself available and accepted God's efforts to strengthen the connection between them, a call to action was implanted within his psyche, and God watered and fed the seedling while Paul waited in prayerful meditation. The concept first occurred to him in prayer, and it so perfectly addressed many of the concerns with which he had been struggling that it seemed as if the tumblers of a safe had clicked precisely into place, and a gift of inspiration that had come from outside of himself appeared in his mind.

Paul raised the issue during his next meeting with Father Matt, who was intrigued. He admitted the possibility that it could represent a genuine calling, and promised to pray for discernment as they considered moving forward. Father Matt returned a few days later, saying that he believed the plan was a good one and Paul had his blessing to proceed. Father Matt added that he had not sought approval from his superiors within the Church but, based on the skepticism with which they had dismissed the account of Father Frank's miraculous intersession, he was wary of their ability to seek instruction from the Holy Spirit regarding this politically sensitive topic. With Father Matt's blessing, Paul began working on the project to which God had set him, deploying his inborn gifts of charisma and communication, and constantly asking God for infusions of humility and empathy.

CHAPTER TWENTY-EIGHT

S am Wainwright's heart raced as he tried to absorb what he was seeing in the Sunday *New York Times* open on the table before him. The speeding of his heart had begun as soon as Sam saw Paul Peña's name below a piece titled "A Rapist Priest's Apology." Sam closed the paper and shoved it away from him with a shudder. He tried to push it out of his mind, and to restore his shattered equilibrium by scrubbing every surface in his already clean apartment.

Eventually Sam acknowledged that, as much as he wanted to kill his curiosity, he would not have any peace until he read what Peña had written. Sam fished the paper out of his recycling bin, took a few centering breaths, and then opened the paper to Peña's open letter.

From the outset you should understand that, left to my own devices, I am a liar and a manipulator. I was a priest who raped and otherwise sexually abused many adolescent students at the schools where I held positions of trust and responsibility. Until recently, I refused to acknowledge that my actions could be considered abuse, and I lied to myself by characterizing my choices as consensual relationships with individuals old enough to choose. These lies and the lies I told publicly at my trial exacerbated the damage my earlier actions had caused to my victims.

I do not ask for or expect understanding or the forgiveness of those I hurt, but recently I've been the recipient of assurance that God's grace and mercy, and the redemptive sacrifice of Jesus Christ, extends even to someone who has done what I have done.

Because I have been given such a precious gift, which is all the more precious because I do not deserve it, I must answer God's call to tell the truth. I thought about trying to contact each of my victims to tell you this truth, but I worry that direct contact without warning might do more harm than good. Hopefully this open letter is a better method of relaying an important message.

To the people I hurt: You have absolutely no responsibility for what I did to you. I used my position and the force of my personality to convince you that some part of you chose a physical relationship with me. You did not choose it. I knew that I held great influence over you. Over time, I carefully and intentionally prepared each of you for my physical advances so that you would believe yourselves to have played some part, and to have as much of a vested interest in keeping quiet about them as I did. Not only did I assault your minds, I breached your physical defenses with drugs and alcohol. Most shamefully, I used your faith as a tool against you. I know that, for many of you, this betrayal ruptured your relationships with God and with the Church.

For years, I did not possess even a shred of remorse for what I did. I'm sure it is painful for you to consider me invoking God, even in this context, and I am sorry for that pain and for all of the other pain I've caused you. Still, I must relay that God motivated this confession by changing my heart and my understanding, and by filling me with compassion for your suffering.

I am so very sorry.

I hope that you are receiving professional psychological help for the hurt I caused you, and I hope the Church is paying for your care. If it is not, and if I can do anything to help get you the care you need, I am willing. My superiors in the Church knew about my pattern of behavior long before it became a matter of public knowledge, and they did not protect you from me. I'm not saying this to deflect my own blame—my choices were mine alone—but to affirm that my case was consistent with the larger failure of Church leadership. The Church has the financial resources to help you, and it should.

I hope it helps you in some way for me to say, as between you and me, all the shame associated with what I did to you belongs to me alone. If you want me to be a part of any process that moves you closer to healing, I am willing to participate. For those of you receiving therapy, I am willing to engage in meetings in any format your therapist believes will be constructive. I have no illusions that such meetings will be a panacea, and again I do not and will not ask for your forgiveness. I will tell you I'm sorry, though. I will listen to you, and I will hear your pain. You deserve at least that much.

May God bless you and keep you and fill you with the peace that passes all understanding.

"But Sam, isn't this exactly what you've been talking about needing?" Angela Sears's small, close-set eyes gazed at Sam intelligently from behind her glasses. Although her cluttered office should have irritated Sam's compulsiveness, the comfort he derived from its homey smell and its interesting, varied textures was one of the counterintuitive mysteries of their long history. "You told me just last week that you just needed *someone* to take responsibility for what had happened to you."

Sam struggled with her question. "No, it's not enough. I was wrong if I thought it would be. I don't know what else I need, but it's . . . more. I feel like . . . I feel like his throwing an apology out into the void is only one ingredient of the medicine, if you will."

Angela looked particularly owl-like as she gazed at Sam while considering her response. She cocked her head and regarded the intricately woven baskets mounted on her wall.

"Have we talked about the work I did in Africa during graduate school, Sam?" she asked.

Sam shook his head. They hadn't talked much about her. Probably best because Sam had paid her for years to talk about him. She pursed her lips tightly as if deep in thought. Coming to a decision, she said, "I hate to do this, but I think we should end today's session early. I have an idea about where we might go from here, but I'd like a little time to look into it. I don't want to talk about it before I can figure out if it's feasible, but if everything lines up, we can discuss it during next week's session. Okay?"

Intrigued, Sam agreed and they confirmed their standing appointment for the following week.

"OKAY," Angela said breathlessly as she rushed into the office where Sam had been waiting for her for several minutes. As usual, her improbably red hair was disheveled, likely a result of her habit of running her hands through it hundreds of times a day, and her favorite Kelly green blazer contained evidence of a coffee mishap. "I did the checking I promised to do and I'm psyched out of my mind."

She settled herself into her chair. "Last week I asked about my work in Africa because I think, maybe, we can use it here. During grad school, I studied the therapeutic benefits to crime victims of having the opportunity to confront their perpetrators, and to have the perpetrators accept responsibility. There wasn't a lot of opportunity to study that dynamic here, because it's just not how our criminal justice system works, but in researching South Africa's Truth and Reconciliation Commission, I interviewed people who had participated in that process. More interesting, for purposes of my specific focus, was what I got to see of the Rwandan *gacacas.*"

She stopped to take a drink of water and Sam asked, "What is that?"

"So, these were informal community gatherings that took place while the country was trying to rebuild after genocide in the '90s. They included both the Tutsi victims and the Hutu perpetrators of rape, murder, and other atrocities. They were completely the opposite of our ideas about protecting victims of crime from exposure to the people who had harmed them. The Rwandan *gacacas* were founded in the reality that, going forward, victims and perpetrators would have to live in the same intermingled communities in which they had lived before the genocide. It would only be possible if both sides really worked at reconciliation."

Angela explained that the parties to the process committed to work toward three pillars of reconciliation: truth-telling, repentance, and forgiveness. Perpetrators had to overcome their guilt and fear of consequences to publicly accept responsibility for the violence they had committed against their neighbors. In response, the victims and their loved ones shared their experiences, perspectives, and ongoing processing of the trauma they endured. After the process of multilateral truth telling, even those who had admitted to raping or murdering their neighbors apologized. It wasn't a magic formula or a perfect process, and it was still necessary to put in more work toward justice, reconciliation, and forgiveness after the *gacaca*, but its positive effects seemed out of all proportion to its simplicity. The approach kickstarted the country's healing and rebuilding in profound and tangible ways.

"This experience is what makes me excited about what Peña's offering. I've seen how, with the right framing and safeguards, real healing is possible. Before floating the idea to you, I wanted to meet Peña, look him in the eyes, and gauge his sincerity. I didn't want to travel down the road of a *gacaca*-like process if there was a substantial possibility that it would do you more harm than good. So—"

"Wait," Sam interrupted. "Are you saying you met with Father Paul since I saw you last week?"

Angela barreled ahead. "Yes! I didn't tell him anything about you that could reveal your identity and I don't want you to feel pressured to do this if you're not comfortable with it. But he's willing if you are, and we could include a couple of other participants, including the prison chaplain and, remarkably, another victim of Peña's who happens to be an inmate in the same prison. I gave them all some literature about *gacacas* to read while you make your decision. I can't guarantee that it will help, but I *think* it will. I never thought I would see an opportunity for something like this here."

In spite of the circumstances, Sam couldn't help but laugh at her single-mindedness and excitement. "All right," he said. "Tell me what it would look like."

CHAPTER TWENTY-NINE

P aul, Joshua, and Father Matt were already present in the fishbowl of a glass-sided room when they saw Angela and Sam approach the glass door. As Sam entered, he looked directly at Paul, and could see Paul's brain working to match Sam's features with a figure from the past. When Sam removed his dark wool coat, there was a collective intake of breath from the three men as they recognized the distinctive white collar that marked Sam as a priest.

The five participants sat around a circular table, and Angela asked everyone to bow their heads as she read a prayer Sam had written to commence the process. The men complied, and Angela began in a low, melodic voice:

Heavenly Father, Lord Christ, cause your spirit to move in us today. Bless our intentions with the purity of your grace and love. Bring your healing and cleansing power into this place, and align our words and actions with the perfection of your will. In the name of the Father, and of the Son, and of the Holy Spirit, amen.

When she finished, Paul, Joshua, and Matt opened their eyes and looked expectantly at Angela. Wasting no time, she inclined her head toward Sam and said, "We agreed that it would be best to start with Sam before anyone else shares."

With the mention of his name, Sam watched as the final gear clicked into place, and the years fell away from his face before Paul's eyes. Paul's inner turmoil betrayed him only in his sudden pallor and in the way he wiped his palms on his pants.

Paul focused his attention on Sam, and in turn Sam stared down at his hands as he began to speak. He was surprised to hear that his voice was low and steady; not even the slightest tremor hinted at his overwhelming anxiety.

"I wanted to be a priest for as long as I can remember. I loved the ritual and mystery of the Church, and the community that flowed from and surrounded it. In my family's lore, most of the stories about my early childhood feature the Church in some way. The story of the youngest version of me that my mom loves to tell happened in Church. I was four years old and, as young kids often are, I was lost in my own world during the service. When a lay reader with a particularly deep voice began to read that week's scripture, my mother says my head shot up from my coloring worksheet, I looked around as if searching for the source of the voice, and then I whispered to my mother, 'Is that God?'

"I always carried with me a sense of God's active participation in my life. I was assured of God's guiding hand over the world, and I was secure in my place within it. My path seemed perfectly clear: I would pursue the calling that allowed me to serve this omnipotent, loving being, and I would guide others to know him better."

Sam lifted his gaze and looked directly at Paul. "When I met you in high school, it seemed like God was smoothing my path to his service. You were charismatic, smart, and funny, and unlike most adults, you seemed genuinely interested in what I thought. I could be honest about how perfectly I was created for a calling within the Church."

"When you did," Sam stopped speaking until he could gather strength to continue, "what you did, I felt so worthless. I thought I had stained myself so deeply that I couldn't keep pursuing what had defined my life. And you did it by using your authority as a representative of Christ!" His voice rose in anger and disbelief that conveyed his still-fresh pain.

"I had learned my lessons well. I would have told anyone else that God's gifts are given to us in spite of our unworthiness. For the first time, though, I understood what unworthiness felt like. Overnight, it became a whole lot more difficult for me to believe that God's gifts were meant for me. You might think the shame would have settled more lightly on me because, unlike many of those you abused, I'm gay. You might think I didn't have the extra layer of confusion that your straight victims felt. You would be wrong.

"At that time, I was still a very long way away from coming to terms with that aspect of myself. My life was centered on a religion that I loved, but that thinks I am fundamentally flawed because of how I was born. What you did made me even more confused and self-loathing, and added years to my journey to accept that I am as I am because God made me this way. To accept that even that aspect of myself is fearfully and wonderfully made."

Sam continued to describe how his experience with Paul drove him into a spiral of seeking sex with other older men who, similarly, treated him like a plaything and then discarded him. To escape his constant feelings of shame, he turned to drugs. Within two years of finishing high school, Sam was living on the street—supporting his habit by whatever means presented themselves.

"Eventually I got on the road to lasting recovery, but it was a long road. It began through a friendship I developed with an Episcopal lay minister I met in a treatment program. As I spent more time in her church and with the Rector, God renewed my dreams of serving him. The path he showed me looked different than it had when I was younger. The gift of renewed purpose and reconnection with God enabled me to commit to recovery and, in time, I was ordained as a priest of the Episcopal Church."

Sam spoke directly to Paul. "It's a strange thing, but I know I'm more capable of sharing God's compassion because of the way my experience with you humbled me. On the other hand, the more I've learned about compassion, and about the holy trust we hold as priests, the more I've understood exactly how terrible you are. The more I've hated your guts. I've prayed, I've worked with therapists like Angela, and I've tried to let go of that anger. I want to let go of it for my own sake. I just haven't been able to move past it."

As Sam finished speaking, Paul remained silent. His eyes moved between Sam and the hands clasped in front of him on the table.

Joshua responded to a cue from Angela. After ensuring Sam was finished, Joshua picked up the thread of conversation.

"Sam, a lot of what you said is familiar to me. I've struggled with the same anger, but in my case, anger turned into violence, which landed me here. I made my own choices, but I was never violent before Paul raped me. Like you, my anger and shame derailed my life. Unlike you, I never got back on track. I still have twenty years before I'm eligible for parole, so there probably isn't a track for me to get back on."

Joshua briefly described his history with Paul, and how seeing Paul in prison, and realizing that Paul didn't recognize him, had felt like a gift—like an opportunity to repay Paul for some of the damage he had caused. He explained how he had seized that opportunity one night when Paul was alone in the showers, and how baffled he had been the next day to hear that Father Frank had died and that Paul had miraculously recovered.

"I don't understand what happened with Paul and Father

Frank. I'd be full of shit if I said it didn't make me rethink what I thought I knew about God being a fraud. It also really pissed me off that God stepped in in such a big way for Paul, but he just sat on his hands while Paul did his best to ruin me, and you, and all those other boys."

This was the first Sam had heard about the circumstances surrounding Father Frank's death, and he struggled to wrap his head around it as Joshua continued.

"I couldn't stop thinking about what they used to drum into us at that fucking school. 'His ways are not our ways' . . . as if that was supposed to magically get us through anything. I always thought it was just more bullshit. But then . . ." he spread his hands in front of himself. "All this happened, and I'm thinking, 'It sure seems like a fucked up way to accomplish anything, but maybe something is breaking loose for the good.'"

Joshua took a deep breath, "After what happened, I was confused and depressed. Depressed because making my fantasy real didn't make me feel better like I thought it would. I wondered why Paul should be protected at the expense of Father Frank. And I felt so small in the face of the kind of power that could make something like that happen.

"For such a long time, hating Paul has fueled me. When Paul apologized to me, it almost made me hate him more. He had shit on my love and trust so much that I had to wonder whether his apology was just some new way to be cruel. I'll probably never be able to fully trust him, but my bullshit detector is better now than when I was a kid. I believe what he said to me and in his letter. It doesn't mean I'm ready to forgive him. I might not ever be, but for the first time I can imagine letting go of my anger. Not for his sake, but for mine."

They all sat in silence as Joshua gathered his thoughts to continue. Father Matt briefly placed his hand on Joshua's shoulder.

"Paul's apology didn't fix me, but it helped me let go of some of my shame along with the anger. I wouldn't have thought he could say anything that had the power to help or hurt me, but as much as I hate to admit it, his words still matter to me. I needed to hear him apologize. More than anything, I needed to hear him accept responsibility.

"I guess the reason I'm here, Sam, is to let you know that you're not alone. I understand your anger like only the other boys Paul raped can."

Angela allowed a period of silence to sink in before she nodded to Paul.

"First, Sam, I've heard everything you said. I'm so, so very sorry for what I did to you. As I'll explain in a bit, I have more insight into what you were feeling than you might imagine.

"I know that you've read my letter, but it's important for you to hear these words from my mouth: I am sorry, Sam, both for what I did to you and for how it impacted your life. I knew what I was doing. Sam, I *know* that part of your guilt is tied up in feelings of attraction you had toward me, which, at the time, you were barely able to acknowledge to yourself. Know this, Sam: you would not have done anything with those feelings. They were an innocent crush, and those feelings would have faded. Even if you didn't say no, you were too young and inexperienced to understand the true dynamics of what was happening, or to consent."

Paul caught Sam's eye and held it, "What happened was not your fault, and you have no share in the shame. It belongs to me alone."

Those words worked their way into Sam. Angela had made exactly the same point, and so had other therapists, but they had never before penetrated in this way. Sam had never fully believed them. Sam buried his face in his hands and tried to hold in the flood of grief he felt for the confused young boy he had been. It was too overwhelming, and his floodgates burst as he gave himself over to silent, violent sobs. Angela soundlessly pushed a package of tissues toward him.

When Sam had finished crying, he looked expectantly at Paul. Paul continued, "Angela thought it would be important for you to understand how I finally came to repentance. It's pretty new. Until recently, I didn't admit there was anything wrong with what I did. If you and I had met shortly after my trial, you would've seen a man with a very different perspective. Joshua, Father Matt, and I experienced firsthand the story I'm about to tell you, but we understand if you find it tough to believe. We're used to skepticism—but we know what we know."

Paul related the dreams. "I carry with me all of those experiences, from the perspective of my victims. I had five dreams about you, Sam. The first time I touched you, you had been excited to give me a beautiful book of Neruda poems because I had mentioned in class how much I admired him. You hadn't even begun to admit to yourself that you were attracted to boys. You had two clear thoughts as I took advantage of . . ."

Paul broke off mid-sentence. "No, that won't do. Father Frank insisted I use accurate language." Paul forced himself to look directly into Sam's eyes, "I raped you, Sam. As I . . . raped you, you had two clear thoughts as you looked at the book of poetry on the desk. First, you thought that you must have asked for what was happening because you gave me the book. You did *not*, Sam. I had planned what would happen that day before you ever set foot in my office with the book. Second, you wondered how you could possibly make confession about doing what you were doing with a priest.

"About confession, I have to hope you've worked through this in therapy and on your road to ordination. Just in case it is not clear: I was the one who needed to confess—not you. In every aspect of our shared history, Sam, you had nothing to confess because I sinned against you. I have made my confession to God. I hope it doesn't cause you more pain to hear that I am secure in knowing that the redemption secured by his son extends even to me."

Sam remained completely motionless, thunderstruck. Finally, Sam turned his entire torso toward Angela. Shocked, he couldn't adjust his expression or his posture more than absolutely necessary. Angela's eyes, wide as saucers, mirrored his. Obviously, Paul's insights had struck home—they had been a topic Angela and Sam had discussed at length in therapy.

Sam shook his head to clear its daze, and replied, "God tells us over and over who he is, but it still blindsides us when he directly touches our circumstances. What you just said has haunted me for years. Hearing those words come out of the mouth of the man I've hated helps me believe that God *knows* me. Completely. He knows the most secret, shameful parts of me, and when he shines his light in those places, he reacts differently than I expected. Instead of convicting me, he moves mountains to comfort me." Sam looked at Paul wonderingly, "What a strange tool to accomplish his purpose . . ."

The guard who had been standing just outside the room opened the door and informed the group that the time the warden had allotted for their meeting was nearly up. Father Matt asked for a few additional minutes.

"We've used a lot of emotional energy today. I'd like to end with a prayer to ask God to renew us, and to give us guidance about what to do with what he's done here today."

As they all bowed their heads, Father Matt's melodic voice invoked the name of the Father, the Son, and the Holy Spirit, and adopted the warm tone of gratitude, familiarity, and adoration characteristic of mystics:

"We are awed by your presence and your perfection, Holy Father. Thank you for giving us eyes to see, ears to hear, and that unnamed sense that recognizes your presence and your movement to foster powerful reconciliation in this place today. Thank you for blessing each of us with the knowledge that we have been willing tools to accomplish your just and compassionate purpose. Thank you for infusing us with your forgiveness and joy, and for your creative genius as the ultimate repurposer. Thank you for using us, just as we are, and for assuring us that we are valuable tools in spite of our wear and decay. We delight in your compassionate mercy, and we find peace in your promise of restoration and your work to refine us into new creations. Thank you for loving us and for making us capable of love. Continue to bring us into communion with you, and with your body the Church, and to inspire us with the will to continue to seek you and to offer ourselves for your use. In the name of Jesus Christ and all your saints, especially Father Francis Muncy, we humbly pray. Amen."

No one in the group spoke as they raised their heads, but everyone, including Father Matt, shared expressions of surprise about the words he had used to close the prayer. As they went their separate ways, each of them replaced their astonishment with the realization that Matt's unexpected words merely acknowledged the obvious truth. Each of them struggled with the implications. Had God actually included an admitted pedophile into his canon of saints?

CHAPTER THIRTY

A s her mentor Andy had predicted, the state supreme court made short work of Veronica's appeal. Her hopes of airing her grievances against the Church's decision-makers in a courtroom, before a jury, were snuffed out fully and finally. Her lawyer's brain, which had primarily thought about justice in terms of the redress available through the courts, and accountability in terms of hitting institutions in the only place they felt pain—their pocketbooks—foundered. Searching desperately for a satisfying outlet for her frustration and rage, Veronica had found an activist group of Catholic mothers whose children had been sexually abused by priests. Most of these devout women believed that the inadequate response must have been a regional communication failure, and that if the higher authorities within the Church—the archbishops, the cardinals, the Pope—simply heard, firsthand, the stories of these mothers and their children, heard their suffering, then surely things would change. Surely the highest levels of Church leadership would be moved to compassion and repent the failure that had caused the abuse to flourish. They would apologize; they would mean it; and they would institute measures to identify and remove predators, and to care for those who had been injured.

Her crusader's vigor renewed, Veronica worked tirelessly with her local group to lobby for a meeting with the archbishop of their ecclesiastical province, to lay their grievances before him, and to ask him to intercede on their behalf. The group eventually became such a squeaky wheel that the archbishop could no longer ignore it and agreed to meet with the women. Women from throughout the three-state ecclesiastical province had booked travel to be present at the conference center the archbishop designated for the audience, and the Colberg chapter had asked Veronica to speak on their behalf.

As the appointed date grew closer, Veronica wrote and rewrote her remarks, practicing tirelessly in front of the mirror, avoiding any statements or body language that could be written off as female hysteria.

The Saturday before the audience, Veronica sat in her favorite window seat puzzling over a paragraph that wasn't sitting quite right with her. As it was wont to do, her hand had traveled up to her scalp, searching for a strand of hair of just the right texture and length. When her fingers found a likely candidate, they separated it from the surrounding strands and plucked it out by the root with a satisfying pop. Still deep in thought, Veronica ran the wiry strand through her pinched fingers, subconsciously pleased by its irregular ridges.

Tom interrupted her reverie by handing her a glass of wine. "Almost finished?"

"Getting close," she sighed, accepting the glass with a smile.

Tom hesitated before saying, "I just wanted to make sure I have your travel plans straight: The audience is supposed to be over by 1:00 p.m. You'll go straight to the airport to catch the 3:00 p.m. flight back to Colberg and will be back in time to drive with us to Avery's graduation ceremony at seven."

"That's right," she said, standing up onto her toes to kiss her husband's cheek. "Worst case scenario, I'll catch the 5:00 p.m. flight and go straight to the ceremony. It's only an hour-long flight and I'm not checking any bags."

Tom nodded. "Cutting it pretty close. Do you think that maybe, um, it would be better to have someone else speak, just to be sure, you know, that you don't miss Avery's ceremony?"

Veronica stepped back and looked at him. Hard. Incredulous.

"I'll be there, Tom. I'm not going to miss it."

"The graduation . . . or the audience?"

"Both! We've worked so hard for this opportunity! I have to see it through!"

"Avery's worked hard to make it to this graduation."

"And I'll be there! Jesus!"

"We need to make sure Avery knows how proud we are of her achievement."

"I feel like you're accusing me of not being a good mother. How dare you!"

Tom's slow fuse finally reached its terminus. "Oh, you're an incredible mother . . . to Sean. The thing is, Ronnie, he doesn't need your mothering anymore. He doesn't know everything you've been doing for him. The girls know, though. They know. And Avery'll know if you're not at her graduation because you need to prove how much you love the child who's not here to feel it."

Veronica doubled over as if she'd been punched in the gut. Suddenly full of regret at what he'd just said, Tom tried to lay an apologetic hand on her back. The instant he touched her, she shrugged him off and bolted upright, furious eyes glistening with tears. "Just because it's been easy for you to move on doesn't mean I'm doing grief wrong, Tom."

He reeled back and stood very still. He forced air out through his nose. He pursed his lips wryly and then nodded slowly, as if he was seeing something he recognized. "You've always had such a knack for hitting the jugular. I know you think you're the only one who grieves for Sean, but he was ours too. Mine and the girls'. You've put yourself out on an island and the girls and I just have to find our own way. You're such a fucking martyr, aren't you? You do all the big, showy acts of anger and righteousness, and you think that means you loved him more than we did. Than I did."

"He was *mine*! He was my only kindred spirit in this world! I never expected it, but that night when he was born, when he and I were alone in that hospital room, I looked down at him and he looked back at me. Those lovely, double-lashed eyes looked directly into mine, and he saw me. We recognized each other and I thought, 'Oh, there's my friend!' And he was my friend, my truest friend, until somebody made him feel too worthless to live." Veronica had been pounding at her chest and was forced to stop speaking until she could breathe again. "I won't stop trying to hold everyone to blame accountable. I can't."

Tom looked at his wife of twenty-seven years with a mixture of weariness and hurt. But still, love. He turned around and started walking away. "Make sure you're there Friday night," he called over his shoulder.

CHAPTER THIRTY-ONE

Veronica's leg bounced impatiently as she sat in the stiff, uncomfortable conference room chair. She looked at her watch again. 2:14 p.m. Only three minutes since she'd previously checked it. She was already too late to make it to the airport for the 3:00 p.m. flight, and the archbishop had yet to make an appearance. Veronica had no idea what the order for the representative speakers was, so she decided to seek out the event organizer to see if Prudie could make sure Veronica was at the top of the list. She would leave for the airport immediately after speaking.

"Ladies," said a voice through the microphone at the front of the room. Veronica recognized the voice as Prudie's. "Ladies," said Prudie more loudly to carry over the din, "thank you for your patience. We've been in touch with the archbishop's office to get more information on the holdup. When we know more, you'll know more. In the meantime, let's bow our heads and pray for the wisdom to say what needs to be said, and that the archbishop will have ears to hear and the will to act."

While everyone prayed, Veronica weaved her way to the

front, until she was near enough Prudie to intercept her as soon as she finished leading the prayer.

Back in her seat, Veronica looked again at her watch. 2:46 p.m. Veronica had practiced her remarks so many times that she knew that if she stuck to the right pacing, they would take seven minutes. To get to the airport on time for the 5:00 p.m. flight, she needed to leave the conference center no later than 4:10 p.m. Assuming it would take five minutes after the archbishop arrived to introduce him and to set the context for Veronica to begin speaking, she calculated that she would only be able to leave by 4:10 p.m. if the archbishop arrived by 3:56 p.m. Seventy minutes. Surely he would make it before then. Veronica closed her eyes and whispered silently, "please, please, please."

At 3:56 p.m., Veronica again glanced anxiously at her watch. She heard a commotion at the front of the room and thought, *Oh, thank God. Cuttin' it pretty fine though, Lord.*

Veronica craned her head and saw Prudie Holmes standing near the podium, speaking to a black-suited priest, looking displeased. Eventually, she held out her arm to direct the priest toward the podium.

He stepped up to the microphone and tapped it a couple of times. Satisfied it worked, he said, "Ladies," in a smooth, patronizing voice. "I'm Father Michael, one of the Archbishop's private secretaries. The archbishop asked me to express his sincere thanks for your efforts to make it here today. He knows how much you have suffered because of a few misguided souls, and he grieves for you and with you. Unfortunately, the archbishop has been called away on urgent business . . ." as if to quell the rising murmurs, the priest pushed his palms down on the air in front of him. He raised the volume of his voice, "and so he is unable to be with you here today. He is very interested in what you have to say, and he has asked me to come in his stead to record our conversation, and report back to him. It looks like the first lady scheduled to speak today," he looked down at the paper in front of him, "is Mrs. Veronica Matthews from the Colberg diocese. Mrs. Matthews?"

He looked around at the sea of faces.

Cheeks burning, Veronica stood. She walked into the center aisle, looking back at Father Michael as he regarded her from the podium. Just as the silence and lack of movement became oppressive, Veronica ripped the quiet with a vulgar hawking sound. She spat on the floor, then turned and strode toward the door at the back of the room, holding her arm up at a right angle as she walked so that her middle finger faced the podium at the front of the room.

VERONICA HAD REDISTRIBUTED her purse to join the strap of her carry-on bag so that she could turn the key while simultaneously pushing up on the door with her shoulder to cajole the persnickety deadbolt. Too late, she realized the door wouldn't be locked. There was a celebration inside.

Rearranging her defeated face into a high-cheeked, openmouthed expression of pride and delight, Veronica turned the doorknob and kneed the door open. She deposited her bag near the collection of shoes by the hall closet, and placed her keys and phone in their dish on the console beneath the family portrait. Her fingers, in their well-practiced routine, moved to her lips and then to the glass over the image of twelve-year-old Sean's face.

Voices, laughter, and clinking glasses led Veronica through the living room and kitchen to the patio doors. She slid the glass frame and stepped through. Avery was smiling prettily, head bowed in blushing modesty as her favorite professor raised a champagne flute toward her and gushed over her talent and work ethic. When Avery raised her glass at the end of the toast, her gaze fell on Veronica. Her smile tightened and her brows drew together. Twitching off her sour expression, Avery fixed her attention on her professor and increased her smile's wattage. At her side, Tom looked over to see what had dampened Avery's mood, and he spotted Veronica near the door.

Tom's jaw clenched as he set his half-full champagne flute on the table behind him and lifted a full glass from the collection remaining there. He eased his way through the celebrants, and thrust the champagne into Veronica's hand without speaking. She started to speak, but he had already started off to return to Avery's side, placing a steadying hand between her shoulder blades.

AFTER THE TOASTS and the cake cutting, Veronica rummaged in the freezer for the pack of Marlboros she kept there. She could leave the pack there, undisturbed, for months, but if ever a day called for a stress-relief cigarette, this was it. Pack in hand, she settled herself on the large, comfortable swing in a dark corner of the yard and tried to light the cigarette with the cheap plastic lighter she had found in the junk drawer. After a few failed attempts, Veronica shook the lighter and discovered it was out of fluid. She threw it in frustration, and it clanged satisfyingly against a planter.

A soft laugh sounded from the darkness behind her, and Veronica turned just as a lighter flared, illuminating a young man's face.

"Here, let me," he extended the lighter toward her.

Gratefully, she raised the cigarette to her lips and leaned forward to meet the flame, inhaling deeply. When the cherry was firmly established, she inhaled the toxic smoke into her lungs, holding it there, simultaneously soothed and revolted. Then she leaned back on the swing's deep cushions, sinking into them.

"Mind if I sit with you for a bit?" Her white knight moved around the side of the swing's frame, lit only by the glowing ember of his own cigarette. Veronica responded by opening her palm and gesturing, Vanna White style, toward the seat beside her. The balance of the swing shifted as it accepted his weight.

"Rough day, then?" he asked.

She exhaled. "The roughest."

They sat silently for a few beats before she asked, "So did you graduate today too?"

"Not this year," he smiled. "I know it's none of my business, but I'm a pretty good listener, if you wanna talk about it."

She returned his smile ruefully. "That's very kind of you, but I think maybe I've talked about it too much. Can't stop talking about it, even when—especially when—people don't want to hear. I've let it take over."

"I know a bit about unhealthy obsession." The weariness of his voice, coming from someone so young, surprised her.

She expected him to expand on the statement, but when he didn't, she asked, "Have you found any tricks that work?"

"I don't know if I'd call them tricks, but yes, I did find help. It might be a little woo-woo for some people, though." There was a compassion and confidence in his voice that belied the self-deprecation.

Curious in spite of herself, Veronica bit. "I'm not opposed to a little woo-woo, if it helps. What did you do, then?"

"I prayed," he answered simply. "I told God it was all too big for me, that I didn't want to put my obsession before the well-being of others, but I wasn't strong enough to fight it alone."

"And that worked, did it?" Veronica could not completely erase the skepticism from her voice. "Easy as that?"

"It was never easy," he pushed back. "But I also asked for constant reminders about why I was fighting and who I didn't want to hurt. Focusing on those priorities led me to keep asking for help."

"Did God take away your obsession?" Fragile hope cracked in her voice.

He waited in silence until she looked him fully in the face. The compassion in his expression broke her heart and she felt seen in a way she hadn't in a long time. Maybe ever. A very old soul peered out from his young face.

"No, he didn't take it away," he said softly. "But he did transform it. And me. He answered my prayer in a different way than I expected. He helped me realize that he could even use my obsession for good, if I gave it to him. I'll pray for the same for you."

The stress of the day caught up with Veronica. Vision blurred, she felt for her new friend's hand. When she found it, she gripped it like a vise and the two continued smoking on the swing in silence.

PART V

CHAPTER THIRTY-TWO

Angela and Sam unpacked their meeting in the prison over the next several sessions. It was clear it would take a long time to understand all of its implications. Sam's mind wouldn't let go of the close of Father Matt's prayer; he needed to know more about the person who had set Paul on his path toward redemption.

Online research didn't yield much, so Sam started reaching out to people who had known Father Frank. Sam spoke with the prison therapist, who shared her perspective about how unique Father Frank had been among the sex offenders she had served, and Dr. Yvette told Sam about her remarkable experience with Father Frank and Paul.

Sam also contacted people who had known Father Frank in his role as a helping professional and community servant. Sam heard, repeatedly, how tireless Father Frank had been in working to improve the lives of all he served, regardless of their religious affiliation, or lack thereof, and how he helped them gain confidence in their own value and purpose.

Even years later, many of them were still shocked by what Father Frank had confessed about himself, and especially because none of them had ever seen Father Frank in the company of children. Sam wouldn't have expected it, but the people who knew Father Frank from before he went to prison were surprisingly reluctant to disown him. His former patients and colleagues were sad and distressed that his secret sexual attraction toward children had been revealed to them, but they considered that the assistance he had given them in combating their own inner demons could only have come from a place of sincere empathy—because he himself was fighting the good fight against his own darkest nature. They just couldn't find it in themselves to condemn him. Based on these conversations, Sam concluded that Father Frank was complex like all humans, comprised of both light and dark facets although, admittedly, his light facets were unusually brilliant, and his dark facets were profoundly inky.

One of the most interesting conversations Sam had about Father Frank was with Tavis Pereira. Years later, Tavis was still working through how he felt about Father Frank, and what he thought of the mystery surrounding Father Frank's death. Tavis had only heard rumors about what had happened in prison with Father Frank, so he was riveted by hearing what Sam had learned about it directly from Paul Peña and others who had witnessed the events firsthand.

"I know. It's unbelievable," Sam agreed. "I had a hard time buying it myself, but I've seen the photos of both men taken by Dr. Yvette Stanwood, and I've spoken with her about what she observed. She's clearly a woman of science, Tavis, not a crackpot or a religious zealot. She herself says she wouldn't have credited the story if she hadn't seen it with her own eyes, but she couldn't be more certain about what she witnessed."

"That's the thing, isn't it though?" said Tavis. "We call ourselves religious and say we believe in a powerful God, but if evidence of that power smacks us in the face, we're convinced it must be some kind of a hoax."

They sat in silence for a bit, and then Sam asked, "Are you familiar with the basic requirements for canonization?"

Tavis said he remembered a little bit from his catechism, but his understanding was murky. Sam relished the teaching aspect of his vocation, and jumped at the opportunity to explain.

"In a nutshell, within the Roman Catholic tradition, saints are those who are recognized as Servants of God; whose presence with God in heaven is certain. Saints are worthy of universal veneration within the Church because their service to God demonstrated heroic degrees of the theological virtues of faith, hope, and charity, and the cardinal virtues of prudence, justice, fortitude, and temperance. Of the two forms of worship, adoration is reserved to God alone, while veneration is honor and reverence appropriately directed toward created beings.

"There are two routes to sainthood, with martyrdom providing a shortcut. Martyrs are those the Pope certifies as having given their lives voluntarily as witnesses of the Faith, or in acts of heroic charity for others. For non-martyrs, also called 'confessors,' it's a long process requiring detailed information about the candidate's witness to the faith by how he or she lived, as well as evidence of two miracles attributable to the candidate's intercession. The miracles are viewed as a sign from God that the candidate is with God in heaven.

"Within the Anglican Communion, we developed a much broader conception of sainthood after our split with Rome. We now extend the term 'saint' to all faithful Christians, and we don't jump through a maze of procedural hoops to recognize particularly Holy individuals."

Tavis wrinkled his forehead. "Okay. Why are you telling me this?"

"Well . . ." Sam stopped, still finding it difficult to say the words out loud even though he and Father Matt, Paul Peña, and Joshua had discussed it several times. Sam braced himself; he still cared, sometimes too much, what people thought about him, but he had promised to serve a God who would sometimes ask him to do difficult and counterintuitive things, so needs must. "Some of us who have been affected by Father Frank's life and service think that he meets the qualifications for canonization. We're starting the process down that path. Because Father Frank lived his life within the Roman Catholic tradition, we thought it important to pursue canonization within that context."

Tavis stared at Sam blankly. The friendliness drained from his face. "You're kidding, right? I mean, I admired Father Frank. It creeps me out that I still admire him even after what he told me—what I heard, from his mouth, with my own ears. Maybe part of the reason I admire him is because he told me even though nobody ever would have known. Because he provided a little bit of justice, way too late, to that little girl. But a saint? Like, people are going to light candles asking for his help? Shit, I don't know, man . . ." He puffed air out of his mouth in disbelief.

"I know, but hear me out. The way Father Frank died was the first miracle. Technically, he should qualify as a martyr on that basis alone. Even if he didn't qualify as a martyr, though, there is a second miracle attributable to him. Admittedly, there's less corroborating evidence. But I'm part of that evidence. The impact of that second miracle changed my life for the better, and there are many others like me."

Tavis's arched eyebrow was sufficient encouragement for Sam to continue. "You know more than just about anyone else how dangerous and unrepentant Paul Peña was." Sam leaned across the table. "I'm sure you know that this man's behavior and attitudes were *deeply* entrenched. He had convinced himself of his own bullshit."

Tavis remained silent, considering. He nodded and Sam continued, "According to Paul, Father Frank appeared to him in a vision after his death and commissioned Paul to be God's instrument of repentance and reconciliation in this area of blight within the Church. Paul says the substitution of Father Frank's life for his own created space for a new humility and change of perspective. More critically, Paul developed genuine empathy for his victims as the result of a long series of vivid dreams. Every night for well over a year, he vicariously experienced every instance of abuse he had inflicted, from his victims' perspectives. He dwelt in our thoughts and sensations, and he experienced our physical and emotional pain. I believe God sent Paul those dreams so that Paul would really understand what he had done. I believe it because Paul knew exactly what I was thinking as he raped me when I was fourteen."

Sam saw that the hairs on Tavis's arms had prickled, and Sam continued to explain how Paul finally accepted responsibility for the full scope of what he had done. After Father Frank's showing, Paul waited for direction about how he could possibly satisfy Father Frank's prediction that he would be God's tool for reconciliation. Sam explained how he had been led to meet with Paul after the *New York Times* letter. Tavis nodded again, remembering.

"I was so afraid to meet with him, Tavis." Sam's voice suddenly wavered. "I was terrified that I would be so overwhelmed by anger that I wouldn't be coherent. I was afraid that, although offering him forgiveness could speed my own healing, I would be unable to forgive him. I had prescribed the antidote of forgiveness to so many of my parishioners who had been poisoned by their own resentment against those who had wounded them, but I wasn't sure I could stomach my own medicine.

"When we met, it was immediately apparent that Paul was fundamentally a different person than he had been when I knew him. He fought through his obvious shame and regret to confess what he had done to me and how he had manipulated me. When I left that day, I wasn't sure how I felt. With some time and space, so many of the negative emotions that had been blighting my life at a static, subconscious frequency, lessened.

"As an acolyte of the Master who led his followers to aspire to his own example of mercy, forgiveness, and reconciliation, it might be less difficult for me than it would be for others to accept that grace and divine intervention had worked such a transformation in the monster of my adolescence. I think it also helped that Paul didn't ask anything of me—not even forgiveness. As I reflected in the days and weeks following the meeting, I realized that something Paul had previously robbed had been returned to me: choice. His apology revealed how his manipulations had once stolen my ability to make uncoerced choices. By unmasking his actions without making demands, he returned that ability to me.

"I was released from my prison of self-blame and shame, but I still held plenty of rage in reserve. But having regained the ability to make free choices, I came to understand that I could either grasp tightly to my anger and allow it to continue eating an acidic hole through my life, or I could experience the joy Our Lord experienced through crucifixion. Having every justification for holding onto his righteous wrath, and being fully defensible in condemning all of humanity for choosing self-gratification over the joy of divine relationship, he chose forgiveness, redemption, and reconciliation."

Tavis continued to listen encouragingly, but Sam could also see that Tavis was still uncertain about the reason for Sam's visit. It was time to bite the bullet.

"Look, Tavis, you are one of the few people who has met both Father Frank and Paul Peña. You know, more than most, who Paul was and what he was capable of."

"Yeah. It feels weird to say it about a pedophile, but I do think Father Frank was a good man. I would need a whole lot of convincing to say anything positive about Paul. It's like saying a tiger can change its stripes. That guy is the most arrogant, manipulative shit-heel I ever came across."

"I get it. Absolutely. Would you be willing to meet with him, to see for yourself whether he's changed?"

Tavis considered, then cleared his throat. "I wouldn't do it for him. I would do it for you, though. But I guess I still don't get why it matters to you if I think he's changed."

"Well . . . those of us who are making the case to canonize Father Frank think it matters. We think that if you see how he affected Paul, then maybe you'll help us with the canonization effort. If you wrote a report, the Congregation for the Causes of Saints would use it to make their recommendations."

"*Jesus!*" exclaimed Tavis, rubbing his forehead with his hand.

"I mean . . ." Sam pointed to his clerical collar.

"Sorry, Father," said Tavis, chagrined. "*Seriously*, though!"

"You don't have to decide this minute. Just meet with Paul, and then pray about it. I get it if you end up not wanting to do it."

Tavis held Sam's gaze for several seconds. Sam did his best not to fidget or look away. Finally, Tavis nodded.

CHAPTER THIRTY-THREE

Veronica stepped back, assessing the flowers she'd just placed near the steps leading to the altar. She bent down and adjusted them, then looked again, finally satisfied.

"They look lovely, Veronica," said a voice behind her. Thinking she had been alone, Veronica startled at the voice that carried in the cavernous acoustics of the cathedral. She turned and smiled as she recognized the speaker.

"Oh, thank you, Bishop. I think they'll do. Are you the celebrant for tomorrow's Mass?"

Bishop Cólima nodded and then, uncertainly, asked, "Veronica, I wonder whether you might take a short walk with me? It's a lovely afternoon and there's something I've been wanting to discuss with you."

"Of course. Just let me run to the ladies' room first. Meet you near the west door in ten minutes?"

"Perfect."

As she washed her hands, Veronica wondered what the bishop wanted to talk about. Considering her lawsuit against the diocese and outspoken criticism of the Church's handling of the clergy abuse crisis, the cordial relationship between the two of them was somewhat surprising. Veronica appreciated, however, that when Bishop Cólima had taken over from his predecessor in the wake of Paul Peña's trial, he had instituted reforms and safeguards even though such measures had not been adopted, or even meaningfully considered, by the global Church. Some of his reforms even ran counter to the Church's formal policies. His employment of Tavis Pereira, for example, and his commitment to report all substantiated allegations against clergy to law enforcement, was implemented at a time when the Church's official mandate was that all allegations must be kept absolutely secret. Only recently, and only in response to overwhelming pressure, had the Vatican released guidance *permitting*, but not *requiring*, Church officials to coordinate with law enforcement when they became aware of information pertaining to sexual assault against children.

Veronica appreciated Bishop Cólima's willingness to flout official policy because it was the right thing to do. He, in turn, appreciated her determination. They had formed an unlikely relationship that was something just shy of friendship.

During the pendency of her short-lived lawsuit, Bishop Cólima had happened upon her praying a rosary in the cathedral. He had sat down next to her, and they had talked after he waved away her warning that, as the current head of the Colberg diocese, he should not interact with the woman who was both the lawyer and plaintiff suing his diocese.

"Let's put that aside for now, shall we, and just agree to speak as brother and sister in Christ?"

She agreed, and they had had an edifying conversation. The bishop explained that, while he held a great deal of autonomy within the diocese, the archbishop heading the ecclesiastical province had demanded consistency in the handling of civil lawsuits relating to clergy abuse. Bishop Cólima speculated that the archbishop had, in turn, received a similar mandate from the Vatican. While the Church's secrecy strictures had only recently relaxed sufficient to allow bishops like Cólima to report suspected abuse to law enforcement, the Church still refused to allow any voluntary sharing of information in the context of civil lawsuits. The upshot, Bishop Cólima had explained, was that his hands were tied with respect to her lawsuit.

"I figured as much," responded Veronica.

"What interests me," admitted the bishop, "is finding you here praying a rosary."

Veronica looked at him curiously.

"So many people in your situation have left the Church. But here you are."

"I guess I'm just not willing to allow one more thing to be taken from me. I grew up in the Church; it's always been and still is a huge part of my life. Paul Peña and the men who enabled him took my boy from me, but they can't take my Church. The Church isn't the men who administer her, it's the body of Christ. I'm still part of that body. I love her. I want the men who act on her behalf to do better."

Bishop Cólima smiled his approval. "You and me both."

VERONICA MET the bishop at the cathedral's western entrance and, after they had walked in companionable silence for more than a block, Bishop Cólima said, "I've been meaning to ask you what you thought about the abuse summit at the Vatican a few years back."

"Too little, too late," responded Veronica drily. "Just more hand-wringing and asking for forgiveness without admitting responsibility or actually *doing* anything about the problem. I'm sure it was some PR phenom's idea, and that's exactly what it appeared to be—a PR stunt.""I don't disagree," said the bishop.

"You probably read in the news that our bishop's conference had planned to develop and implement detailed procedures the year before the summit, but the Vatican told us to stand down. We were told that the summit in Rome would result in some kind of unified approach from the global Church. I'm sure you can imagine our disappointment."

After several paces in silence, Bishop Cólima blurted, "Veronica, there's something I wanted you to hear from me. First, we've known each other for a while now. Do you think I'm a man of conscience?"

She did not need to think about her response. "Yes. From what I've seen, you do what you think is right even if it might make it more difficult to advance in your vocation."

"Good. I'm going to tell you something you're not going to like, but I've prayed about it, I've agonized over it, and my conscience is convinced it's the right thing to do."

She looked at him expectantly, head cocked.

He plowed ahead. "I don't know how much you've heard about Father Frank Muncy, the circumstances of his death, or the influence he's had on Paul Peña."

"Not much," she admitted, wincing slightly at the mention of Peña's name.

Bishop Cólima told her the broad outlines.

"The thing is," he said, "that Sam Wainwright, prison chaplain Father Matthew, and several others plan to begin the process seeking to canonize Father Frank. They need a bishop to sponsor the application, so they came to me. I knew Frank. He was obviously a complicated man, more complicated than most of us knew. The short story is, I've decided to sponsor the application. I wanted you to hear it from me."

She did not explode. She breathed deeply and stopped walking. She turned to face him. He turned toward her.

"Thank you for telling me," she said, looking directly into his eyes. "Sincerely. I'm sure it was no picnic, but it's more evidence that you are a man of integrity. I'm not sure how to feel about this. I'll need some time with it. Who knows, maybe I won't need to *do* anything because the Congregation for the Causes of Saints will shut down the application right away. You have to admit, recognizing a pedophile—an *admitted* pedophile—as a saint is a pretty preposterous idea."

His sheepish smile acknowledged her words.

She said, "Like you, I'll need to pray and think and, ultimately, listen to my own conscience to figure out if, or how, I should respond."

Her deep laugh lines, long rusted with disuse, creaked around a smile that reached her sad eyes. "Thank you, Bishop, really, for telling me. Do you mind if I walk back on my own?"

He reached over and patted her back. "Of course not."

CHAPTER THIRTY-FOUR

Sam tried to capture the attention of the assembled members of the Congregation for the Causes of Saints. "Gentlemen, like the rest of us who are asking you to canonize Father Frank, Tavis Pereira has been a firsthand witness to so much of the damage caused by priests who commit sexual offenses against children and other vulnerable people. He has prayed for God's guidance, and listened to what God called him to do. He decided to appear before you today because he saw how God used Father Frank as a tool for redemption and healing—starting with Paul Peña.

"I've spent most of my life hating Paul Peña for what he did to me. When I learned how many other boys he'd hurt, the tree of my hatred grew. I chose a life in an institution that professes the availability of forgiveness and newness of life for all, but I didn't really believe it applied to Paul. I couldn't fathom forgiving him, or myself, and so I couldn't imagine a God that could forgive us either.

"God strengthened my sight so that, through my haze of pain, I could see the truth of Paul's transformation. A complete transformation was the only explanation for how he was able to offer his apology to his victims even when he knew he would be met with hatred and rage. I learned that he was able to continue sharing his repentance because he had learned to rely on a strength greater than his own.

"His experiences made it impossible for him to doubt that God was actively working in his life. He had endured the pain of a serious physical attack, and the marvel of overnight healing and of being the object of such compassion from someone who loathed him but was willing to assume his injuries. . . even unto death. Father Frank's willing substitution for Paul illustrated, in a way Paul's extensive religious education never had, how Christ's sacrifice of love can transform us.

"The gospels teach it, but not until his experiences with Father Frank could Paul internalize that Christ's sacrifice was given not only for the righteous, the mistaken, or even the moderately bad—but for *all* of us. Even for the worst of us. Even for those of us who knowingly and willingly choose to sin against God, our neighbors, and our neighbors' children. Even, as Paul finally understood without room for doubt, for him.

"Paul's miraculous physical healing was just the beginning, and his calling to repeated expressions of repentance was refined through the painful fire of experiencing firsthand the injuries he had inflicted on his victims. It was clarified by Father Frank's posthumous visit. These experiences changed a cruel, selfish man into a flawed but willing tool of Christ's ministry of reconciliation.

"Before meeting Paul in that prison, I had worn my fury like a comfortable garment. Afterward, despite receiving reassurance that I would be within my rights to continue harboring hatred toward Paul, I was surprised to realize that I wanted *to want* to forgive him. It was a slow process that led me to several other meetings with Paul where I aired my anger and tried to understand how he had changed.

"As draining as those meetings were, we began to discuss

how to boost the signal of Paul's repentance to the many others who needed to hear it. Obviously, Paul's ability to act independently was limited, so I started visiting those of his victims that had participated in the criminal proceedings against him, and explained my recent experience and how meaningful it had been for me to hear Paul accept responsibility for his actions.

"Several of the men I visited told me to fuck straight off. I fucked off, as requested. Some of them said they needed time to think, and I haven't heard from most of them since then. A few, though, chose to attend facilitated meetings with Paul.

"It's a powerful medicine to hear a person who has hurt you accept responsibility and express remorse without deflection. It's a medicine that's almost never offered to victims of childhood sexual abuse, and the effects were profound.

"Many of the men were neither ready nor willing to move toward forgiving Paul, but the transparency with which he told the truth about the way he had manipulated each of them led to an even more important forgiveness—to forgiving themselves.

"During this same period, Paul began receiving overtures from some individuals on the other side of the equation: people who had sexually abused children or adolescents, and who had been moved to offer the same apology to their own victims. We formed a team of mental health professionals, ecumenical clergy, and newly empowered abuse survivors to carefully screen these offenders and discern their motivations. Our team has worked hard to ensure that victims never come into contact with their abusers until we've completed rigorous preparations to safeguard the victims from further emotional harm. So far the screening system has been effective.

"Once past the screening process, the offenders who have participated have been surprised by their own transformations. In some cases, they came to us with their regrets fully formed and in other cases, they were led to our program by a niggling tap of curiosity working through their conscience. Paul Peña's own road to Damascus, so to speak, has prepared him to guide even the merely curious through a frank appraisal of past actions—building an understanding of the victims' perspectives —and examining the consequences of the abuse. They've seen the mysterious alchemy through which light transforms guarded, secret shame into guilt and repentance."

Sam paused, took a drink of water to soothe his parched throat, and then dove in again. "I hate what Paul did to me and to so many others, but I love having such a great seat for witnessing how Christ has used even that pain to spread the beautiful seeds of his love and forgiveness. Many of those who have suffered in the same or similar ways are angry that my response has been to advocate for the canonization of Father Frank. I understand their anger. I understand how it feels like a betrayal. But, really, the way God used Father Frank is the perfect example of how God's capacity for forgiveness, for transformation, and for using each of us as we are rather than waiting for idealized versions of ourselves, transcends our own understanding. Father Frank belonged to a category of individuals that our culture sees as the very worst example of deviancy and sinfulness. We deny their humanity, we feel justified in making them the butts of our crudest jokes, and we actively and gleefully wish them harm.

"If Paul had died from that beating, many people, including me, would have thought his punishment was just. But God, in his creative, redemptive brilliance, led Father Frank to prayerfully intercede on behalf of the person who embodied his worst fears about himself. God accepted the obedience Father Frank offered, stoked it like a fragile, glowing coal, and then used it to overwhelm Paul with a raging, purifying fire of compassion, clarity, repentance, and forgiveness.

"God paved the way for some incredible healing through what he did with Father Frank and Paul Peña, but I'm sure you know that not everyone agrees. Our movement has gained momentum, but there's also a powerful opposition. If I hadn't been personally impacted by what happened with Father Frank, I'm sure I would have identified with the opposition movement.

"When taken at face value, most people think the fact that you are seriously considering our request to add an admitted pedophile to the canon to be an example of the Church's astounding lack of a reality touchstone in the priest sex abuse crisis. If they take the time to learn more, though, they would observe the awe and gratitude of the countless survivors and offenders who are able to describe the positive changes wrought in their lives. In the presence of such gratitude, many naysayers can't help but reconsider their earlier dismissal of the possibility that a member of that most hated caste of society could possibly be rightfully named to the canon of saints. They begin to believe that maybe God is calling the Church to this action precisely because it radically highlights the unknowable vastness of God's capacity for seeking, forgiving, and reconciling even those whom their fellow humans find impossible to forgive.

"Saints are particularly important in the Roman Catholic tradition because, unlike God, they are not all powerful, all knowing, and unsullied by human imperfections. They bring hope in believers' daily lives often *because* of their imperfections. The apostle Paul inspires us because his story reveals how the presence of the godhead in the person of the resurrected Christ could transform even ardent persecutors into willing champions of faith. Saint Francis of Assisi continues to touch hearts because he demonstrates how the joy of Christ's promise can outshine the glitter of great wealth.

"Others are led to Christ because of the story of saints like Saint Vladimir of Kiev, who performed human sacrifices, or the Blessed Bartolo Longo, who was a Satanic priest before converting to Christianity. These examples help all of us believe that God can use and love even someone who has committed the deeds that lurk in the darkest corners of the psyche. The sexual abuse of children has always existed, but we live in a time where it is not always concealed and ignored, but sometimes comes into the light where, rightfully, those affected can grieve.

"In the middle of this, God, in his quietly insistent way, asks, 'Remember when I said I came, not to the righteous, but to bring sinners to repentance? I meant even those who do the things you hate the most. I despise their actions, but they too are my precious lost sheep, and I will go to great lengths to find even them in their wilderness. I am who I am, and my grace is sufficient . . . even for them. My redemption includes . . . even them.'

"Obviously, it's complicated, and I get it. I understand all of the arguments against canonizing Father Frank. Although I believe I'm doing what God has called me to do to demonstrate the power and creativity of his redemption, it's dangerous to claim to know God's will. I could be wrong. I'm hoping the Holy Spirit gives you the discernment to make a recommendation consistent with God's will.

"I don't anoint saints. In spite of its processes, rules, and traditions, neither does the Church. If you're honest with yourself, gentlemen, you'll know that you don't either. Neither does the Pope. No, *God* chooses his saints, and he shapes and tempers them to be what his Body needs at the time it needs it. God used Father Frank as a tool to accomplish miracles that furthered his purposes. I am simply responding to a call of the Holy Spirit to seek official recognition of the status God himself bestowed on Father Frank.

"I think the Church should do this precisely *because* it's complicated and politically unsettling. On its face, the optics are terrible, and I'm sure the media will capitalize on that fact with headlines guaranteed to drive revenue. Scratching deeper, though, the thrust of this story is not the canonization of a pedophile. It is the canonization of a flawed but obedient servant who answered God's call, gave his most wicked and persistent inclinations to his Redeemer, and opened himself fully to be used as an instrument for the people most wounded by the nature of his sinfulness.

"I am an example of the healing power of Father Frank's decision. So are the many survivors who have received a greater measure of peace than they ever hoped to have because of Father Frank's obedience and how his spiritual gifts paved the way for God's transformation of Paul Peña and, in turn, for the movement of reconciliation Paul has led.

"The power of the Holy Spirit within this movement is why I'm not just a lone wing-nut advocating for the canonization of Father Frank. We receive plenty of vitriol from people who focus on, and hate, the idea of making a pedophile a saint. I'd be lying if I said I don't care what those people think. It hurts when they describe our efforts as pedophile advocacy or when they suggest that we must be pedophiles ourselves. But I also know those people have certain ideas and expectations of who God is, and their assumptions about his ability to work in the world are limited by what they think they know. Their anger is not just painful, it's terrifying. Even so, the call to this task, which began as a small, easily ignored voice, has become an unmistakable command, and Our Lord fills us with the strength to pursue it every day.

"Gentlemen, please think about what I've said today. Pray about it. Give it to the Holy Spirit. Then make your recommendation according to your conscience."

CHAPTER THIRTY-FIVE

From across the chamber, Veronica watched Sam Wainwright conclude his remarks while the assembled members of the Congregation for the Causes of Saints jotted notes. The Devil's Advocate now approached the lectern, and Veronica picked up the earpiece supplying her with real-time translation of the Italian spoken by the Devil's Advocate, who was tasked with presenting the case opposing the canonization of any candidate for sainthood. In many ways, the process was similar to a jury trial, with the presentation of witnesses for both sides, and the members of the Congregation serving as a sort of jury that would submit recommendations to the Pope for his ultimate decision.

The case in favor of canonization had rested with Sam's remarks and, listening, Veronica had found herself moved in spite of herself. When she first heard about the canonization efforts from Bishop Cólima, she had been gun-shy about putting herself out there again, but after a great deal of prayer, she had concluded that her conscience required her to speak out. This time, she had moved forward with open eyes, fully understanding the likely futility of her renewed efforts to make

Church leadership inhabit the perspectives of the thousands upon thousands of children and families who had been wounded by the culture that bred the clergy abuse crisis.

"And so, *signores,*" continued the Devil's Advocate in Italian, "I encourage you to listen to Mrs. Veronica Matthews from the Colberg diocese, the very diocese where Frank Muncy lived and worked. She explains, better than I ever could hope to, why canonizing Father Frank would be a terrible decision."

As Veronica approached the lectern, those members of the Congregation who did not speak fluent English re-inserted their earpieces.

"Gentlemen," Veronica began, making eye contact with each member of the Congregation in turn, a technique she'd often employed to persuade courts and juries. "Mr. Wainwright and the other witnesses testifying in favor of canonization did an impressive job describing their long road here, to speak in front of you, and of Father Frank's long spiritual journey. I don't know Mr. Wainwright personally, but I do know and respect two of the other witnesses in favor of canonization—Bishop Cólima and Tavis Pereira. I also know both of these men have given their testimony out of a genuine belief that canonizing Father Frank is the right thing to do. Perhaps in another time, in another context, I could agree with them. But in the current time, and the current context, I know you will make a grave mistake if you recommend canonization. A mistake that further fractures, perhaps fatally, the already injured Church we all love.

"My sweet son was one of the boys Paul Peña abused. He was younger than most of Peña's victim's—only 12 years old. Sean was so much more than just a victim, but what Paul Peña did to him reduced Sean, in his own mind, to a handful of bewildering experiences. His father and his sisters and I, and really everyone who knew him and loved him, tried to make him understand how special he was. Even as an infant, he was remarkable. He wasn't even a year old when I fell pregnant again, and a little while later, I miscarried. One day I was having a hard time with the loss, and this kind child, who hadn't even taken his first step, crawled over to me, touched the tears on my cheek, and gave me a kiss. He wasn't even a toddler and he was comforting and encouraging me!" Veronica's throat caught her sob.

"It's easy to dismiss such examples as a parent's overenthusiasm about her child, but he just continued to grow in loveliness. His older sisters have always bickered with each other, but they never bickered with Sean. One year he had received a big gift certificate to a toy store for his birthday, and there was nothing in particular that he wanted, so he spent it all on a big gift for his closest friend. *That* is who Paul Peña stole . . . not just from me, but from the world.

"Sean and I were close. Once he finally started talking about what happened to him, he shared a lot of details with me. I can tell you that the physical injuries from his rape healed in the blink of an eye compared to the damage Peña did with his manipulation. No amount of therapy or love from the people who cared for my Sean could heal that hurt. While Paul Peña went on with his life, Sean carried the shame with him for years —until he just couldn't carry it anymore."

Veronica mesmerized the Congregation with her tale of Sean's life and death, of what she had learned about how Paul's superiors had enabled him and obfuscated the danger he presented to the body of Christ, of how she and countless others had been frustrated by how the Church had prevented them from seeking justice through the courts. She told them how she and other families had been denied even the catharsis of being heard by representatives of the Church hierarchy.

"The irony is not lost on me, and I hope it's not lost on you: after years of trying to make myself meaningfully heard by senior Church officials, my opportunity finally comes when the Church is deciding whether to elevate a pedophile priest—the very category of individual responsible for the rift between the body of the Church and its leadership.

"The Church has broken the hearts of the faithful and the suffering again and again. Instead of protecting our communities of faith, Church decision-makers almost always erred on the side of protecting accused clergy, referring them to unproven and ineffectual treatment programs, and then unleashing them on new communities without warning.

"When journalists began uncovering the extent of this practice around the world, the Church hired PR firms to protect its image and when they *have* engaged directly with victims, they've retreated to their entrenched positions of defensiveness and justification.

"Even now, the Church is too afraid of impacting its wealth and status to offer a meaningful apology to those it hurt. What we want, what our pain demands, is not an apology that generally expresses sympathy for the suffering, but one that encompasses how the institution and the individuals in leadership failed us. And then they need to show us exactly how they're going to prevent this from happening again. Without that kind of sincere repentance, there can be no reconciliation.

"I've heard all of the reasons Frank Muncy is different: he never actually touched anyone underage; he didn't have the technological capability to view the child pornography in his possession for years before he turned himself in; he did so much good for the community; and he chose to hold himself publicly accountable for his actions. Good. Fine. I hope those mitigating factors help him with God, but they do not erase the fact that he admitted to seeking out and viewing child pornography, and he admitted that he was sexually attracted to children."

Veronica's incredulous outrage broke through her attempt at dispassionate persuasion. "And we're supposed to venerate this guy? Those of us whose lives became hell because of priests like

Paul Peña who used their positions to manipulate children to make them believe that *they* were sinful?"

"So you see, gentlemen, that the decision about whether to canonize Father Frank can never be made in a vacuum. If you do this, you will lose many more of the faithful than you've already lost. Many more who, like me and my family, have continued to love the Church even though the failure of her leadership. But if you do this, regardless of how nuanced and eloquent your justification, you will be sending a message to the abused children and their wounded families. The message is: 'The clergy *is* the Church. We alone decide what is right for the Church. We choose our own over you.' I urge you not to send that message. Recommend that for once . . . for *once* . . . the Holy Father choose the body over the institution."

CHAPTER THIRTY-SIX

"Gentlemen," said Sam, again addressing the Congregation, "I appreciate this opportunity for rebuttal, and I'll make my remarks brief. In short, it won't be much of a rebuttal because I've heard Ms. Matthews's challenges before and, for the most part, I agree with them.

"Before delving into the flaws with the Church's handling of the crisis that Mrs. Matthews pointed out, I, and many others, had perceived the Church to have apologized for its role in the damage done to so many of the youngest, most innocent members of its flock. However, as Mrs. Matthews says, the substance of such 'apologies' leaves much to be desired. In fact, under scrutiny, the Church's statements would not satisfy even the most accommodating priest in the confessional.

"The Church repeatedly has issued the kind of pseudo-apology beloved by older siblings: the passive-voiced 'I'm sorry you were hurt' rather than the active-voiced 'I'm sorry I hurt you.' While good parents require their children to own their behavior by amending their apologies, no one has been able to hold the Church or its leaders to such account. The Church continues to make mealy-mouthed statements, expressing sorrow for the effect of suffering without acknowledging its own participation in the cause.

"In researching the Church's response, I've been horrified by the impressive skill of the Church's public relations professionals. Misleading headlines have given the Church the benefit of accepting responsibility without the reality of having done so. A headline reading 'Roman Catholic Leaders Apologize to Child Victims' reveals only that leaders 'expressed sorrow for some priests' inappropriate contact with children, and regretted that the manipulative habits of such offenders allowed them to continue their shameful behavior under the noses of their superiors.' The Church's public statements have relied heavily on euphemism, substituting 'inappropriate behavior' and 'boundary issues' for 'rape' or 'sexual assault.' Additionally, rather than acknowledging that, for decades, Church leaders systematically and knowingly covered up allegations and transferred known offenders to different geographical areas where they continued to injure children, the Church's PR machine characterized the leadership's failures as 'negligence,' 'lack of realization of what was happening,' or a 'failure to respond.'

"I appreciate that the current Pope, as the holder of the Church's highest office, has at least publicly acknowledged the problem and its effects. Obviously, this is an improvement over his predecessors' avoidance of the issue. Media reports cite the Pope's private meetings with small numbers of abuse survivors as parts of broader visits around the globe, and then the Church's public relations machine releases generalized statements about the fruitfulness of the meetings and the Holy Fathers' commitment to improving processes that would eliminate the problem for future generations of the vulnerable faithful.

"These statements are masterpieces of legalistic tightrope walking—conveying sympathy without expressing remorse and requesting forgiveness without actually accepting blame. They do not accomplish a fraction of what Father Frank or Paul Peña have accomplished by accepting responsibility for their actions. The victims chosen to meet with the Pope are always carefully vetted in advance to ensure they will not express rage or ask uncomfortable questions. In this way, the Church hierarchy is insulated from direct exposure to the rage and despair the abuse crisis had engendered in much of the rest of the global body of Christ.

"As Mrs. Matthews told you, victims' groups receive no satisfaction, and their members often feel their injuries have been compounded by the leadership's refusal to acknowledge that such widespread damage has not been caused by a couple of bad apples alone, but that the rot has permeated the barrel. The institution's leaders have, in this area, led so badly that they bear significant responsibility for how victims' shame continues to be fed by the darkness of secrecy.

"I suspect that people rarely say these things directly to you, gentlemen, as holders of high offices within the Church, or directly to the Holy Father, but somebody should. This is the context in which you are making your recommendation about Father Frank. If you decide that he should be admitted to the canon of saints, many people will be justifiably angry. When I shut out the noise and wait for God to guide my actions, his call is faint but clear. It compels me to urge you: Do it anyway."

CHAPTER THIRTY-SEVEN

" S o, to answer your primary question, the expectation is that the Holy Father will announce his decision regarding canonization during next week's event. I don't know what that decision is and I'm not sure whether the Holy Father has even made up his mind at this point, or even which direction he's leaning."

Pope Dillon, the 268th man to hold that title, and one of only a handful who had declined to change his name upon ascending to his position, paused in the hallway leading into the great room. One of his personal secretaries was speaking animatedly into the telephone. Curious, Dillon delayed entering the room so he could hear more of Nathan's thoughts that, certainly, Nathan would have heavily filtered if he had been speaking directly to Dillon.

"I don't envy the Holy Father this decision. If he hadn't committed to making an announcement, the wise political move would have been to punt and either leave it to a subsequent Pope or allow the issue to fade with time. He's hamstrung himself by removing that choice . . . and I don't see a win either way. He'll either be seen as choosing glorifying abusive priests over their defenseless victims in a gesture of breathtaking insensitivity, or as caving to politics and ignoring what many perceive to be an unmistakable movement of the Holy Spirit toward healing and reconciliation."

Nathan, silent, listened to the voice on the other end of the line.

"Of course. 'No' is the pragmatic choice. If I were advising any other head of state, there would be no doubt." When he continued, his voice trembled with confusion and sincerity, "But he's not just any head of state. We rely on him to be particularly sensitive to the Holy Spirit . . . It's tough to reconcile political wisdom with the way Father Frank died . . . and with what certainly appears to be the fruits of the Spirit that have resulted. So, I just don't know what decision is best. But I'll spend the next week praying for God to bless the Holy Father with wisdom and discernment."

Dillon entered the room and Nathan acknowledged him with a small bow of his head. "All right, Staci, I'm going to need to let you go. I'll make sure you get a press pass and I'll see you next week in Colberg."

"Press pass?" Dillon inquired after Nathan had hung up.

"Mmm-hmm," Nathan answered. "Staci's an old friend from college and she's covering your visit for the regional paper."

"Right," Dillon said. He placed the stack of papers he'd been carrying under his arm on Nathan's desk. "These are the reports gathered by the Congregation. I've read them and made some notes. I'd like to make sure they're with us in the States next week, so please pack them."

"Absolutely, Your Holiness. You have a meeting with the Senior Communications Advisor in a little over an hour. Would you like tea first?"

"No, thank you, Nathan. What I *would* like is a laptop loaded with the video of the arguments made before the Congregation for the Causes of Saints, a pitcher of water, a glass, and 24 hours. I'm afraid you'll have to cancel all my meetings between now and this time tomorrow afternoon."

Nathan's brow puzzled over this announcement. Pope Dillon was known for exercising an unprecedented degree of control over his own agenda, but also for his reliable participation in the rigorous schedule he set for himself.

"Of course, Holy Father. May I ask . . . where will you be?"

Dillon nodded toward the smaller room that served as his private office. "I'll be in there. I need time to fast and to pray."

IT WAS SHORTLY after 2:00 a.m. Dillon had watched and re-watched the video of the arguments before the Congregation for the Causes of Saints. He had read and re-read the materials submitted in favor of and in opposition to the canonization decision, as well as the recommendation of the Congregation.

Listening to the arguments of Veronica Matthews and of Sam Wainwright, Dillon acknowledged he had fallen prey to a shortcoming of his predecessors: decrying, in general terms, the actions of those who physically perpetrated sexual abuse against children, while remaining conspicuously silent about the complicity of the Church as an institution. Like his predecessors, Dillon had actively defended some accused priests against whom an unassailable mountain of evidence had later accumulated.

Dillon remained undecided regarding the proposed canonization of Father Frank. On the one hand, he found the stories of the redemption and transformations of both Father Frank and Paul Peña to be deeply compelling, particularly poignant examples of what Dillon had taken to calling "God-sized forgiveness," which he defined primarily by comparison to human-sized forgiveness. He considered that reasonably enlightened humans could usually forgive a multitude of hurtful actions, including lies, assault, theft, and adultery. In contrast, there were certain transgressions that touched such a deep nerve that they seemed unforgivable.

Dillon imagined forgiveness as a solid, immutable object, like a diamond. Depending on the perspective, or facet, through which one approached the concept, forgiveness could be offered through the purely human mechanism that indwells in souls with the propensity to crave peace and reconciliation over conflict. Others approached forgiveness through their tendency to hold fast to the memory of injuries sustained, and for them forgiveness usually required the heart softening of divine intervention. Still a different facet came to mind when Dillon imagined God-sized forgiveness. It was the facet through which even people pre-disposed to reconciliation considered the circumstances of an offense to reveal a perpetrator so filled with malice and disregard for the traumatic consequences of satisfying their deviant desires, that they could use the very defenselessness of a child to accomplish their sexual gratification. Through this facet, Dillon could understand why someone like Veronica would find it impossible to forgive both the man and the institution that had willfully and fatally injured her son. In those circumstances, Dillon did not imagine that forgiveness and reconciliation could be possible without divine intervention.

The faith to which Dillon was a lifelong adherent held that no crime placed its perpetrator beyond the power of Jesus to redeem, and no offense was beyond the power of the Holy Spirit to reconcile and even use in accomplishing God the Father's good purposes. If it could be believed, the story of Father Frank and Paul Peña demonstrated this truth because it revealed that the Great Shepherd can, and does, pursue in love even these most bedraggled of lost sheep. This pursuit impressed believers with a sense both of God's unfathomability and his proximity and willingness to aid in carrying our heaviest burdens. His pursuit of Father Frank and Paul Peña, with a perfect love that demanded both repentance and accountability, evoked the security of resting in the care of wise and loving parents: clear expectations, proportional discipline, and a return to good grace after the penitent worked toward restitution.

In contrast with the intractable anger Veronica had demonstrated so eloquently during the hearing before the Congregation, other similarly situated parents had submitted materials supporting Father Frank's canonization. One father even admitted that he had once formulated a plan to kill Peña. Nonetheless, some of these righteously enraged people had been able to speak with such sincerity and even joy about the manner in which choosing to forgive Paul had enriched their existence and acted as a balm to soothe their pain. It had motivated them to lend momentum to a growing wave of reconciliation.

It was this glimpse into the benevolent motivations of an unfathomable deity, and into the commitment of his son to tenderly restoring even the seemingly irredeemable, that stirred healing victims and humbled-but-hopeful perpetrators alike in seeking to honor Father Frank with recognition of sainthood. They each considered him to be God's instrument for their personal metamorphoses. Dillon could not fault those who held fast to their anger, but he had to acknowledge the power in the demonstration of God's creative repurposing.

Dillon continued to consider these conflicting perspectives. Thinking deeply on these issues did not make his choice any clearer. Sighing, he hauled himself to his feet and allowed the pins and needles in his legs to settle before stepping gingerly to the private restroom attached to his office.

Exiting the restroom, he clicked off the light and headed back to the glowing fireplace, settling himself back onto the pillow he used for meditation. He was usually an early-to-bed, early-to-rise kind of person, but his fast had enhanced his focus and banished drowsiness. He had no escape from the irreconcilable perspectives about Frank's canonization. Hoping to return to the state of meditation, he prayed silently, *Please, Lord God, for the sake of your son Jesus Christ, lend me your hand. There are so many ways to go wrong with this decision, and if I try to make it by myself, I will make the wrong choice. Help me. Lead me, by your Spirit, to the choice you would have me make.* Anguished, and feeling more alone and uncertain than ever, he continued in silence.

"Stop feeling sorry for yourself," chided a gentle voice nearby.

Startled, Dillon looked up to see a man sitting in a chair near the fire, smiling at him. His face was the one Pope Dillon had seen in the files he had been poring over all night.

"Hey, Dill," said the man. "Mind if I call you Dill?"

A LITTLE MORE THAN 24 hours after he had entered it, Dillon emerged from his office, smelling a little stale but looking bright-eyed. He moved with an energy that Nathan wouldn't have expected for someone who, in the past 24 hours, probably hadn't slept and definitely hadn't taken in anything other than water.

"We have a lot of work to do, Nathan, and not a lot of time. I'm gonna need you to push your logistical genius like you've never pushed it before. And no more calls to Staci—everything from here needs to be kept in the strictest confidence."

CHAPTER THIRTY-EIGHT

The day of the Pope's audience dawned gray and cold. Although the audience was limited to 300 specifically invited attendees and a few journalists, the Pope would be appearing later in the day to greet a throng of congregants at the local stadium. Unsurprisingly, traffic was abysmal and parking was impossible.

Sam Wainwright had arrived early, and he sat with a group of other survivors who had similarly supported the canonization of Father Frank. Only minutes before the Pope's scheduled appearance, Veronica Matthews entered the room and, making herself small and unobtrusive, took a seat near the front, but on the aisle as if to give herself a ready escape route, should she need one.

At the precise minute appointed for the event, two sets of doors near the front of the room opened, and a procession of bishops, archbishops, and cardinals filed in, each robed in highly ornate vestments that varied to reflect the geographic location over which each prelate held spiritual authority. As the richly robed men processed with slow dignity and stopped in front of the chairs that had, apparently, been assigned to them, members of the press pool exchanged puzzled glances. They had believed they were covering a semi-private papal audience for select proponents and opponents of the effort to canonize Father Frank, but the high-level and wide-reaching representation of members of Church leadership suggested something else was afoot. They were surprised to note the presence of Cardinals Verguenza and Aibu, both of whom had famously dismissed complaints about bishops and priests within their respective spheres of authority as little more than extortion. Also present was Cardinal Callum, a lifelong friend and confidante of the Holy Father who, like the Pope, usually dressed in the modest raiment typical of the Jesuit Order from which both men hailed, and who looked supremely uncomfortable in the baroque robes in which he appeared on this day.

The heavy wooden doors closed behind them, and the room stood in expectant silence. The audience was overwhelmed by the cacophony of color and textures in the congregation of elite Roman Catholic clergy at the front of the room. Sam feverishly worked to identify and catalogue specific faces and, as he did so, his astonishment grew.

Once again, the ornate doors opened, and they framed the Holy Father in the most formal trappings of the highest Church office. His eyes were closed, and his prayerful posture enabled those present to observe the full glory of his vestments and the Papal Tiara that sat heavily upon his brow.

Eyebrows raised in surprise, Sam struggled to make sense of the significance of what he observed. To his knowledge, neither this Pope nor any of his recent predecessors had worn the Papal Tiara, consistent with his preference for eschewing the material trappings of his office in favor of asceticism. Virtually every photograph of him, even at the most significant events, depicted a holy-looking man dressed simply in a white alb and chasuble, with only his plain white zucchetto to set him apart as Rome's highest Pontiff.

It was particularly stunning that this ascetic Pope had chosen to wear the tiara because it had long been out of favor with even the more epicurean of his recent predecessors. In fact, Pope Dillon had once publicly criticized the historic tradition of the Papal Tiara, citing with approval Pope Paul VI, who had ceremonially laid down the tiara, and the human glory and power it represented, on the altar at the Second Vatican Council in 1964, then symbolically sold one of the ornate headpieces and used the proceeds for charitable causes.

The Pope began a slow, stately stride towards a raised dais in the front. After installing himself on the dais, he remained silent for several moments as he examined the faces of those who had come to be near to him and to what he represented. This period of silence deepened the already unsettled atmosphere, and highlighted the stark contrast between the groups of people in the cavernous room. There was the Church hierarchy on a staging area physically higher than the audience it faced, its representatives regal in their exquisitely made vestments of exorbitantly expensive materials in deep, rich hues. The formality of their robes encouraged the wearers to display their most exemplary posture, and many wore expressions of a stern, haughty dignity.

In contrast, those standing in the recessed portion of the room, whether supporting or opposed to the canonization of Father Frank, were plainly subject to the authority of the gathered clerics, whom they regarded with awe. Although most of the lay attendees had made an effort at respectability by donning formal clothing, even the most well-turned-out congregants could not hope to match the peacockery of the clergy. Beyond the garments, the divide was also emphasized by the room's topography, which forced the laity to look up at the gathered ministers of God. It was no wonder that many of the upturned faces displayed reverential expressions.

Reverence was not the only nor the most common expression on display, however. A degree of wariness inhabited the faces of many of those present. The wrinkled brows and cocked heads conveyed puzzlement over the significance of such a gathering when they had expected "only" the presence of the Holy Father and the small team with which he usually traveled. Of course, the presence of the Pope alone would have been a once in a lifetime event for most of those in attendance, but the added appearance of so many other leaders of the global Church raised it to a new plane of importance. They were unsure how to interpret the imposing scene unfolding before them. At first glance, it almost seemed like a calculated show of force against those who had challenged and criticized the Church.

The Pope allowed the silence and tension to build until it was palpably oppressive. After making meaningful eye contact with what seemed like each and every member of the audience, he then closed his eyes as if in a silent bid for strength and divine aid, and in English tinged with the Strabane County accent of his youth, he filled all the corners of the room. Even without a microphone, his voice spread easily over the assembled crowd. His carriage conveyed conversational ease, with none of the physical strain that ordinarily accompanies an effort to project one's voice in a large, populated space. The room was so quietly riveted that even those at the greatest physical remove were able to hear clearly.

"In the mystery of Our Lord's perfect timing and ability to transform even our most sinful choices and destructive decisions into tools to further the peace and love of his kingdom, one of the reasons we gather today is to formally acknowledge that his ability to forgive and to redeem is greater than our own human capacity to forgive. In each era, he has shown his love by transforming examples of that age's most reviled kinds of villains into holy vessels of his mercy. We acknowledge that he continues to work in this way and to directly participate in our lives.

"There can be no doubt that Our Lord calls on us daily to deny ourselves, to take up our crosses, and to follow him. His Word is full of examples of wretched, despicable lives that he transformed when they accepted the opportunity he offered. Our canon is an ode to the transformative power of Christ's love and redemption. He came to call not the righteous, but sinners to repentance. And yet we continue to react with skepticism when he does what he says he'll do, and we're filled with niggling doubts that some sins may be greater than his powers of redemption.

"Our Lord defeated death. There are no sins greater than his power of redemption." The Pontiff paused to allow his words to descend on the crowd with their weight. "No sins," he repeated.

"Father Frank Muncy struggled with the most hateful and insidious of demons. Upon realizing that his sinful nature was greater than his ability to control it, he asked Our Lord to help him bear the burden, and in gratitude for this answered prayer, he devoted his life to the service of Christ and his fellow sufferers. He was not forced to expose his deepest sins, but he responded to the demand of the conscience that Christ Jesus instilled within him.

"If it were up to me, I would have chosen a less complicated object of veneration, but Our Lord chooses his own saints, and he delights in turning our comfortable sense of decorum on its head. Father Frank Muncy offered his shame and fear to Christ Jesus, who, by the alchemy of forgiveness and redemption, alleviated Father Frank's terror of earthly consequences and enabled his obedience to Our Lord's calling for his life. My own calling in this situation, while uncomfortable and certain to draw worldly disapproval, does not require nearly as much courage as Father Frank displayed. This morning I directed the Prefect of the Congregation for the Causes of Saints to promulgate a decree including Francis Stephen Muncy in the canon of saints." As soon as he said the words, the Swiss Guards lifted the cloth covering an easel on the platform to reveal Father Frank's seminary portrait.

Rather than pausing to allow his pronouncement to sink in, the Pope's voice carried over the shocked murmurings of the gathered crowd, and the assembly's ingrained reverence for his position quickly silenced them again. "Although it is not one of the miracles that formed the predicate for his canonization, we have reason to hope that Father Frank's intercession will lead to a new era of justice and reconciliation within the Church we love. We know, at least, that he brought all of us into this room today."

At this point, the Pontiff did pause, and a door slammed at the back of the room, an audible expression of one congregant's disappointment in the Pope's decision. Veronica, seated near the front of the assembly, had lost all color. She stared, mesmerized, at Father Frank's portrait. Every image she had seen of Father Frank depicted him toward the end of his life, in middle age. The young man in the portrait looked like a different person, and Veronica recognized the smoking companion who had offered her compassion and hope when she had needed it most.

The Bishop of Rome's posture was upright as ever, but his haggard expression conveyed his sensitivity to every ounce of the physical and symbolic weight of his vestments.

"Brothers and sisters, Our Lord has seen your suffering," he began, "and he longs for reconciliation between the members of his body that comprise his holy Church. He longs to reunite us: you, the faithful, with us, the clergy, who have undertaken the sacrament of Holy Orders to share his light and grace in the world."

With these words, the Pope paused as if checking in with a decision he had previously made and then, apparently finding it as sound as he had found it before, he gave an almost imperceptible confirmatory nod as he moved toward the shallow stairs that separated the stage on which he stood from the seats that held the wounded faithful. Observing the potential danger, several members of the highly costumed Swiss Guard started as if to intercept their charge. Waving off his guardians with an economical display of his palms, the Holy Father gathered his heavy robes in his hands to avoid tripping over them as he descended the stairs, and then he walked down the center aisle until he stood in the midst of the lay assembly.

An eerie silence descended as the Pope once again unhurriedly searched the faces of those who had gathered to meet with him. Each person present had a brief but intense experience of recognition and acknowledgement. To facilitate his survey, the Pope slowly rotated in a circle until at last, after several silent minutes, he had made a full revolution.

Without the raised platform, the Pope's diminutive size was more apparent, and he approached in height the men surrounding him only as a result of the tall Papal Tiara that rested heavily on his brow. Any disadvantage of physical stature, however, did not linger in the observer's mind, which was occupied instead with the Pontiff's undeniable and ineffable charisma that combined humility with a quiet confidence. The Pope walked back up the aisle toward the platform but, upon reaching the first row of the audience, he turned around once again and faced the lay assembly, dropping to his knees. Again, the Swiss Guard started forward in alarm, and again the Holy Father waved them off.

The lay people, clergy, and press representatives universally displayed brows furrowed in confusion, which then converted almost simultaneously to round-eyed, slack-jawed surprise at the Pope's next action. Still on his knees, he reached up and removed the Papal Tiara, then set it on the floor beside him. Then the Holy Father closed his eyes, raised his hands with palms out until they were parallel with his head, and bent forward at the waist until his forehead met the floor. The stiff brocade of the most elaborate official robes of the most powerful institution in the world seemed to resist the movements that were unnatural to the position, but the Holy Father was not deterred from prostrating himself before the gathered sufferers. While the leader of the Holy Roman Church remained bowed, those present looked around in shock.

When the Pope finally lifted his head, rather than settling into a more comfortable kneeling position in which he rested on his lower legs, he kneeled in a more formal position that required him to continuously flex his quadriceps, hamstrings, and gluteal muscles. Disregarding his physical unease, the Pope again spoke in the deceptively quiet tone that somehow carried clearly to every ear in the room.

"Fellow believers," he began in a voice of unflappable purpose, "I kneel here at your feet to say long overdue words: As both a man, and as the head of our Church, I have sinned against you." Gesturing to the religious royalty seated behind him, he continued. "The institution of our Holy Church, represented by the leaders you see here, has sinned against you. We are truly sorry and we humbly repent."

With these words, the Pope again hinged forward and pressed his forehead to the ground. Uncertain of what was expected of them, the elite clergymen on the raised platform cast about themselves as if searching for a clue. With an expression of peace, Cardinal Callum followed the lead of his superior and friend, and sunk to his knees, pressing his forehead to the floor. One by one, nearly all of the other clergymen on the raised platform followed suit, with the exception of a few rigidly erect holdouts, who looked at the spectacle with expressions of horror.

As the import of what they were witnessing hit home for each of those gathered, the Church's walking wounded expressed their profound reactions in unique ways. Some simply remained wide-eyed and standing, as if frozen. Others burst into ungovernable weeping. Still others sat heavily on their nearby chairs, with silent tears running down their faces.

Eventually, the room quieted again and the Pope raised his head from the floor and motioned for both the audience and the clergy to be seated.

"We have existed too long in a state of division," he said. "We ministers of God have not acted as ministers of God, and we have not heeded the voice that guides us to act according to Our Lord's holy plans. When our failures were exposed, we retreated even further into the trappings of worldly power. Into lies. Into secrecy. Into evasions. While it is true that to err is human and to forgive is divine, we requested and expected your forgiveness without acknowledging or confessing even the rough outlines of our guilt, and without repenting in the manner we require of those who turn to us for spiritual leadership. We never communicated our sorrow for failing to love you and our God as we should. We lacked even imperfect contrition, and our responses continuously revealed that we sought only to avoid the worldly consequences of our sinful actions.

"We wielded our spiritual power with an arrogance that made our claimed authority meaningless. We relied on the worldly influence and wealth our institution has accumulated instead of on the source of our true authority: the Christ who disdained pretension in favor of humility and institutional might in favor of radical love.

"We forgot that we are mere men, and we encouraged you to forget, too. We forgot that our leadership is dependent on a commitment to continuously seek alignment with the author and perfector of our faith. When we rely on our own judgment, and on power emanating from sources other than the One we serve, we are as flawed and broken as the rest of the world.

"Beautifully, Our Lord does not demand or expect perfection—even from us—but he does insist that we strive to adhere to the principles he taught, especially during instances of inevitable failure. And we have failed. Too many of us failed as individual men, by abusing our power in order to take physical gratification from those over whom we exercised extraordinary influence. Even when we did not personally commit physical assault, we failed. We can no longer call our failure negligence or ignorance. It was much more blameworthy. We failed . . . we sinned . . . by enabling and by keeping the secrets of our fellow clerics at the expense of the health of the communities we were called to serve. As has become clear in recent years despite our efforts to conceal our sins, both types of failure extended so high up in our tree of authority that they are institutional sins.

"Even when our secrets were being dragged into the light, we dug in our heels and retreated into defensiveness and legalism. Rather than accept Our Lord's scriptural direction to confess and renounce our sins, we denied our blame, and our denial increased your pain."

"In reflecting on this black stain on our integrity, both as men and as component members of an institution, I considered *why* we have failed to follow Our Lord's teachings in the midst of this crisis. The immediately apparent answer is that we avoided light and truth for the most human of reasons—to avoid just consequences.

"Rather than acting as the representatives of Our Lord on Earth, and teaching by example his priceless message of repentance, confession, absolution, and reconciliation, we, as an institution comprised of human, and therefore fallible, men, acted in accordance with our human natures. Terrified that the power and wealth of our storied Church would crumble on our watch, we doubled down."

Here the Pope winced slightly as if his kneeling posture had finally taken its toll on his aging knees. Rather than altering his position of supplication, however, the Holy Father straightened his back and continued.

"Saint Francis Muncy exemplified the triumph of divinely

attuned conscience over fear of consequence. We, as the men who purport to lead this institution that devotes itself to community with the divine and with the entire Body of Christ, and who must, by virtue of our callings, aspire to embody the teachings Our Lord so lovingly bestowed, can do no less.

"In this spirit, on behalf of myself and the Church, I unreservedly apologize to you and to all who have been raped, assaulted, threatened, manipulated, ignored, and disbelieved. We failed to protect you when we could and should have done so. We wronged you in these and in countless other ways. We are truly sorry and we humbly repent. *I* am truly sorry and I humbly repent."

The Pontifex Maximus again sought the gaze of the individuals surrounding him and said, repeatedly, clearly, and firmly, "I am so very sorry." The effect of the sincere and humble personal apology was compelling. Although some cried, most of those to whom the Pope spoke remained stock still, as if rendered immobile by declarations they had desired but never expected to hear. It was magnificent to behold the transformations in their faces, as their expressions moved from hopefully wary to unexpectedly fortified.

Returning to his address, His Holiness said again, "I am sorry," and then he continued, "In the past, our acknowledgement of any blame has been implied rather than overt. We skipped a key component of reconciliation by asking for forgiveness and prematurely demanding a mending of fences without explicitly laying down our defensiveness and examining our sins in the light of truth. As many of you know from what we have demanded in the sacrament of confession, there can be no absolution or the resultant restoration of communion, of *relationship*, which is the hallmark of reconciliation, without unvarnished truth-telling and repentance that includes a genuine commitment to stop sinning.

"We must stop holding ourselves to a lesser standard than

we demand of all of you in the confessional. I do not ask for your forgiveness today. If that happens, it must be in your hands and in God's hands. Without pressing the weight of that expectation on you, I say again: I am sorry. We have sinned against you; we have sinned against Our Father in heaven; we have betrayed our charge as God's ministers on Earth. We are truly sorry and we humbly repent."

Allowing this repetition of the words to sink in, with the grace of a much younger man he rose from his knees to his feet in a single, fluid movement. "As I said," he continued, "a necessary component of repentance is a sincere resolution to alter behavior and to accept just consequences. Going forward, we in Church leadership will no longer employ public relations experts to guide our response to allegations of abuse at the hands of priests and inquiries regarding the actions that were taken to cover up credible claims. We will do, instead, as we should do with all aspects of Church governance: we will prayerfully seek God's perfect will, and humbly request his guidance in shaping our actions to do justice. Let me be clear: we will not abandon our human brothers who have sinned, but neither will we deploy a shroud of secrecy to protect them from the just consequences of their actions. We will, instead, in the light of day, remind them of Our Lord's mercy that is as much for them as for all of us when we confess our transgressions. We will remind them of Saint Francis Muncy, and of what is possible when we rely on Our Lord's strength rather than on our own.

"As an initial step toward accepting just consequences for our transgressions, I pledge a full 10% of the Church's assets to supporting those who have suffered as a result of sexual abuse at the hands of priests."

A rush of murmurs followed his startling announcement, and the Pope pushed down the air in front of him to silence the crowd.

"This is not an attempt to pay off those who have been harmed. Rather, it's simply a start to demonstrate our commitment to righting our priorities. But it's not where we stop. For those who exercise their rights to pursue compensation in the courts, you will find our approach to be altered significantly. Our focus no longer will be on protecting the worldly wealth of the Church, but on reaching a just result. Justice requires full knowledge of the facts. Accordingly, while we cannot, as a practical matter, offer substantial amounts of money to each person who alleges abuse, we will no longer rely on what have been two of our most significant legal shields. First, we will not invoke statutes of limitation to avoid liability. Second, we will not rely on legal maneuvers to protect documents in our possession from requests for relevant information. If justice requires truth, as we know it does, then we will resolve any future litigation with both sides having access to as much information as can be made available.

"Equally important to making restitution, we will protect today's children, and tomorrow's children, by reassigning priests accused of offenses against children to roles that remove them from all contact with children until law enforcement and the Church complete their respective investigations. Corroborated allegations will result in expedited laicization."

"I hope these steps will lead some to regaining trust in our sincerity and that they will work with us toward reconciliation. Many others, however, understandably, will consider their relationship with our Church to be hopelessly severed. I will pray that such people find Our Lord through other avenues. I anticipate that at least some will be dissatisfied with the idea of settlement, and will seek to hold us to full account through their day in court. This is their right, and it is an aspect of our renewed commitment to justice for which we must be prepared. It will test our new dedication, but we must not waver," and here his gentle voice increased in volume and rang with steely resolve, "even if faithfulness to this principle results in the Church's utter financial ruin."

As the room once again erupted, some of the loudest reactions came from the gallery of elevated clergy behind him, with the fish-lipped and red-faced Cardinal Verguenza sputtering to his neighbor in a particularly animated fashion. The Holy Father turned his gaze to his fellow clergy, and he climbed back up on the platform to face and address them.

"Brothers, I know this approach seems antithetical to what we were taught in seminary and within our institutional culture. We've been impressed with the duty to safeguard the wealth and reputation of the Church that has accumulated over two millennia. Well, we've already largely failed with respect to the reputation. Regarding the wealth, while we do a great deal of good for God's kingdom with those resources, perhaps we've become too much like the man who stored up his grain in silos. We rely on accumulated riches rather than existing in that place where we *must* rely on Our Lord's direct providence to accomplish his works. We are called by a master who eschewed riches, and who stated that worldly wealth obscures the path to Him. There is no justification, then, for safeguarding the material treasure of the Church at the expense of justice and reconciliation. If this course leads our Church to worldly bankruptcy, so be it. Like any good parent, we will be leading our flock by example, and we will return to the very principles of humility so lovingly taught to us by the author of our faith."

During this address, several members of the assembled clergy had been unable to contain their outrage, and they had stood and left the room as quickly as their unwieldy garments allowed. Others looked about in confusion. In other eyes, though, glossy with welling tears, shone a light of love, admiration, hope, and even relief.

Many of those present would not have believed what happened next if they had not experienced it for themselves, and they later struggled to describe it. At the end of the Pope's words, after the only open doors in the room had closed behind the last angry cardinal, a refreshing wind began at the back of the recessed portion of the room containing the lay assembly, and it moved forward through every corner of the space, ruffling hair and blowing about skirts and lapels. As it moved through those gathered, the assembled faces transformed into a unified expression of deep and resonant joy. The quiet rustling of the supernatural wind was interrupted by an elated laugh of spontaneity and hope ringing out from the audience. It drew the attention of all present.

The congregants looked for the source of the sound, and when their eyes landed on Veronica Matthews, they had the same sensation of delight as one feels when caught by an unexpected spring shower when the sun is shining brightly and no clouds are in sight. As tears flowed down her cheeks, Veronica laughed with the infectious enthusiasm of an infant. Veronica's laugh opened the floodgates of emotion, and the rest of the room joined in.

Veronica moved purposefully toward the edge of the raised platform where the Pope stood and bent to lift the hem of the Holy Father's alb and kiss it. But the Pontifex Maximus, with tears on his cheeks and the afterglow of laughter coloring his face, removed his hem from her hands and brought her hands to his lips. A breathtaking look of love, acknowledgement, and forgiveness passed between them, and he raised his thumb to her forehead, where he made the sign of the cross as he whispered a blessing for her ears only.

For a book club guide to Every Saint A Sinner, visit
www.pearlsolas.com/bookclubguide

ACKNOWLEDGMENTS

Many thanks to the friends and family who talked through this idea for too many years to count, and then graciously volunteered their time to read and provide feedback about early drafts. I'm looking at you, Jen, Coral, Gina, Dwight, Demi, Heather, David, Yvette, and Elizabeth. Thank you also to the professionals who guided a novice novelist from early drafts to a finished product of which I am proud: Sarah Elaine Smith, Emma Borges-Scott, Marissa Frosch, Brooks Becker, and Alexandra Amor. Owen Gent, I am in awe of your talent and am delighted with the cover you created. Thank you.

This work would not have been possible without my parents, siblings, in-laws, and nieces and nephews. *I* would not be possible without my husband and our boys. Thank you for loving and supporting me, and for teaching me every day how to be a better, more authentic human.

ABOUT THE AUTHOR

Pearl Solas's writing reflects her interest in the breadth and depth of the human spectrum, and in the contrast between cultural narratives about categories of people and the lived experiences of people within those categories. Pearl lives in the Pacific Northwest of the United States with her husband, children, and two dogs.